THE RESISTANCE BOOK ONE

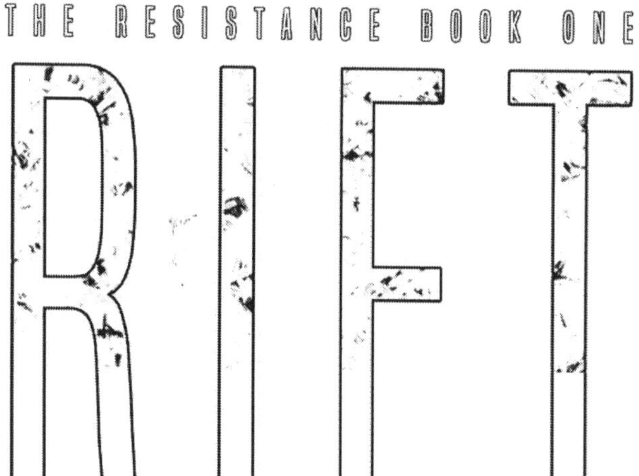

Books By Nathan Hystad

The Survivors Series

The Event
New Threat
New World
The Ancients
The Theos
Old Enemy

The Resistance Series

Rift
Revenge
Return

Red Creek

Keep up to date with his new releases by signing up for his Newsletter at www.nathanhystad.com

Cover art: Tom Edwards Design
Edited by: Scarlett R Algee
Proofed and Formatted by: BZ Hercules

ISBN-13: 9781794233577

1

Jish

Grand Admiral Jish Karn rubbed her temples, trying to ease a relentless migraine. She wanted to close her eyes, but every time she did that, her captive's beady black eyes stared mercilessly at her. Her hand trembled as she thought about him, and she was relieved when a nasally voice broke her free from the sudden onslaught of dread.

"And that's where we're at, Grand Admiral. Clearly, we need to increase production at the mines in order to keep up with the new demand for our fleet." The man stood at the end of the table, his arms active as he spoke. Councilman Tob was resourceful, but Grand Admiral Jish Karn found him a dreadful bore.

She'd heard enough for today. She'd already sat in silence for two hours, listening as the team rambled on about the costs of running Earth Fleet, the projections on colony repairs, the logistics of growing their fleet of ships, and countless other things she didn't want to discuss.

"Which mines are currently step one in the supply chain?" Jish broke her silence, hardly even aware that she'd spoken. Over the years, she'd grown accustomed to allowing her brain to formulate questions she thought the subordinates wanted her to ask.

Tob went right into it. "Uranus' moon Caliban for the hulls, and most of the metals used in the carriers and EFF model fighters. Mercury for armaments, and of course, the assembly plant orbiting Mars."

Jish thought about how terrible the prisons could be. Mercury was made for the worst of the worst: men with no chance of rehabilitation, forced to spend their remaining days creating weaponry for the fleet. None of the ammunition was produced there, so the likelihood of danger was decreased, but every now and then, one of them would find a way to create chaos, oftentimes only killing themselves in the process.

Phobos was possibly easiest on the prisoners, since they were mostly dissidents or white-collar criminals, many who spoke out about the Fleet or tried to embezzle funds from the government. Jish had spent some time touring the production facility, and was impressed with how clean an operation it was.

Caliban was another story. She'd never visited it. The idea of a prison deep under the surface of a tiny rock disturbed her. She much preferred the openness of space to the confines of an underground hell like that. Plus, there was a nagging discomfort in the back of her mind that if she stepped foot in the women's mine, she might end up stuck there, slogging through the smelter process with the other female prisoners.

"Very well," Jish said, realizing she'd been staring blankly out the window for over a minute.

"Very well what, Admiral?" Councilman Tob asked.

"Proceed in accelerating the production schedules of the prisons. We'll make funds available where needed. As always, keep everything from this meeting to yourselves," Jish said, scanning the three faces at the table.

She often wondered how much to tell the small group. Obviously, she wasn't able to offer them all the Earth Fleet secrets, but she was finding it harder and harder to keep everything under wraps. She used to rely on one man to discuss things with, but he'd disappeared from the face of the solar system.

The three Fleet members stood, and Jish asked one more question before they parted ways: "Any further word on Councilman Fairbanks?"

She saw Tob flinch just enough to tell her he might know something. She'd pry it from his cold dead hands if she had to, but instead of letting on, she smiled at him as he spoke. "No, Admiral. We've probed all our contacts across the system, and no one's seen or heard from him. I think he might be gone."

"Gone?" she asked, raising an eyebrow.

Councilwoman Neve spoke now. "He was last seen on Mars Minor. It's not a safe place for any ranking officers of the Fleet to be spotted, is it? Our theory is this: Councilman Fairbanks went there and never left. He's likely been thrown into the incinerators, like all the dead bodies found on Minor."

"Dead? You think he's dead?" Jish was laughing now. "That old badger will never die. Thank you, you're all dismissed."

The three glanced at each other before leaving Grand Admiral Jish Karn alone in the boardroom. She'd have to deal with Councilman Tob, and soon. He was leaving out something about Fairbanks, and she couldn't afford to be out of the loop. The existence of their race depended on it.

Jish crossed the room, smoothing a wrinkle from her uniform as she stood by the bar. The clear bottles called to her, and she poured a glass of Europa Scotch, sipping it at first before swallowing the rest in a quick, burning gulp. Her eyes watered at the sensation. She hated the stuff but was finding it more necessary every time she went to see *him.*

She wanted nothing more than to go to her quarters, take a hot steam shower, and listen to some old-world jazz. Instead, she fought the urge and entered the ship's halls. Her feet led her past some lingering officers who saluted her as she went by. She ignored them. Eventually, she found herself close to her destination, and she advanced into the elevator.

She peered back down the hall, checking for witnesses. With the tap of her fingerprint, a second window opened on the console, one only she could activate aboard her vessel, *Stellae.* The doors closed, and Jish scrolled until she found the hidden floor in the bowels of the large exploratory vessel. She selected her option, and the doors to the elevator locked in place. It wouldn't stop on any other floors until she was off.

Jish thought about avoiding the encounter tonight. She'd had a long day, and there was always tomorrow. The elevator slowed, and the doors opened to reveal a narrow hall. Her shoulders brushed the sides of the walls as she entered the cramped space. The elevator closed behind her, and she heard it hum as it lifted away, leaving her alone on the hidden level.

Turning to a side panel in the wall, Jish once again used her fingerprint to open a secret compartment. Inside she found a stunner, and she took it, feeling the metal of the handle dig into her firm grip. It was cool in her sweaty palm.

The hall was a hundred feet long, and she now walked with purpose, determined to get this over with so she could be in her quarters, washing the day away in less than half an hour. The door at the end of the corridor opened as she approached, her biometrics programmed into it. No one else would be able to enter this space without her alongside them.

Her heart beat hard in her chest as her boots clanged down on the metal floor grating inside the open room. As she entered, dim lights flickered on, casting ominous shadows across the walls. The energy field at the opposite end of the room glowed a light blue, and Jish couldn't take her eyes from it.

Each footstep echoed loudly in the chamber as Jish approached the cell. Even though she knew there was no way for the prisoner to reach her through the barrier, being this close to him always sent shivers down her spine. Her uniform felt tight, constricting.

Jish stood a few yards from the humming energy field, and saw the form get out of his crouched position in the corner. He stretched, his long arms hitting the ceiling with a bang. She jumped, chiding herself for being such a baby. She was a sixty-year-old woman, a powerful admiral at the top of the Earth Fleet, but this creature sent her back to a childish fear of the unknown. As she watched him approach the barrier, it was as if she were looking at the bogeyman under her bed.

"Stand down!" Jish yelled at him, but he did no such thing. He stared at her mercilessly, his black eyes shooting countless unspoken threats. "Are you ready to talk yet?" she asked in as big a voice as her small frame had bottled up inside.

He didn't reply. Instead, his shoulders slumped; he walked back to the far corner of his cell and crouched back down in the shadows.

"Talk to me, damn it!" she yelled, letting the creature get the best of her. He always did, and he seemed to know it. "What do you want with us? Why are you watching us? Tell me!"

He didn't move, and she knew there was no getting

through to him tonight. The Scotch had hit her, and she suddenly felt wobbly in the knees. *You have to stop doing this to yourself,* Jish told herself. He'd only used the console once, to point to where the Rift opened on the map; otherwise, he refused to communicate.

Jish watched him for several minutes, wondering if it would be better to just kill the being. Selfishly, she knew it would ease her own mind; she wasn't even thinking about its pathetic existence, stuck in a cell deep in her ship for the last thirty years. At one point, she'd felt sorry for the creature, until she remembered how dangerous he was. Before her sat the biggest threat to humanity ever encountered. He was proof of alien life, and humans could never learn they weren't alone in the universe.

Her boots clanged against the floor as she left the room, the lights snapping off as she closed the door behind her. She meandered through the narrow hall, her shoulders bumping the walls as she arrived at the elevator.

Tomorrow, she wouldn't come down here. It was over.

Jish smiled at the thought but knew she was only lying to herself. As each day passed, they were coming closer to August second, and the countdown felt like her own life's clock ticking away.

Grand Admiral Jish Karn stepped into the elevator when it opened and headed back to her quarters, where she could sleep so she could do it all over again tomorrow.

Flint

Flint sat back and took in the room. He'd been in this particular bar countless times before, but it had an off-kilter vibe today. The patrons were a remorseful bunch: dome workers with too few hours to themselves here on Mars, and even fewer credits. Flint's drink remained untouched, even though he'd ordered it half an hour ago, and when the waitress came to check on him, he covered the top of the glass with a hand.

"I'm just leaving," he told her. She scanned the chip in his hand, giving him a humorless smile before moving to the next table.

The place was sullen, too quiet, even though synth music from the Moons drifted through hidden speakers. Flint was getting tired of waiting for his contact. He had places to be and hated being stood up.

A stranger entered. He had the look of a government man: straight-backed, and even though he'd dressed down to fit in, Flint saw through it a mile away. He mentally urged the man to leave, and got a sinking feeling in his gut when the man locked eyes with him before casually averting his gaze.

The guy ordered a drink at the bar: something thick and purple poured by the overweight tender, splashing down the side of the gray metal cup. Flint started to get up when two Mars patrol guards sauntered past the bar's front doors. But he plopped back down, covering his face with a hand, trying to look like the rest of the lifeless bunch drowning their endless sorrows before doing it all again the next day.

The chair across from him grated on the floor as it was pulled back, and Flint peeked through his fingers to see the new stranger sit down.

"Seat taken?" he asked, his accent unplaceable. A New Earth metropolis, maybe?

"Go for it," Flint said flatly.

The stranger glanced over his shoulder at the patrol

guards, then back at Flint. His face was friendly, with soft eyes and a long, straight nose. "Are you waiting for someone?"

"What makes you say that?" Flint asked, finally taking a small sip of his drink. He raised an eyebrow. "Is it that unusual for a man to be sitting alone in a bar?"

"Clark's been detained," the man said casually, taking a long draw from his cup. He dabbed some of the purple drink off his lip with a napkin.

Flint's heart hammered in his chest, and he glanced toward the exit. Guards were still standing there, their backs to him. "Why are you telling me this?"

"Because my employer has a job for you, and I don't want to see you detained as well," the stranger said, smiling widely.

"I don't need any more jobs." Flint got up, but the man grabbed his wrist with the speed of a cobra, pulling him closer. The stranger spoke into Flint's ear, the drink's potent fumes carrying into his nose.

"You won't want to miss out on this job. Ask for Benson. That's me." He slipped something into Flint's pocket then stood up, patted Flint on the back like they were old buddies, and left the bar.

Flint waited a few minutes after the stranger had left, and saw the patrol guards leave as well, continuing down the corridor to the next establishment. With deft fingers, he pulled the object from his pocket and held it flat in his palm, where no wandering eyes could see it.

It was plainly a message, but he couldn't activate it here. If Clark wasn't coming for their meet-up, his time on Mars was over. Flint crossed the room, past the thinning crowd, and entered the corridors of Mars Major.

The city was falling apart. Once, it had been the mecca of humanity's future. Now it was a sad realization that space was a killer. It slayed hopes and dreams as much as it had destroyed the early colonists. Long ago, the rich had wanted to venture onto the other planets. They'd wanted to create something new and revolutionary. Flint looked around and thought it was anything but. The only thing the government did properly here was seal the cracking domes when necessary. Otherwise, the residents were left to fend for themselves amidst the dust-covered wasteland.

Every now and then, he'd see an old propaganda poster on the wall, faded until he could hardly make out the smiling faces of the models, or the green trees and crops they'd added for color. Flint laughed at the audacity of such advertising. Earth Fleet. *Join the Stars.* What a bunch of crap. He'd once been drawn in by the propaganda and counted his blessings every day for breaking free from the corrupt group.

He proceeded down the concrete hallways, avoiding eye contact with any of the shop owners, who were desperately hoping someone would stop into their boutiques to purchase something they didn't need or couldn't afford. Flint walked with purpose, and just the right amount of speed, until he reached his destination.

He passed through a corridor, a glass tube that connected Mars Major with the hangar. Here he stood in a short line, with two people in front of him. These days, flights in and out of Mars were few and far between. No one but traders and supply freighters traveled there, and only a limited number of residents could afford to leave.

When it was his turn, he flipped up his credentials. His face and the name *Trent Brand* showed up on the guard's viewer. Flint smiled at her, his grin matching the photo. She waved him through. "Go ahead, Mr. Brand."

His nerves were steel at this point, and he walked

through, heading for the connecting tube leading to his ship. It was light outside, the sun glaring through the clear two-hundred-foot dome. Flint reached his ship's sealed access port and tapped in his code. The door hissed open, and soon he was back inside his ship; his home. Once the hatch was closed again, he took a deep breath and let out any remaining anxious energy.

"What's the word, Kat?" he shouted as he walked into the ship's belly. Shelving lined the cargo bay; crates of various shapes and sizes sat strapped into them.

A voice called over the speakers: "Flint, something's wrong. You better get up here."

He jogged through the ship, passing the small crew quarters and the kitchen before making his way to the bridge of the freighter. "What is it?" he asked, looking at the young woman in the pilot's chair.

Kat cleared her throat and glanced back at him, worry evident on her face. "A message came through. Port guards are telling everyone to stay grounded."

"Damn. My contact didn't make it, and I was told he was detained. They're looking for us, or for what we have on this ship." Flint paced the small bridge, trying to figure out what to do. There was only one option. "Move over. We're getting the hell out of here."

"They'll shoot us down," Kat said, her face etched with concern.

"Have you ever seen them actually use those old-world guns? They probably don't even work," Flint said, forcefully sitting in the pilot's seat. The engines whirred to life, and the ship rumbled as the thrusters opened up.

Warning messages flashed across his terminal, but he ignored them. "Kat, if we don't leave, we're going to rot in one of those mining prisons. Is that what you want?"

She shook her head and started flipping switches beside him. "Give me two minutes."

Flint looked out the viewscreen, only to find rovers steadily advancing. "We don't have two minutes." He rammed the throttle forward and pulled back on the thruster lever, sending them lurching upwards. They rose higher and higher, exiting the thin Martian atmosphere. Rail guns began firing at them from the surface, and he grimaced when his sensors said they'd been hit.

"I'm on it." Kat ran from the bridge, her footsteps clanging loudly down the hall.

When they were high enough, Flint flipped a switch, sending all the energy from the fission engine to the rear thrusters. He let out a whoop as they raced away from Mars, past an unused planetary station, and into the darkness of space.

A patrol ship chased them from the surface below, but Flint watched as its blinking icon dropped further and further behind as his advanced engines worked their magic. No one expected a freighter of this size to have any guts, but this was no regular hauling vessel. This was Flint Lancaster's baby.

Kat arrived back on the bridge an hour later, abruptly waking Flint. It had been a long day, and the excitement had spiked his adrenaline, sending him into a crash shortly after.

"Seriously?" Kat asked. "You're sleeping at a time like this?"

"What? What's the big deal?"

Kat rolled her eyes and peeled off greasy gloves. "The big deal is, we can never go to Mars again. You realize that really limits our *trading* potential, don't you?"

"I was beginning to hate that dive anyway. Plus, we can always get new ID tags and badges." Flint pulled his badge from his pocket, tossing it to the ground. "What kind of name is Trent Brand anyway? It sounds like a supervillain from an ancient comic book." He saw something drop to the floor beside it and bent down, picking up the message from the stranger in the bar.

"What's that?" Kat asked, sitting down beside him. Her hair was pulled back into a tight ponytail, and he wiped a blotch of grease off her nose with his index finger.

He didn't answer her right away. "No issues patching this girl up?"

"It's fine. She had a few holes, but she's almost as good as new." Kat stared back at the small device in Flint's hand.

He plugged it into his console, unsure of what to expect. Words scrolled out on the screen slowly.

"Where did you get that?" Kat asked, her voice a low whisper.

Flint gulped, blinking intensely, wondering if the number he was reading was a mirage. "Some guy at Dino's bar handed it to me. Said he had a job."

"Then why doesn't this explain the job?" Kat asked.

Flint was wondering the same thing. It displayed an access code for fifty thousand credits and an address for one of Jupiter's moons.

"They didn't need to explain anything. Not with fifty thousand credits." Flint thought about taking the money and heading to Earth. He could finally afford a place on the beach... for a while.

"If they're giving you fifty now, there must be more once the job's done." Kat's eyes were wide, and Flint smiled at her.

He tapped in a few commands on the console, transferred the funds to his account, and set a new destination into the autopilot.

"We're going to Europa."

"I don't like that look in your eyes," Kat said, but she was grinning from ear to ear.

Ace

Ace was cold. His stomach growled as he wrapped the thin, worn blanket around his lean torso, but it did little to keep his body heat in. As he lay there in the abandoned building's doorway, Ace wondered if it was time to finally head south, where it was warmer. The trip would be difficult, especially since he had no credits and would get thrown in prison, or worse, if he was caught.

His head rested back on the hard ground, and he fought to keep tears from falling down his cheeks. That would just make him colder, and he already felt them threatening to freeze on his face. He tried to remember when he still had dreams of a happier time, but once he closed his eyes, all he saw were the beatings from the orphanage and memories of his dad passed out in the bathroom of their old cramped apartment.

His dreams had stopped a couple of years ago, and Ace didn't think they were ever coming back. A few rangy men walked by him, glaring as they passed. They likely didn't see anything of value and kept moving, searching for something… anything.

A noise carried to him across the cool evening air, and he searched the skies for the source. Finally, he caught it out of the corner of his eye. The thrusters shot out blue energy as the ship rose higher. A second ship followed, then a third.

Earth Fleet ships. He'd seen the videos on screens in storefronts. Heroes sent to space to guard the solar system from any threats, only Ace had never heard of any real threats out there. There was no such thing as aliens, or beings from other planets. Just humans. But they were bad enough.

Ace closed his eyes and imagined being in one of those flight suits, the cuffs tight on his wrists, gloves fitting perfectly. His feet were snug in the custom boots, and his hand gripped the fighter's throttle with purpose. What he wouldn't give to join the Fleet. He'd always be warm, fed, and have a reason to get up in the mornings.

But he was a nobody, too young to enlist. Ace slid a solitary playing card from his breast pocket and stared at the ace of clubs for a moment. It was the only possession he had of his family's, a constant reminder of a terrible father and his own loneliness. He put it back and patted it before settling in for sleep.

For the first time in two years, he dreamed. The visions were full of Earth Fleet logos and a fighter vessel with an ace of clubs decaled on the side.

The next night, Ace sat with his back against a brick wall in downtown Old Chicago. It was the one place he could beg without being beaten. The rich didn't come to the old cities any longer, not since the brand-new cities had taken over. They lived their opulent lives in high-rises overlooking oceans that covered what used to be the West Coast.

He recalled a lesson from his orphanage about a state called California. They'd shown a video of a rotten white sign, deep under water. It had read *Hollywood*, but Ace hadn't known what that meant.

He looked around, trying to keep an eye out for trouble. There had been a few murders recently – which wasn't unusual for Old Chicago – but specifically near this street, which worried him. It was the only place he had any luck getting credits for food, and if he lost this spot, he was as good as dead anyway, so it was worth the risk.

A middle-aged couple walked by, far better off than he was. There was an old-world play happening tonight down the street, and people milled about, wearing their best clothing, pretending to be something they weren't for a night.

Ace held out his hand. The woman gave him a sad smile and tapped her wrist, sending him ten credits. He mouthed a thank you, and she kept moving, arm sliding back under her date's.

He had enough to get some food. Most people gave a credit or two, and he couldn't believe his fortune. He could eat for three days with this. He decided to press his luck and stay for a while longer.

As the crowds began to thin, the show starting, it grew quiet and dark. Snowflakes fell from the sky, softly at first, then increasing in size and quantity. Winter was early, and Ace hated it. He wasn't sure he could survive another one in his current situation.

Pushing the dread aside, he got up and made for the street vendors, hoping to cash in on the play patrons. As he passed a dark alley, he heard shouting from within.

"Do what he says, Edgar!" one man's voice called.

"Listen, I'm Earth Fleet. You don't want to mess with me!" a slurry voice shouted.

Someone mumbled, and Ace knew he should keep walking. It was none of his business. But hearing the words *Earth Fleet* caused his feet to stop as if he was glued to the sidewalk.

"Well, I can't show you my badge, because I'm only a new recruit. But I'm going to be famous…" The drunken bravado was cut short as two pulse blasts lit up the dark alley. Ace froze, standing in the middle of the alley entrance. He saw a silhouette hovering over two dropped bodies. It turned toward Ace and lifted the gun.

Ace felt his throat tighten, though he wanted to shout out for help. But no one would help a street rat like him, even if he found his voice. The gun lowered and the shadow disappeared, footsteps quick down the alley, away from where Ace was standing.

"Are you okay?" Ace found himself asking, knowing the answer as soon as he neared the fallen men. They were dead, eyes wide open in surprise.

Life was hard on the streets. Ace knew this more than anyone, and even though his gut told him it was wrong, he rifled through the corpses' pockets. He found some hard credits and nimbly pocketed them before seeing the man the other had called Edgar. He was slight, around Ace's height. His hair was the same color; he had brown eyes. He'd said he was an Earth Fleet recruit.

Ace was desperate and saw an opportunity. He looked around the dark lane, and when he felt no one was watching, he grabbed his flip knife out of his worn sock. With a flick of his wrist, he sliced into Edgar's hand. He tried not to gag as the blood pooled out. The chip was the size of a fingernail, and Ace stuck it in a secret pocket on the inside of his shirt, near his heart.

"I'm sorry, Edgar," he said, noticing a small plastic card in the dead man's front pocket. It had half-fallen out, and Ace snatched it up, seeing the digital logo of the Earth Fleet: a fighter vessel with the sun in the backdrop. It flashed between that image and an address with a date and time.

Ace's heart thrummed in his bony chest. He only had a week to prepare. He had to convince the Fleet he was Edgar Smith.

Every one of Ace's possessions was now inside his ratty pack, slung over his shoulder. Door chimes rang as he entered the small shop, and a greasy fat man watched him from behind a counter at the far end of the room.

"Whaddaya want, kid?" the man growled.

Ace almost turned around and left, but he didn't have a choice. It was either this or fade away, another dead street kid no one would miss.

"I hear you're the man to speak with about…" Ace looked around nervously, but they were alone in the shop. "...swapping ID chips."

The man twirled a toothpick in his large mouth and grimaced at Ace. "What's it to you, kid?"

Ace stood firm, looking him straight in the eye. "What do you charge?"

The man crossed his hairy arms, trying to look imposing. "New ID is three hundred credits, plus da surgery… make it an even five hundred."

Ace's heart skipped a beat. Five hundred! Even with begging non-stop for six straight days, he'd only managed to scrounge up eighty. "I have the ID already. Don't need a new one."

The man raised both eyebrows in surprise. "And jus' where did you acquire dis other ID?"

"Traded for it," Ace lied.

The man just nodded. "Two hundred, then."

"I don't have enough." Ace looked around the shop, seeing how rundown and messy it was. He didn't assume the shop owner was a wealthy man. He'd bargain. They all did. "I can pay you fifty."

"Fifty! Dat's outrageous!" the fat man bellowed, his breath wheezing out, turning into a coughing fit.

"It's all I have," Ace said softly.

The fat man set a meaty palm down on the glass countertop. "Kid, you're a royal pain in da ass. I can do it for seventy-five, but yous got to be quick about it. I has other clients waiting for me."

Ace doubted there was anyone else waiting, but he was grateful he'd taken a chance on negotiating. "Deal." Ace transferred half the funds, and when the man questioned it, he said he'd give him the rest when it was done. He knew how these charlatans operated.

The man went to the front of the shop, locked his door, and led Ace to a rear room, where a dim light bulb hung from a chain over a rusty chair. Ace saw the tray of tools and hoped he wouldn't die from infection. At least in the Fleet, he'd have medical care. As the man cut into his hand without using any numbing agent, he closed his eyes and pictured himself in uniform. His growing body filled it out with strong muscles from training and a proper diet. His life was going to change forever after tomorrow.

"All done," the man said, dropping Ace's ID into a metal tray. "Jus' gotta sew you up."

By *sew*, the man meant cauterize with an ancient tool. Ace fought the urge to pass out. When it was over, the skin looked almost normal, just a pink line letting Ace know he'd had the surgery at all.

"Test it," Ace said.

The man scanned Ace's hand, and Ace read the display on the tablet.

Edgar Smith

DOB 05/18/2457

Residence: 3750 Alderberry Way, Old Chicago

Credits: 2014

He stopped reading there, his jaw dropping.

"Traded for it, eh?" The man shook his head. "Better

make it da full five hundred, kid. When da patrols come sniffin' around, I's never seen you. Here, take these now so you don't die before you leave my shop." He handed Ace a small plastic bag filled with pills of various sizes and shapes. Ace cringed but did as the man said. The casings tasted wrong, maybe long expired, but he knew the alternative was much worse.

Ace instantly sent the funds and stumbled up, almost running from the shop. The chimes clattered behind him as he set out onto the snow-covered streets as Edgar Smith. He hated the name, but what choice did he have? He didn't even remember his own given name. His old ID chip had said Ace Club, and he'd been given that at the orphanage. This was as good as any.

2

Wren

Wren tightened the straps on her breathing mask as the fumes from the smelter leaked out of the machine. She motioned for the site supervisor to come over and inspect the broken seal.

"Good catch, 5589. Get back to work." The uniformed android pointed to the other side of the room, where prisoners were stacking recently cooled sheets of metal.

Wren crossed the hot space, painfully aware of her aching feet with each step. She got to the stack, lifting – with a partner – sheet after sheet of the heavy material until the piles were moved onto carts. From there, they pushed the carts down a series of corridors. She knew machines could do this work much more easily and efficiently, but that was what the prisoners were for. Manual labor.

Her partner, Monika – or 3351, as the stitching on her black uniform read – was muttering under her breath during the whole trip to the warehouse, and Wren didn't attempt to communicate with the woman. She'd tried on several occasions, receiving nothing but contempt in return.

They rolled the heavy cart into the large room. Hundreds of rows of tall skid shelving lined the area, most filled with metal sheets much like the ones they'd brought in.

An android walked up to them, scanned their IDs, weighed the load, and ordered them back to the smelting room for another run. This made ten treks so far, and Wren would have at least twenty more before her shift was over. Like every day, it was going to be a long one.

"You're kidding me," Mara said between bites. "You aren't seriously telling me you're starting to enjoy this food, are you?"

Wren shrugged and scooped up another bite of the gray mushed slop in her spoon. "Beats going hungry, I guess."

"How do you do it?" Mara asked quietly.

"Do what?" Wren asked.

"Keep smiling every day. I mean, I get it, most of us are here for a good reason. But you…" Mara stared back at her plate.

"What's that supposed to mean?" Wren asked.

"You're actually innocent, aren't you?" Mara's hand covered her mouth.

Wren used to talk about it. She'd fought for an appeal, but since she hadn't been allowed a lawyer in the first place, it had fallen on deaf ears. She'd shouted at the androids until her throat was raw, but that was two years ago. Now she smiled at Mara and made an almost imperceptible nod.

"Then how do you do it?" Mara asked, her eyes wide. The younger woman was pale, much lighter than Wren's own caramel skin, and a hint of color flushed her cheeks as one of the android guards walked past, casually telling them there were five minutes left before they were to go back to their cells.

"I'm no different than anyone else in here," Wren said softly. "Not anymore." She finished the meal and carried her tray over to the trash chute. With practiced motions, she cleared it off completely, as instructed, and set it down. Mara stayed close behind her.

"You're wrong," Mara said into her ear.

"About what?" Wren countered as they walked single-file down the corridor that would lead to their cells.

"You are different. Everyone can see it," Mara said, and this sent a tingle down Wren's spine. The last thing she wanted to do was stand out, especially here. She'd kept her head down for two years, and had avoided many altercations because of it.

They entered the round foyer: the cell section of the women's prison circled the space. Wren looked up, scanning the twelve stories; her gaze settled above, where four androids were huddled around someone.

"Who's that?" Wren asked Mara, who shrugged.

The visitor was on the fifth story, looking down into the crowd of prisoners. It was a man. A real man. Wren hadn't seen another human, outside the other female prisoners, in two years. There were only androids running the show here. He must be someone important to be inside here with them. Her stomach sank, the gruel suddenly threatening to come back up. If he was important, that made him dangerous.

Wren kept her eyes on the man as she stood on the circular lift in the center of the room. It stopped at the second floor, a guard led the prisoners back to their cells, and then it rose to the third floor, and so on. Wren watched the man with the androids around him closely, feigning a casual interest. Their eyes locked, and he frowned before looking away, checking something on a tablet. He had a nice face, almost familiar.

They stopped at the seventh floor, and Wren stepped off, heading slowly toward her small cell. The android guard buzzed the energy-field barriers open, and they each marched into their cells. The android did something she'd never seen before. It walked over to her cell, keeping its back to her. She stood by the buzzing barrier, curious what it was doing.

"Have a pleasant evening, Wren," it said with a tone unlike the other guards. They all sounded the same: monotone and angry. This one just spoke to her with care and used her real name, another thing never done by a guard before.

She didn't know how to respond, so she just said, "You too." It walked off with purpose, awaiting the lift's return. It held a pulse blaster in its robotic hand and didn't move for a full five minutes, until the lift came back.

Wren watched the guard closely, and as it exited onto the lift's platform, it stole a glance in her direction before disappearing below. She shook her head and sat down on the hard cot, peeling her boots off. Her feet throbbed, and she wished she'd had a chance at a hot shower. What she really wanted was a hot bath in her old clawfoot tub.

She closed her eyes and fought the images flooding into her mind of her previous life. Her laboratory. Her fiancé. Their house overlooking the lake outside New Dallas. As the lights dimmed, her face pushed into her pillow, and for the first time in two years, she cried herself to sleep.

CD6

CD6 lowered to the ground and holstered his weapon. He'd noticed the man on the fifth floor and wondered at his business in their little prison. He'd do some digging to find out. He cursed himself for being so bold as to say goodnight to Prisoner 5589, but she was special. He'd read her file and didn't believe the charges for a minute. Biological warfare didn't seem like a hobby of hers.

While the other prisoners traded supplies for favors, beatings, protection, and coupling together, 5589 stayed out of it all. CD6 had been stationed at the Uranus Mining Prison for Women for forty years, and only once before had he spoken so to a prisoner. She was dead a week later, quietly killed in her sleep. He didn't think it was his interaction that had caused it, but CD6 had vowed to stay away from the humans since then. Something about Wren drew him in, though.

As they marched in timed steps to their recharge stations, CD6 tried to not think about his brothers. They were so single-minded, and as far as he knew, not one of them had the freedom of thought he did. It was unnerving. He'd tried to talk to CB9 about it once, and it had nearly ended with a memory wipe. He'd decided to be more careful after that.

CD6 entered his charging station, stepping on the plate that sent energy through his wiring and into the source sitting in the center of his chest. It glowed softly, an ambient green, and he watched the others charging around him, wondering if any of them hated what they were doing. Slave labor at prisons was as old as time itself, but to CD6, it felt wrong. The Earth Fleet used the metals for war machines, while these women each ended up dead from exertion, from inhaling fumes, or from killing each other.

A few of them got to leave each year, but none ever made it back home. They were blasted into space to die a frozen and breathless death. Even a sentient android could understand this was cruel. They released one every few months to give the prisoners hope that they, too, might one day be released. If they only knew the truth – but you couldn't have your workforce refusing to do the work. Then the Fleet would have to find workers to pay, and that wouldn't be a cost-effective way to build more ships.

CD6's mind raced after speaking with Wren. Could he talk with her again? What would he get out of it, other than a chance she'd be killed, and then he'd be wiped? It wasn't worth it. Still, what was it all for? Why was he different, if not to help someone get through their torment?

He considered this for an hour, and eventually couldn't take it any longer. He set his timer and deactivated himself. His chest glowed green, but his orange eyes dimmed to black.

Jarden

Councilman Jarden Fairbanks sat behind his large mahogany desk, sipping Scotch from a crystal tumbler. His wall was made from a clear, impenetrable resin that gave him a sweeping look at the ship under construction beside the small station tucked away in the Kuiper Belt. Sensors wouldn't pick them up out here – he'd ensured that – but it didn't keep him from scanning the distance for signs of incoming Fleet ships.

The ship was a masterpiece, and as he watched the final touches being put to it, he felt every year of his age. Maybe a few more alongside them. It had been sixty years since he'd seen the Watchers. That day stood as the most glorious and tumultuous day of his life, until today. Today, his ship would be ready, and all he needed was the pilot.

Jarden leaned back in his chair and considered how monumental an event he was creating by constructing this ship. The Council was adamant they stop all experiments and attempts at communication with the newcomers, and that was one of the only things he could agree with them about. Jarden knew he'd hang for his crimes if he was found out, but when it was all over, they'd make statues of him. His face would adorn art for centuries, maybe millennia.

He smiled to himself and took another sip of the smooth brown liquid. His desk vibrated slightly, and he saw there was an incoming call. His line was encrypted five ways to tomorrow, and he tapped *accept*, a holographic display of Benson's head appearing before him.

"Is it done?" Jarden asked his right-hand man.

Benson nodded. "I gave him what you wanted. He nearly got himself shot down by the Mars patrol in the process."

"Where's his contact, Clark, now?" Jarden asked.

Benson's holographic face smiled. "Somewhere no one's going to find him."

"Will he come?" Jarden asked, knowing Benson would have gotten a good read from Flint Lancaster. Benson always read people well.

"He'll come. Mark my word, he'll come."

"Then be sure to head straight for Europa. I want you there when he comes to answer the call." Jarden leaned forward, his voice low. "Benson…"

"Yes, sir," Benson answered.

"Don't let him get away," Jarden hissed between

clenched teeth.

"I won't, sir."

The display cut out, and Jarden was once again alone with his thoughts. He threw on a jacket and decided to do one more walkthrough of the new ship.

Twenty minutes later, Jarden was stepping off the small transport vessel into the bowels of *Eureka.* While it wasn't the largest ship ever created by Earth Fleet resources, it was the most advanced. The only one larger had left sixty years ago, and Jarden was anxious to learn what had happened to it.

His soft-soled shoes touched down on the hard surface of the ship's hangar, and he took a deep breath, reveling in the scent of the ship: cleaning chemicals making it sterile, with a hint of grease.

First Officer Heather Barkley greeted him, her hand extending in the traditional shake request. He obliged, noticing her hands were ice-cold, but she smiled widely at him and spoke in rushed, terse statements.

"Councilman, we're so thrilled to show you the latest results. The engines are completed to spec, and the Shift drive can be tested as early as next week. Come, I'll take you to engineering." She turned, and Jarden grinned to himself. It was nice to see the crew so excited about a project, even if they were far from home with no communication capabilities. They likely expected they were going home when the ship was completed. The ones akin to Barkley wouldn't want to leave the ship, and he was counting on that.

"Very well. Show me to engineering." Jarden followed her, the Scotch warming his belly as he toured *Eureka.*

3

Jish

Jish scanned through the series of reports filling her desk's holoscreen. It was always the same: government officials on the colonies demanding funds for things they'd never receive. She couldn't believe how far Old Earth had gone to spread out among their solar system. Mars had been the first, and she wished her predecessors had given up on the expansion after the first two rounds of colonists had perished out there. The rock was a desolate wasteland three hundred years ago, and it still was to this day.

Anyone with common sense and a dime to their name had already returned from Mars, and the rest were forced to manufacture for the Earth Fleet under the threat of starvation and oxygen deprivation. The Fleet never actually came out to say it in those words, but the powers that be understood the undertones to their conversations. Every now and then, an official like Prime Minister Gane would threaten a strike at all Mars facilities if they weren't given what they asked for.

In this case, it was extra food rations. Their greenhouses were underperforming, and they'd had a rough year and a half on Mars. Jish used to care more about issues like this. She used to visit the colonies and have her heartstrings tugged as she saw dirty rugrats clutching their mothers' dusty pants legs as she walked by, waving at the crowds. Now she didn't have time for them.

She sent a terse reply to Gane on Mars, hoping he would get the point.

No food is incoming. The Earth Fleet is under a frozen budget for the foreseeable future, as all funds are tied up in the continued construction of New Johannesburg. Continue to make do with what you have, and as always, the Earth Fleet is grateful for the work the Martians are doing.

She grinned as she typed the response. Gane hated being called Martian. Hell, the whole planet hated it, but she still used it. A well-placed passive-aggressive slight was all she could do in a non-encrypted message to a government official like Gane, so she did what she had to do.

She kept scrolling through the countless requests, wondering why so many made it past her team of assistants. With a sigh, she tapped the holoscreen off and leaned back in her chair.

"Captain, when are we arriving at the destination?" she asked, her finger tapped down on the comm-switch to the bridge.

"We'll be there in just over five hours, Grand Admiral," Captain Stevens said quickly.

Good. They were close.

"Thank you, Captain." She ended the link, and a second later, an incoming call glowed orange on her desktop. She tapped the comm-switch again. "Go ahead."

"Grand Admiral." It was Councilman Tob. That was the last thing she needed. Her head already hurt enough. "What is it, Tob?" she asked, her patience stretched thin.

"I have some news. Do you have a moment?" Tob asked with a hint of excitement. His voice rarely held anything but stress and boredom. It must be important to the little man.

"Fine. But it better be good," she said, ending that call too.

What did it matter? She had five hours to get to their goal, and she was too wired to sleep anyway. Her computer announced someone at her door, and she let them in.

Tob stood there. His navy-blue uniform was wrinkled, and he had deep purple bags under his eyes.

"What the hell have you been doing, Tob?" Jish asked, unable to hide the disgust from her voice.

He didn't even register her insult. "Grand Admiral, I found him… well, not quite found where he *is*, but I have a trace that might lead us there."

"What are you stammering on about?" Jish motioned for Tob to sit across the desk in one of the two seats. He obliged. With the push of a tablet icon, her holoscreen flashed to life, and reports scrolled to life.

"That's all I need. More reports," she muttered under her breath.

"What's that?" Tob asked, his gaze finally making contact with hers. Red lines raced from his irises, as if they were trying to escape.

"Nothing, Tob. Care to explain what I'm looking at?"

"Sure. Councilman Jarden Fairbanks was last seen two years ago on Mars, correct?" Tob asked.

She waved a hand, indicating he should hurry up.

"From there, he vanished, but not before liquidating his immense fortune. How he managed to accrue so much wealth is beyond me. It wasn't from the Council's wages, I'll tell you that much." Tob added a dig at his own salary, as if Jish cared about his income.

"Fairbanks wasn't a dummy. He invested at a young age and came out on top far more often than not." Jish remembered a few times she'd invested in a company because Jarden had suggested it. She'd made a fortune because of the man, not that it really mattered when you ran the Earth Fleet. She hadn't paid for anything in over a decade.

"Yes, clearly. Some think he took a private vessel from there to Neptune, but we never had proof, and the trail had gone cold." Tob smiled now, and a few years washed from his tired face as he did so.

"Are you telling me you found Fairbanks?" she asked, knowing he would have said that outright if he had.

The thin man shook his head three times. "No. What I did find was some classified project being funded by the Earth Fleet out beyond the Kuiper Belt."

She raised a finger to her lips. She had personally authorized countless classified projects around the solar system, and didn't want Councilman Tob to start sniffing around too much.

"Leave the details with me. I'll look over them." Jish stood, causing Tob to stand up himself.

"Don't you want to hear…?" he started.

"You've done a wonderful job here, Councilman. It hasn't gone unnoticed. But I fear your other tasks have been suffering because of the focus on Fairbanks."

"But you…"

She cut him off and smiled, a sight that seemed to startle the man. "And I thank you for being such a great friend and diligent member of our council. Please don't dig into this any further. I have it from here."

Tob looked ready to argue the request, but the air deflated out of him; he got up, gave her a weak smile, and exited the room. Jish looked through the documents over the next few hours and saw exactly what Councilman Tob had seen. Money was funneling from their special projects funding to a site she'd never heard of. The money snaked through countless avenues to end there, but if you knew what you were looking for, you could always follow the money. It never lied.

"Grand Admiral? We're arriving," the captain personally called to advise her.

"Thank you, Captain Stevens." Jish ended the connection and stood, looking out the window of her office. The sight sent a shiver of elation through her veins.

Dozens of EFC-03s, the newest model of Fleet carriers, sat in space, each connected to the large round station in the center of the construction area. Inside each carrier were a hundred EFF-17s, the fighters they'd need if her predictions were going to come true. If only she'd been able to convince the rest of the Fleet sooner. Jarden had been lying to them for years, and only after his disappearance had the Fleet board listened to her.

She hoped the recruits they had training at their five facilities around the system would be enough to turn the tides. Someone had to fight the enemy.

Ace

The line was long, and Ace sweated profusely in the chilly outside air. He was wearing new clothing –used, but nicer than anything he'd ever owned before. His boots were soft and pliable, his hair chopped short like Edgar's had been. It felt strange after having it long for the past few years, but he was glad for the change. Dressed like this, with a haircut, he felt like a new man. Edgar Smith, to be exact.

The Earth Fleet office was smaller than he'd expected. It was a couple miles from downtown Old Chicago, and the signs were fading, in desperate need of painting. Was this what he was signing up for? He scanned the crowd and saw a group of eager boys and girls much like him, awaiting their exciting future with the Fleet.

Ace rubbed the line on his hand, hoping no one would notice. He wondered what they'd do if they determined he'd implanted a dead man's ID into himself. The line moved and he shuffled forward, almost to the doors now.

A few minutes later, he was inside, where a tall imposing Fleet officer looked down at him. "Name?" he barked.

"Uhm… Smith, sir. Edgar Smith." Ace reached his hand out, and the man scanned him without much preamble.

"How old are you?" the man asked, not looking at his date of birth on the screen.

"Nineteen, sir." Ace used Edgar's age. He was only sixteen, or at least that was what he assumed. He wasn't actually sure how old he was.

"You look younger." The man squinted, looking Ace up and down. "Skinny too. Guess we'll have to fatten you up. Go ahead. Ship's out back. Grab your package from the next room and get changed first."

Ace smiled despite the frown he was getting from the officer. The promise of a uniform and food was the best news he'd ever heard, ever. He was so lost in his own thoughts, he didn't notice the girl in front of him until he bumped into her. She stumbled forward, letting out a string of curses. He'd grown up on the streets, and her phrasing was enough to shock even his seasoned ears.

"I'm sorry," Ace told the young woman. She spun around, taking in his tiny frame.

"It's okay. What, did your dad lose you? Do you want me to have them buzz your mommy?" she asked, using a condescending baby tone.

Her hand rested lightly on his forearm, and he shook it off. "So funny for someone who looks like she just stepped away from a New City gala," he said, trying to sound older than he was.

She looked ready to punch him for the jab, glancing down at her clothing. She was dressed nicely; obviously, she was well off or playing the part. Instead, she laughed, giving him a light tap on the arm. "You're all right, kid. Usually I leave them stammering in a puddle, but you were quick. I like that."

Ace wasn't used to any attention from other people, especially not older girls with dark curly hair like this.

"What's your name, kid?" she asked, walking forward as the line kept moving toward the next room.

"Ace…" He silently cursed himself for not thinking clearly. The girl had him too distracted. "I mean, Edgar."

She looked at him like she was trying to determine the next move in a complicated puzzle. "Edgar? I'd stick with Ace if I were you. What, did your parents see you squirm out of the womb and think, 'We need a name to match the face'?"

"Go on, I've heard them all. And just what name shall I call you?" he asked, finding himself having fun just speaking to another human without being embarrassed or thinking about food.

"You may call me Majesty. Everyone else knows me by Serina." She stuck her hand out, and he shook it. Her hand was warm, her grip firm.

"Very well, Majesty," he said, and was delighted when her light gray eyes lit up in surprise.

"Next," a woman called, and Serina turned around. The Fleet woman looked Serina up and down, took a scan with a handheld device, and chose a pile of clothing from a shelving unit behind her.

"Next," she said again, and Ace watched Serina disappear into one of the many makeshift changing stations that ran along the room's long wall. She gave him a quick grin before ducking behind the flap of cloth.

He felt the clothes pile hit him in the chest, and he stuck his arms out, just catching it.

"Next."

When he finished changing, Ace tucked his new "used" clothing into a bag, and another Fleet worker scanned his hand, taking the bag and tossing a sticker on it. It pained him to watch them take his sack of new possessions away, but it would be fine. They'd return it, but who needed it anyway? He looked down at the uniform, a beige jumpsuit that fit too loosely. He didn't care. It felt perfect at that moment.

He was heading to boot camp. He was going to join the Earth Fleet and become a famous pilot. It was in his cards, and his deck was stacked with aces, so he couldn't lose.

Ace felt a hand shove him forward as he stood inside the doorway, gawking at the line approaching the nearby landed ship. It was much larger than he'd expected, clearly fitting hundreds of new recruits. He looked back when the hand pushed him again, and saw a mouth-breathing giant, eager to make enemies. Ace had seen a million guys on the street like him, and he did what he always did to survive. He didn't react.

"Get out of the way, Tiny," the bully said, getting a laugh from the two other guys behind him.

Ace stepped sideways, waving his hand in the air, welcoming the tormenter to have his spot.

The oaf looked dumbfounded at the action, and hesitantly walked forward, taking Ace's position. The other two goons protested, and Ace let them sneak ahead of him too.

"Told you he was a pushover, Ceda," the widest one said to their evident leader.

An Earth Fleet officer, this one with three stars on his collar, walked down the line toward the ship. "Sorry, everyone. This one is almost full. Another is right behind it."

Ace dreaded a long wait with these three just ahead of him, but just when he was about to find a spot even farther back in line, he saw Serina waving him forward from right in front of the ship's entrance.

He wasn't sure she was directing her attention at him, so he pointed down to his head and mouthed the word 'me?'. She nodded, and the three-star officer waved for Ace to come to the front of the line.

Ace did his best to bite his tongue as he walked past the goons to the front of the line, where he followed Serina aboard for the last two spots. It was clear she had some connections, and Ace couldn't believe his luck.

He beheld the huge gray exterior of the Fleet transport ship, and stepped within it. He'd only ever dreamt of being inside a ship, and he was the ultimate blend of nervous and excited.

"Come on. Let's find our seats," Serina said, walking onto the ship with an air of authority.

Flint

"Didn't we already count all of this?" Kat asked, looking down the cargo bay wall with a frown.

"We did, but since we couldn't offload anything at Mars, we're going to have to make contact with a few buyers on the Moons." Flint didn't mind Jupiter, or at least not the Moons. Some of the smaller ones were home to exotic housing for the rich, and Flint had spent a few days on such a moon last year, staying with one of his customers. He never understood their fascination with Old Earth antiquities. They paid his bills, but if he was that wealthy, he wouldn't care about having some relic from a thousand years ago on his mantel.

"Let's start with this side. Here's the manifest" – he left out "if the Fleet boards us" – "and here are the *real* manifests." They were coded, but Kat had the ability to decipher them. She'd actually created the code after he'd nearly ended up in prison a couple of years ago. She still brought that up far too often.

They spent the next few hours going through everything, item by item. Hidden away were various mood enhancers, and Flint tucked them back into their hiding places. He hated moving product like that, but Clark had assured him there was good money in it, and he had the right contacts. Now that Clark was detained, Flint guessed he'd never see the man again. Once the Fleet heard about a drug trafficker, they typically ended up dead. On Mars, that meant buried in the middle of nowhere, amidst the rock and dust.

Flint tried to not care what he was hauling, as long as it wasn't people. He was many things, but a murderer or kidnapper he was not.

"What's this?" Kat asked. Her fingers were holding an old comp plug-in stick.

Flint shrugged. "Hell if I know. What do we care?"

"I don't, but it was hidden at the bottom of a package. The only reason I even looked inside was because of the scan code on the outside of the box." Kat turned the metal box on its side, and Flint used his tablet to scan the code square.

"Item: Mineral Sample. Year: Urgent. Destination:

Unauthorized." Flint read off the lines, confused by a few things. "You're right. Something's wrong here." He glanced at her hands, which still held the small object. He wanted to tell her to stick it back in the box and to forget she'd ever seen it.

"Flint?" she asked, eyes wide with worry. "What do we have here?"

"It's probably nothing." He said the words, but his gut was telling him otherwise. Against his better judgment, he said, "Let's just take a quick look to be sure."

They left the room as it was and headed back to the bridge. Flint prided himself on his nerves of steel, but there was something about this old-era data stick that was breaking him down. He took the pilot's seat, Kat beside him.

"Here goes nothing," Flint said, until he realized he didn't have the proper receptacle for such an old stick. They fumbled around the bridge, looking through drawers for an adapter, and after ten minutes, ended up back at the console, Flint's nerves fully fried.

He plugged it in, scanning it for any virus before allowing it to open. The first thing he saw was the date stamp. It read *2385*.

"Flint, this thing is over ninety years old!" Kat shouted in surprise.

"It appears that way." He kept looking at the file. There were some encrypted notes he'd look through later, but what piqued his interest were the video files.

He swallowed through his dry throat, accessed the first video, and sat back. The image appeared on their holoscreen, large across the front of the bridge. A date was stamped on the lower right corner: August 2nd, 2385. He stole a glance at Kat, who was staring at it in tight-lipped silence.

The video subjects were clearly on a ship's bridge. Earth Fleet uniforms adorned the man and woman. The man looked too young for the four stars on his collar, denoting him an admiral. The woman had three, but she did the talking.

"*We're awaiting the arrival. If they come as expected, it will be in less than five minutes. This marks the seventh time that we've seen them arrive. Speculation among the group is that they've been visiting for far longer than that. That every thirty years they briefly appear, before retreating back to where they came from. Anomalies have been recorded in this region from as far back as the twenty-first century, so the speculation has merit.*

"*We have yet to try communication because we're not ready for them, should they prove hostile. Admiral Kane, would you like to discuss today's mission?*" The woman sat back, giving way to the young leader.

"What are we seeing?" Kat whispered, but Flint didn't answer. He was wondering the same thing.

Kane's voice was surprisingly deep as he spoke. "*We've done our best to stay off their radar, though we don't know how far it stretches. Our ship will power down all functions, to emit no frequencies and limit our energy readings. We've never been this close to them before.*" Kane looked like he'd seen some action; pain burned in his hard brown eyes, but he seemed nervous. Tense.

"*We have a surprise today. We'll be firing probes through the Rift. Fifty of them, each with a programmed trajectory once through the jump. We hope to learn what's on the other side, and where they come from.*"

Goosebumps raced up and down Flint's arms; the hair on the back of his neck stood straight up like a startled cat's. "What the hell is this?" He wanted to think they'd stumbled on some sort of film, fiction for the masses, but this was real. He could feel the authenticity.

"We're about to find out," Kat squeaked.

The female officer began hitting buttons and flipping switches. "*The Rift is opening,*" she said, and the camera switched to an outside view. Flint couldn't tell for sure where they were, but he estimated deep space, outside the Kuiper Belt. A blue light started glowing in a small dot, and soon it had spread wide open. "*Our power is off. We'll be shutting down the camera feed in a moment.*"

Flint leaned forward, his arms hitting his knees as he watched a ship emerge from the blue light. The front end was square, boxier than anything the Fleet ever came up with, even the early models. On each side, a large cylinder shape protruded parallel with the ship, and Flint guessed them to be immense thrusters. Just as it was halfway through, dozens of tiny probes raced toward the Rift. They each glowed with green light as their small thrusters burned. The camera feed ended.

Flint stared at the black screen. Sweat dripped down his forehead, nestling on his eyebrows.

"Is this real?" Kat asked.

"The bastards have been keeping this from us all these years!" Anger coursed through Flint's veins. The damned Earth Fleet was hiding the fact that there was other life out there, and no one had a clue.

"If this video's ninety years old, and they said it was the seventh event, then the Fleet has known about these 'visitors' for three hundred years." Kat stood, walking to the viewscreen. Her hand touched the surface of it, the video still showing a static-covered black image. The picture snapped back on, startling her. She stumbled back, catching her footing as they began to talk again.

"*The probes made it through!*" The woman was grinning from ear to ear; Kane, her superior, even had the decency to crack a smile alongside her. "*Getting readings… wait. This can't be right. They're all disappearing from our sensors.*"

The video was showing a split scene, and Kane frowned as he tapped on a console. "*The Rift, it's closing.*" His voice was panicked.

Flint watched, now noticing the blue opening still there in the center of the camera view, showing otherwise empty space. It started to open larger, and the nose of the ship poked through. The feed went dead.

The video was over.

Flint sat back in his chair, unsure what to think.

They weren't alone in the universe.

4

Wren

"Prisoner 5589. What are you doing?" the android guard asked.

Wren thought it was pretty obvious. She was staying hydrated. "I'm just having a drink of water." She was sweating fiercely; the smelters felt like they were on overdrive today.

"You have reached your maximum water intake for the shift. Please proceed to your work station." The android stuck an arm out, and Wren flinched back, moving away from the fountain. She'd never heard of a limit to their water intake, but it pissed her off. Most of the workers at the prison moved like they were half-dead, while she overexerted herself to do the work. No one noticed or cared that she did twice as much labor as the other women.

She backed away from the guard and stumbled into another prisoner.

"Watch where you're going," Slicer said. She was a head taller than Wren, and half again as wide. Wren didn't know her real name, but her nickname was an apt descriptor. Rumors were she'd cut her husband into a hundred pieces before throwing them off the roof of a skyscraper in Old Boston.

Wren raised her hands in the air, ready to apologize, when the other woman's fist flew at her. Wren strained to avoid the impact, but she was too late. The meaty paw caught her cheek, and her eyes flashed red before she saw flickering stars. Wren's hand flew up defensively, but the next shot hit her in the side. Air pushed out of her lungs in an instant, and she felt her knee give way to a kick. The floor found her face, and she curled into a ball while the beating took place. It happened quickly, but the guards weren't there soon enough. Eventually, they arrived, breaking it up.

Every inch of Wren ached, and she painfully opened an eye to see Slicer being dragged away by an android. The large woman's body went limp. Another guard came to Wren's side, brandishing a needle. She felt a small prick penetrate her skin, and all went dark.

She woke in an unfamiliar room. Where was she? Had she fallen in her laboratory? Her injuries were numb, and her mind floated around, trying to recall exactly what happened. Then it hit her. She was in prison. Dread dripped down from her brain, enveloping her body, and she started to cry. The tears turned from sadness to full-on grief as her body was racked with heavy sobs. Her life was over, and for what?

It was the first time she'd let herself think about it since she arrived, and she cursed the drugs for letting her have this moment. She needed a barrier to separate who she used to be from who she had to be now.

Eventually, she stopped, the tears dried up, and she could feel the once-wet streaks tighten on her face. She felt empty; devoid of feeling. The room was dim, soft lights glowed from strips on the walls, and she noticed her feet were strapped to the table now: loosely, but enough to keep her from going anywhere.

The door slid open, and light footsteps entered the room. They weren't the heavyset stomps of the androids, and for a moment, Wren thought Slicer was back to finish the job. She found the energy to lift her drugged head, and saw a man wearing a suit casually standing a few feet from the end of the bed.

"Hello, Wren Sando." The man's voice was smooth, like he'd modified it to sound that way.

"Hello," she managed to croak out. Her throat was dry, and he moved to her side, passing her a thin tube attached to the side of the bed. She sucked on it, cool water hitting the back of her mouth.

"I'm sorry it had to go down like that," he said, and she didn't have any idea what he was talking about.

"What..." She cleared her throat. "What do you mean?"

"The altercation. I only told her to hit you, not try to kill you." The man's eyebrows were upturned, like he was trying to look concerned. He needed to work on his acting skills.

Wren tried to grasp what he was telling her. He'd set up the attack? "Why?" she got out.

"I needed to talk to you, and this way, it wouldn't look out of place," he said, as if that redeemed him from arranging her beating.

Her sadness was gone, quickly replaced with hatred. She stared daggers at him. "What do you want?"

"You are Wren Sando, correct?" he asked.

She managed a nod and took more water. "Doctor Wren Sando." As if the title gave her any more power.

"Then I want to speak with you. You worked in New Dallas as a biotechnologist?" the man asked.

"Who are you?" she countered.

"I know what you found. I know why you're here. I

can help you," he said, but the words fell cold. His face was too eager, and she focused on him now. He was older than his body was showing her and was clearly well-off or well-funded, because he'd had countless modifications. His eyes belied the truth. They were those of an eighty-year-old, not the forty-something he appeared.

"How can you help me? I don't even know who sent me here," she said, not allowing herself to feel hope.

"The testing you were working on. You know what it was. The vaccine he had you creating…" The man stopped as Wren cut him off.

"I was a biologist," she said, shaking her head. "No. I *am* a biologist, and it wasn't a vaccine."

He looked surprised. "Then what was it?"

She didn't want to talk about it. That was her old life. But what if he could help her? She decided to play along. Her situation clearly wasn't going to get any worse. "A weapon."

His eyes widened, and he nodded, as if some pieces to a mysterious puzzle fell into place before him. "Yes. That's it."

"What about it? How can you help me?" Wren asked, her heart beating fast.

"And you spoke out about it, correct? Who did you tell?" The man's hand came up, and she noticed something in it for the first time.

"Are you recording this?" she asked.

He looked abashed, as if she'd caught him doing something wrong. "I am. It needs to be. Otherwise, we can't stand against him."

"Who is 'him'?" Wren asked, but he shook his head.

"I asked you first. Who did you tell about the weapon they were having you build?" The smooth candor was gone from his voice. It was heavy now, rushed.

"Fairbanks. It was Councilman Jarden Fairbanks." It felt good to say his name. Wren had pictured the old man's face countless times over the years but hadn't said it out loud.

The man smiled widely. He clicked the recording object in his hand and slid it into his inside breast pocket. "It seems our paths align, my dear." The door slid open and he turned from the room, leaving her alone.

"You said you could help me!" she called from the bed. An android guard stepped into the room, walking to her side, and she felt the now-familiar sting of a needle biting into her shoulder. "Help me," she managed to get out before everything went dark once again.

CD6

CD6 scanned for 5589 as he stood at the edge of the dining hall. She was nowhere in sight. This was her confirmed time to be eating, and Prisoner 3659 was sitting by herself. They always ate together. CD6 didn't know how to feel about this. Being in a prison, one got used to the routines. He liked watching 5589 as she kept her eyes down, smiling when she spoke to her friend.

CD6 wondered what that was like, having a friend to talk with. He glanced over to BE13 at the other end of the dining hall and saw nothing but a cold, impassive android. Why was he different? The doors opened, and two guards stepped through with a prisoner between them. Her feet shuffled, and she stumbled to the line, where mechanical arms dumped food on a metal tray as she held it under them.

5589 wound her way through the tables, and the entire room of three hundred went silent. Each dragging footstep was accentuated in the silence, and 3659 met her beside the table, helping her to sit. Wren's face was puffy, a bandage wrapped around her forehead. CD6 worried for her. He knew that emotions weren't something he was supposed to concern himself with. It was a biological response to a situation, but regardless of his programming, he felt it.

The visiting man had left the day prior, and CD6 hadn't been able to determine who he was. He'd sneaked off in the night to attempt to dig through the prison's records, but none had been made about the stranger. He'd had to hide as a patrol guard walked by him, and CD6 had never been so afraid in his life.

Life. He wondered why he even considered what he had here a life. He was worse off than the prisoners.

He stood still, watching the room, but secretly focusing on Wren Sando. Her head was down, facing her plate as she ate slowly at first, then with feverish hunger. CD6 felt sorry for the woman and made a decision there and then. He read his internal clock and started a countdown until power-off time for his rotation.

Ace

Ace had never left Old Chicago, let alone Earth. The trip took a few hours, and the whole time, Ace sat on the sideways-facing bench beside Serina, strapped in like everyone else, wearing the exact same uniform as the rest of them. He looked to the left and then to the right, and realized he was now part of something much bigger than he'd even dreamed. These were now his people. He hadn't been a part of something like this since he was a little child, and even then, he couldn't consider his family a blessing.

Twice he slid the ace of clubs from his pocket and

idly rubbed the top left corner of it with his thumb. The second time Serina glanced over at him, looking like she was about to say something, then stopped herself. He'd left it in his pocket since then. Now he fidgeted with the seatbelt, his nervous energy threatening to make him explode.

An officer – a lieutenant, if he was reading the stars on her collar correctly – walked down the aisle, telling them they were about to land on the moon base. Ace felt his heart thrum, and he smiled wide at Serina. He couldn't get a read off the girl. She was too good-looking and obviously too important to talk with a scrub like him, but she didn't dismiss him like everyone else did. She looked back at him with kind eyes, as if she'd sat in a Fleet drop transport carrier her whole life.

Then it hit him. She had.

Serina was the daughter of someone in the Earth Fleet. It seemed so obvious now, but Ace decided to ask her about it later. He couldn't wait to hear her stories of the excitement and adventure her childhood must have brought.

As the ship lowered, he wondered at his own back story. He didn't know much about Edgar Smith. Would the authorities find his body in the alley back home and figure out his identity? Even though he'd removed the ID, Ace knew there were other ways for them to find out who it was. He was banking on the fact that it was in a rough neighborhood, where people ended up dead all the time. The patrols didn't have the time or resources to solve every random death, and Ace hoped that was true for this case.

He'd have to think up some story, because he couldn't tell them he was a sixteen-year-old street rat. His head began to pound as he worried he'd be caught. Up until then, he'd been running on adrenaline and the thrill of getting into the Fleet. He chided himself for not having a better plan. If he was going to make this work, he needed to be smarter, more careful.

The ship touched down, and his seatbelt automatically released. "Everyone stay seated. We're getting off in single file," the lieutenant shouted.

Serina set a hand on his arm. "This place is such a dump."

Ace was surprised. "What? The moon base?"

She nodded. "This is the only place the Fleet can torment the new recruits without any prying eyes. Did you know that only twenty percent of recruits make it to the next stage?"

Ace hadn't known that, and he shook his head, which went from a small headache to a pounding drum as she told him this.

"You'll be fine. If you're serious about a career, work hard. That's what my mother always says. 'The cream always rises to the top' is her favorite saying." Serina looked forward, her eyes going unfocused.

"Why are you doing this?" Ace asked her quietly. The recruit on his other side looked from Serina, then to Ace, and rolled his eyes. Ace lowered his voice more so no one could hear him. "Why are you being so nice?"

Serina turned, locking eyes with him. "Because you remind me of someone."

"This row, on your feet. We march out. On three," the lieutenant shouted, and Ace fumbled up, his legs half-asleep after the long ride. He didn't have a chance to ask her more as they stepped off the large ship into a see-through corridor connecting the ship to a massive dome. He'd heard about the colonies but had only seen a handful of images during his time on the streets. He'd never had access to the Interface, so his knowledge of the outer worlds was limited to what he'd heard, which consisted of rumors from drunken street thugs.

Beyond the corridor's clear resin, he could see the surface of the moon. The dust and rock were beautiful in their dull tones, and Ace thought he'd never seen something so special. He was on the moon, joining the Fleet. He wanted to pinch himself but worried he'd wake up cold and hungry on the doorstep of an abandoned church if he did.

They marched, a clumsy attempt to stay in step with each other through the tunnel and into the massive dome. He didn't know how large it was, but the edges had no end from where he was standing. It carried on in all directions for countless miles. He didn't even want to know how long it had taken to construct such a thing.

The recruits were standing in rows, directed by two-star officers, each wearing a frown. Ace took a quick count and guessed there were a hundred and fifty of them standing there, each fresh-faced and gawking at their surroundings. There were hovering vehicles and squat buildings nearby, looking much more advanced than the boot camp he'd been picturing. They stood there until the next ship came, doubling their numbers to three hundred recruits.

Ace spotted the goons cockily walking into the dome, one of them catching his eye before getting in line.

One of the vehicles floated from a large flat-roofed building, and the officers all saluted the man who stepped off it onto the ground. Ace saw three full stars and a half-moon on his collar, and saluted the commander with the rest of the recruits.

"Welcome to the Fleet, recruits. I am Commander Evan Bryenton. This is the moon, where you'll be conducting your introduction to the Fleet. Think of this as a tryout. You've all been through school before, so you have a basic understanding of what a curriculum is. Here we have classes, and you will be graded on them." The commander spoke loudly and clearly, as if he'd said the same speech a hundred times before. He was an older man, Ace guessed in his sixties, but he still looked fit and dangerous. His eyes were dark and deep-set; his brow cast a shadow over his upper face.

Ace was excited. He couldn't wait to start whatever it was they were about to go through. He hoped his malnourished body would be able to sustain him through it.

The commander continued. "We want to see what each of you has to offer us. There are many divisions of the Fleet, so think of this as an aptitude test. You've all heard the numbers, so look around and know that out of five of you standing here, only one will make it through."

Ace looked around him, and saw the shuffling of feet followed by nervous whispers. Commander Bryenton let it go and kept talking. "Out of three hundred, we'll invite sixty of you to join the Fleet in some capacity. This number isn't firm, but it is realistic. Which of you has what it takes to be Earth Fleet?" he asked, and Ace raised his hand. For a second, he felt foolish, but the rest of the recruits soon joined him, until all three hundred arms were in the air. The commander locked eyes with him for a moment before breaking into a thin smile.

"Good. Then we'll start by running. Lieutenant Ford will lead you. Follow him. Do the run, and we'll get you fed and find you a bunk. Welcome to Earth Fleet boot camp." Commander Bryenton saluted them and turned, leaving in his hovercar.

Serina was still beside Ace, and she leaned to speak in his ear. "Pace yourself. This is going to hurt."

Lieutenant Ford, a younger man with sparkling white teeth, smiled widely at them from the seat of a hoverbike. "Recruits, with me. This isn't a competition, but I've been doing this for ten years, and the first one to complete this run has made it through boot camp one hundred percent of the time. It will also determine your squadrons, so do your best." With that, he revved the bike and advanced forward, along the left edge of the clear dome.

Ace started out in the middle of the pack; Serina ran ahead, easily dodging through the crowded throng of runners. He'd run enough in his short life, but usually from someone, not for a competition. He was glad he'd eaten a lot for breakfast that morning, indulging on Edgar's credits before leaving Old Chicago behind.

Ace thought about the advice from Serina and slowed down, his legs moving with less urgency now, in a rhythm. He glanced outside the dome as he ran along its edge. The sun was beyond, glaring brightly, and Ace noticed the dome had a tint to it. He wondered if it auto-adjusted the tint depending on where the sun was facing.

The other recruits were pulling ahead now. He had no idea how long this race would go on, so he kept his slower pace. After a mile or so, nothing outside the dome had changed, and he started to look inside it. At first, there had been buildings, barracks, and other military offices. Now he saw testing fields: tracks, target shooting, and various other setups ran deep into the dome.

There were no other recruits around him, and he glanced back to see the herd thinning, many people falling to the side. He passed one girl who was bent over retching. Ace averted his gaze and kept moving. After a while, he saw runners ahead. A few of them ran smoothly, but more were wearing out. His recently-issued boots were starting to chafe his feet, but Ace kept going. They were much better than the taped-together shoes he'd been wearing two days ago.

Ace tried to gauge how far they'd run, but he couldn't. At his best guess, it had been four miles. His legs were burning, his chest on fire, but he kept moving. He wasn't there to be an inactive participant. He wasn't there for a few weeks of free food, only to be sent back home with nothing to show for it. He was going to make the Earth Fleet.

There were more structures on the ground now. Four-story complexes rose up from the rocks, and he even saw grass and trees. Another mile, and he saw something that surprised him. Crops. There were rows and rows of greenhouses, water dripping down the glass ceilings as he trudged by. His breaths were coming long and deep now as his lungs fought for air, and he could smell the fresh loam and soil, rejuvenating him.

The moon base was quite the spectacle, and Ace wondered if the Fleet made them do this run so the recruits could get a good look at their temporary home. Of course, they'd have to work for it.

Ace looked back to the path and had to jump to avoid a fallen runner. The man looked five years older than Ace, and he had a light beard. He saw the guy stumble to his feet and press a hand against the dome, trying to keep moving.

Ace was beginning to wear out. He couldn't keep going forever. His feet ached; blisters were forming, but he didn't stop. This was different for him than for most of the recruits. He knew he'd be dead if left to the streets much longer.

It had been at least an hour and a half by the time he saw the end. He'd passed countless recruits; some were out, sitting on the ground, others walking slowly. It was only when he crossed a line with a few Fleet officers standing there, marking things down on tablets, that he realized he was done. He kept running for a minute, his legs not accepting his brain's command to slow.

Seeing Serina leaning against the dome convinced his worn body to halt. He tried to stay on his feet, to look like a tough guy in front of the girl, but his legs betrayed him. He stood grinning at her one minute, his chest heaving; the next, he was on his face in the dirt.

"What took you so long?" she asked, kneeling down beside him.

"How did I do?" Ace croaked out.

"You didn't win, if that's what you want to know," she said.

Of course Ace hadn't won. That thought hadn't even crossed his mind. The only thing he wanted to do was finish, and not in last place.

Serina helped him to his wobbly feet as an officer came over. "Nice work…" The officer scanned a tablet. "Smith. You finished ninth. Good enough to be in the top three percent. You're with Blue Squadron." She passed a patch to him, and Serina smiled, flashing her matching blue patch at him.

The officer left the two of them standing there while more people crossed the finish line. Serina clapped him on the back. "Looks like we're on the same team, Ace."

5

Flint

"What are we supposed to do with this information?" Kat asked for the third time that day.

Flint didn't answer her this time. "Wait. Did you check for hidden files?" Why hadn't he thought of that? With the obvious video file on there, he'd assumed that was all they could find on the stick. Now he wasn't so sure.

Kat shook her head. "I didn't. You don't think..." She left it unsaid. She got up and crossed to the console they'd been working on the day before. "These old sticks had backdoors. It was a flaw in the original design, and often people used them to keep the real files from finding the light of day. Not many knew about the issue. Eventually, the manufacturers fixed the glitch, and you couldn't hide a file any longer."

Flint was aware of this and was furious he hadn't thought of it earlier. They'd hardly slept the night before; the video they'd seen appeared every time he shut his eyes. Aliens were visiting and had been for a long time. Were they hostile? What did it mean?

"Anything?" he asked, hoping she came up empty-handed. He wasn't sure he wanted any more details.

Kat didn't say a word for a moment, but her deep intake of breath gave her away.

"What is it?" he asked, moving behind her.

"There's more here." Kat tapped a video link, and a similar setup appeared before them.

This one was date-stamped August 2nd, 2415. "That's thirty years later," Kat said, and they watched with heavy concentration.

Again, a man and a woman were on the feed. The man spoke. "*I am Commander Fairbanks, and this is Admiral Palmer.*" He motioned to the elderly woman beside him. The ship's bridge was much like the previous one, but a newer model. Flint recognized it from videos and museums he'd seen. The sound cut out, and the two of them watched the video's subjects' mouths move with no audio. The image flickered a few times, brief clips of their voices coming through. "*…hidden… probe… home…*" But as quickly as the sound came back, it was gone again.

"What's wrong?" Kat asked.

"Old feed, or some distortion when they were recording." Flint paused the video, closing the program and restarting it. The results were the same. Soon the image blacked out, and when it came back on seconds later, the shot had changed from the bridge to a ship in space. It had Earth Fleet symbols on the sides, and Flint couldn't believe how large it was.

"Wow," he whispered as the massive vessel flew slowly by the still camera angle. He wasn't sure just how large it was, but he guessed at least two kilometers in length. Maybe longer.

"Are they going into a battle?" Kat asked, worry sewn into her tone.

"That doesn't look like a warship," Flint answered.

"Then what? Exploratory?"

Kat was on the right track. Flint tapped the video into reverse and smiled to himself. "It's carrying people." He flipped to a different screen, tapping keys until the Interface was open. "Remember hearing all those conspiracy theorists going on about the odd happenings at the Ganymede colony after the turn of the century?"

Kat nodded along.

"Follow me here. The colony disappeared, leaving it empty. How many people was it again?" Flint found the resource on the Interface and opened the file. His finger ran along the screen, and he tapped it. "Over two thousand men, women, and children vanished" – he snapped his fingers together – "just like that. No one ever knew what happened to them. The government said it was a virus, trapped within the domes and killing everyone before a cure could be found."

"What about it?" Kat asked.

"Don't you see?" Flint found a different section of the file and showed her. "They never had any bodies. They backed it up with some story about needing to keep the corpses for testing, and a few weeks later, they told a story about having to incinerate them all in space to keep the infection from spreading past the colony on Ganymede."

"Are you suggesting those people didn't die? That they were… what, used in a government cover-up?" Kat asked.

Flint went back to the video and pressed *play*; the large vessel rolled across space in front of the camera again. "That's exactly what I'm suggesting."

The video cut out, and Flint cursed. He wanted to see what happened.

"This is insane." Kat took his seat as he stood, and Flint could tell she was trying to see if there was a way to repair the damaged file.

"Did you see the date?" he asked her, now pacing

across the short bridge.

"August second, 2415."

"And what's the date today?" he asked.

She looked back at him with understanding in her eyes. "June thirtieth, 2475. That means…"

Flint nodded. "It means another sixty years has passed since that video. If what they said in the first one still stands, then the aliens come every thirty years." Just what had happened sixty years ago on that video? And what had happened the last time, thirty years earlier still? More importantly, as he headed toward Jupiter, he somehow felt connected to what was about to happen in a month.

"I don't like this, Flint," Kat said softly.

"I don't either. Keep playing with the files, and see if you find anything else," he said.

"What are you going to do?" She sounded nervous.

He started to walk back to his quarters, a comp tablet in his hand. "I'm going to find out everything I can on this Fairbanks and Palmer. There has to be something that can fill in the blanks."

Jarden

"Activate the drive," Captain Young said, lifting a hand in the air before quickly dropping it to his side. Councilman Jarden Fairbanks sat on the edge of the bridge, letting the crew do what they were paid to do. He was content to be a silent witness to the test jump.

Only the slightest vibrations in his seat's arms told him anything had changed on the ship. Jarden smiled wide, baring his pearly white teeth. Yes. He was so close. The drive had worked once before, and he was going to make sure this one would as well. The amount of time and resources that had gone into getting those initial colony ship blueprints had been astronomical.

He'd called in every favor, every back scratch and bribe he could; all the while, no one knew what he'd really been after. Even now, the rest of the Fleet and the government had no clue that Councilman Fairbanks was out here. He smiled again, thinking about the guile needed to pull off something of this magnitude. He wasn't an arrogant man, but he did appreciate his ability to get a job done.

"Drive is ready, sir. Prepare to launch. On your mark." First Officer Barkley stood at a console and glanced back at Young, awaiting his command.

"Now. Launch." Young briefly glanced to Jarden, a look of pride on his face. Fairbanks was going to love replacing him. Young was a tool, and not one he wanted to keep in his toolbox for the extended trip.

The viewscreen covered in blue energy, and now the ship vibrated fiercely. Something was wrong! They didn't have time for an issue now. There was only a short window before they needed to make the real jump.

As Jarden sat, concerned over the errors someone in engineering must have made, the viewscreen flashed white and blinked. When it flashed back, they were a thousand kilometers in front of a large asteroid, the very same they'd set as their destination.

It worked… Jarden stood up, his hands shaking. His hand found purchase on the arm of the chair, balancing him. "It worked," he whispered. The bridge was silent: the ten officers on board didn't move, let alone dare to breathe for a moment. "It worked!" he shouted now, the rest of the crew joining him in congratulations.

They were happy, but little did they know just how a big a step this was for humanity. Jarden walked up to the captain, his legs working once again, the initial surprise shaken from his old body. "Well done, Young. Take us back the long way. I don't want to risk damaging anything before we run an analysis."

"Yes, sir," Young said.

As Jarden left the bridge, he heard Young shout out a series of commands, but Jarden hardly heard them.

"I'm coming. I'm coming." He kept repeating the words under his breath as he worked his way off the bridge.

Wren

Wren was surprised at the special treatment. She'd seen inmates suffer from beatings, but they always arrived from the infirmary days later and were thrown right back into the work schedule.

"Are you sure? I don't want to break any rules," she said to the android guard. It held a tablet and pointed to it, showing her number highlighted in red.

"You are not assigned to work detail until tomorrow. Vacate the area or you will be assigned a demerit." The monotone voice stopped talking, indicating the conversation was over.

Wren turned on a heel and walked back down the hallway, expecting a guard to stop her. None did. The door opened, allowing her back toward the common area, where inmates could relax for short periods throughout the day when they weren't working, eating, or locked in their cells.

A few others were there, their shifts different than hers. Truth was, Wren didn't know if she worked a night shift or a day shift. There really wasn't such a thing out here, and it took a while to get used to.

An older woman, with frown lines so deep they looked like scars, motioned her over. "Sando," she said, her voice dry and raspy.

"West," Wren replied.

"No one's seen Slicer," West said, and Wren found herself shrugging.

"What do I care? She attacked me." Wren felt the fresh cut on her forehead pucker as she frowned.

"Kinda strange, ain't it?" the old lady asked.

"I just want to mind my own. Have a good day." Wren walked away, crossing the room. She passed the empty tables and chairs, heading for a small, worn sofa at the end of the space. It was quiet over there, no one to bug her. She sat down, feeling the tender bruises from her beating, and tried to determine what had happened.

Slicer wouldn't have attacked her without reason, or at least Wren didn't think so. Things had been so blurry while she'd been in recovery, but she was certain a man had come to visit her. Had he arranged the beating so he could talk to her? Then she recalled the name she'd given the man, and how quickly he'd left after she'd shouted the councilman's name.

Wren's head pounded, and she closed her eyes, trying to ease the pain. Traces of medication still lingered in her bloodstream, and she found herself drifting off as she sat there. Dreams came fitfully as she slept: of a life long gone and a future she would never have.

When she woke some time later, her eyes darted open fearfully. She breathed a sigh of relief as she found the open room empty of prisoners.

A mechanical noise coming from beside her caught her attention, and she turned to it, her head going light at the sudden movement.

"Hello, Wren," the android said without looking at

her. His hand rested on his weapon as it always did, but only one guard had ever called her by her real name.

She sat up, feet flat on the floor. She stared forward as she spoke, not wanting to draw attention to her conversation in case watchful eyes were prying. "What do you want?"

"I want to help," came the reply.

"Help with what? I can't be helped," Wren said, her looming headache coming back in a flash.

"You don't belong here. I want to help." The voice was even, but she could still sense the intensity behind it.

"Who are you? I don't understand. You're an android. One of *them*. Who put you up to this?" Wren spat out the series of inquiries.

"I am CD6. No one has put me up to anything. I can tell you shouldn't be in prison. I shouldn't be here either," he said.

"Why not?"

His answer came quickly. "Because I don't belong here. I'm different from the other guards." His voice was low, and she glanced back at him. He was still staring forward.

Her heart raced, pain shooting into the back of her eyes with each fast pulse. "What do you expect to do?"

He didn't answer right away, and she almost hoped he was done with his contact. After twenty seconds, he replied, "We can leave. I've found a way."

Her throat closed as tears formed in her eyes. Leave? How could they possibly leave? It was impossible. But maybe… with the help of an android… "How?"

The door opened, and another guard entered the room, followed by the newly-ended shift workers. These ones came from the processing plant and were wearing light brown jumpsuits. He moved now, speaking softly as he went by her. "Be ready."

His words rang in her mind as he strode out of the room, past the other guard and through the doors, out of her life as quickly as he'd appeared.

"Where were you today?" Mara asked at dinner time. Her younger friend's cheeks were red, her eyes sad and puffy.

"I wasn't on the work schedule." Wren poked at the lumpy food on her tray and felt something other than hopelessness for the first time in two years. She felt hope, and from the words of an android. She shook her head and ran a finger over the bandage still wrapped over her forehead. She must be crazy. There was no way a guard had actually talked to her. She was going insane. Still, even with her half-thinking she might indeed have gone off the deep end, she clung to the feeling of hope, like a life vest in the middle of the ocean back home.

Mara looked up at her, scrunching her nose. "That's strange, isn't it?"

Wren shrugged.

"Where's Slicer?" Mara asked.

Wren was getting tired of the incessant questions but didn't want to yell at her only friend inside the prison, so she forced a smile. "Hopefully out the airlock."

Mara's mouth formed a surprised O, and then she laughed too. "Wren, stop it. What did you do to get her angry with you?"

"Nothing. I bumped into her."

Mara appeared to think about this as she sculpted a volcano from her powder-turned-slop, and didn't respond. They sat in silence for a few minutes, Wren finally eating something off her plate. Once she started eating, her healing body demanded she finish.

"Guards were talking about double shift starting tomorrow." Mara let out a sigh, air billowing her cheeks before sending a few pieces of slop flying.

"Double shifts? They've never done those before." Wren was uncomfortable with all the changes recently. First she saw a man in the prison; then an android spoke to her like she was a human, not a number. Then the beating, followed by the drug-infused interrogation, and now this. She felt like she was a tiny cog in a much larger wheel, and she wondered what the big picture was.

"West said this happened thirty-odd years ago. Earth Fleet demanded more material for their ships. Prisons produce eighty percent of the metals used on their fleet ships. Or at least, that's what the guards told us once." Mara pushed her plate forward and dropped her utensil in the center of the slop pile with a splash.

"They're ramping up production for something," Wren whispered to herself. Mara didn't seem to notice, but Wren put the pieces together. The special project she'd been in charge of at New Dallas was part of it. This much was clear. But if she was working on a theoretical virus to wipe out a specific type of DNA two years ago, and the military was increasing their ship production, then…

Wren's tired eyes sprang open. They were preparing for something.

She saw the helix in her mind's eye. She'd had nightmares from the brief time she'd seen the images on Darnel's monitor. Of course, that was the same time her laboratory had been compromised. She could still close her eyes and see the bullet entering Darnel's head as the Patrol walked in behind the Fleet troops.

She remembered arguing before being thrown in

handcuffs and dragged away. She knew she would have been dead beside her assistant if the Patrol hadn't shown up. The Fleet were there to take her lab results and cover up the project; of that she had no doubt.

Now it all came clear. Her study wasn't hypothetical or theoretical. It was real.

Earth Fleet was preparing for an invasion.

6

Ace

His bed was small, and most of the others had complained about the size of their cots. Ace had quietly cried into his pillow the first night and the second: happy tears that he was sleeping on a mattress, regardless of its diminutive size. His luck had changed so drastically, and no one would ever understand where he'd come from. To them, he was Edgar Smith, a kid who grew up in Old Chicago but had gone to school, had a home and a family.

The idea that the real Edgar Smith's family would be grieving their missing son helped his tears flow that first night, but he couldn't do anything for them now. He'd stolen the boy's ID and wouldn't go back. Never. By the third night, he was too exhausted to cry, and he fell asleep as soon as his head hit the lumpy pillow.

When morning came, which was somewhere around 5 AM, he was woken by the sounds of his squadron's drill instructor. Time didn't seem the same on the moon base. Lieutenant Deso was an imposing character: thick arms and legs, and a barrel chest. His gray jumpsuit looked like it was going to explode at any moment.

"Get your sorry asses out of bed. Do you think this is Saturday morning back home? Are you waiting for your mommy to call you down for cereal and holotoons? Get to it!" Deso yelled, and Ace found himself smiling. This was his ideal Saturday, and he didn't ever remember waking up on a weekend to feel safe and comfortable without a care in the world.

"What's up his butt?" Buck, a young recruit in the bunk below Ace's, asked as he swung down to the floor, landing softly.

"Just doing his job," Ace said, slipping into his jumpsuit. He wished he could sleep in it so he didn't have to change in front of his squad. He was by far the smallest one here. The runt of the litter. He glanced over to Serina's bunk, which sat across the small room. She was standing there stretching, her jumpsuit folded down to the waist. Ace felt a rush of heat, and he quickly averted his eyes.

Buck wasn't done. "I still think he's a jerk."

Ace didn't respond. They formed a line, Serina at the front. She'd been voted squad commander the first night, and it didn't have anything to do with the fact that she was the only one who'd volunteered. Ace knew no one else had wanted to go against her. She'd won the race, and that was enough for them all to establish her as their leader.

They marched in unison, heading out of the small bunk and down the halls, where other squadrons were getting in line and funneling outside at the same time.

In a couple minutes, they were under the dome, and Ace found himself staring above. Nothing but space all around them. Outside that dome was certain death, and he shoved the fear back inside. He wasn't going to make it into Earth Fleet with worries about dying in space. He had more immediate things to concern himself with, like surviving until breakfast.

"Good. Nice of you all to make it," Lieutenant Deso

shouted to his squad. Ace could hear the other lieutenants doing the same routine, and he blocked their yells from his mind. He'd focus only on Deso. "We have a game this morning. If you finish, then you can eat. Clear?"

"Yes, sir!" Blue Squadron shouted in near-perfect unison.

"I can't hear you!" Deso shouted back.

"Yes, sir!" they repeated, this time fully in sync.

"Good. Capture-the-Flag is an age-old game, used for years as a training tool. We have our own version." Deso opened a box beside him and pulled out a gun. Ace's heart beat faster in his chest as he watched Deso tap a button by the trigger. The gun was slightly larger than a pistol, and the side lit up green as he brought it to life. "This is a stunner. Shoot someone with this gun, and they're frozen in their footsteps for ten seconds. Who wants to volunteer?" he asked.

When no one stepped forward, Ace glanced to the right, where he saw another recruit from another squad being shot with one. It didn't look so bad.

"Shoot me, sir!" Ace bellowed, and the recruit in front of him stepped to the side.

"Smith. Very well." Deso didn't give warning; he just fired, hitting the recruit in front of Ace. The girl, Casey Keller, had raised a hand out in front of her, and she was now frozen in place, a green glow surrounding her. "No one said I was a good shot. If I was, maybe I wouldn't be teaching a bunch of snot-nosed kids on the moon."

Ace's heart slowed, and he found himself fighting back a smile. In a few seconds, Casey was free from the pulse, and she coughed, her hand flying to her face. She stepped back in line, though Ace could tell her legs were wobbly.

"Thank you, Recruit Keller. Everyone grab a stunner

and get into the transport. You'll be facing Yellow today. Remember, there's no prison in this game. You get stunned, you're done. Got it?" Lieutenant Deso handed out the guns, and Ace held one in his hand, the weight strange in his grip.

"Ace, where are you?" Serina's voice carried through the headset.

His back was pressed against a tree. They'd been brought to a forest. Ace couldn't believe it. A forest on the moon. It was amazing. He quickly forgot about it as the game began. Then he was on a life-or-death mission to capture Yellow's flag, which turned out to be a glowing yellow orb sitting on top of a barn-like structure deep into their end of the forest.

Barriers were set up, and Ace could see another game going on twenty yards to his left. Green versus Purple. He watched as a Green female recruit was sneaked up on and stunned. He took a deep breath and replied to Serina.

"I see the flag. There are at least three of them guarding the structure. If I can get close enough, I think I can get up there, but I need some cover." He leaned around the tree and spotted two of his own team: one behind the barn, and Serina across the field to his right.

"We can give you cover. Get the flag, pass it down, and I'll run for it." Serina's confident voice carried through.

Buck announced himself as the recruit behind the barn. "I've got your back, Ace."

They'd stuck to calling him by his nickname, Serina doing him the favor by using it first. Whatever she did, the rest followed. He owed her again.

"Fire to the right, I'm coming in from the left." Ace moved around the treeline, avoiding detection in the open field where the opponents were watching. Green blasts shot out from Serina's location, then from Buck's. Return fire blasted at them.

Ace was now just at the edge of the barn, and he spotted footholds along the building's side. The coast looked clear, and he sprinted for the wall. A Yellow raced toward him from around the wall. He'd been hidden from Ace's vantage point. Instead of randomly firing like the incoming recruit was doing, Ace dive-rolled and ended on his belly. His attacker kept coming, but his legs were moving too fast for him to stop, and he tumbled to the ground five yards in front of Ace.

Ace watched the guy's stunner fly from his hand, and he didn't waste any time. He fired at him from close range, seeing the boy's eyes widen and freeze. He hurried back to the wall, and his feet found purchase in the slots, easily scaling it to the roof.

"I'm up," he whispered into the mic.

"They found me!" Buck called, and went silent. It was just Ace and Serina left.

"Get it, Ace. I'll enter the field in twenty seconds," Serina said. "There's still one down here. I dealt with the other."

Ace scrabbled up the pitched roof, his feet sliding on the tin sheets. He raced toward the yellow orb and smiled. They were so close.

He saw Serina's form running from the cover of the forest, and into the open space in front of the barn. A Yellow recruit stepped from the trees in what looked like slow motion. She hadn't seen him.

Ace panicked and sealed his own fate. "Up here, you ugly bastard!" He waved his arms, jumping up and down behind the prize flag.

It was enough to grab the opposition's attention. Stun fire coursed through the air toward him, and he ducked, grabbing the orb. It was the size of a soccer ball and weighed next to nothing. Serina was running now, away from the barn, and Ace lined up the throw, putting what strength he had in his small body behind it.

Just before the orb left his grip, the stunner blast hit, freezing his body and taking him out of the game. His frozen eyes watched as the orb sailed through the air, into Serina's outstretched hands. She ran like the wind, heading back for their own camp.

Ace unfroze as she disappeared into the forest, and he slumped to the roof, lying on his back on the tin. In a minute, he heard the lieutenant's voice carry through his headset. "Congratulations, Blue. You have defeated Yellow."

"That was amazing, Ace." Buck's eyes were wide as Serina told the story of their victory to the surrounding tables. She was up on her feet as the rest ate a late dinner, the excessive training done for the day.

Ace shifted uncomfortably in his seat, shying away from the attention. "I got stunned, so I don't know how special I was."

Serina was the one to bring the spotlight back to him. "You climbed the roof, took the fire from their guard to protect me, and threw a perfect pass. It doesn't get better."

He shrugged, and the tables around them went back to their meals, a few people from other squadrons even slapping him on the back in congratulations.

When it was just Buck, Serina, and a few other Blues left at the table, Ace lowered his voice. "Where does this put us?"

Buck grabbed a spoonful of steamed vegetables and shoved them in his mouth, continuing to speak. "In the rankings?"

Ace nodded. Each squad was tiered in their training challenges, but he'd been avoiding looking. He wanted to do his best each time and not worry about scores. At the end of boot camp, the Fleet told them, their personal fate wasn't determined by their squadron's final rank.

Serina answered. "We're tied for first with Orange." She looked across the room full of recruits. They were allowed to make noise tonight, let off a little steam, Sarge had told them: no booze, no sex, but they could talk amongst each other for the first time. Ace followed her gaze to Orange. They were silent at their tables, eating food, otherwise sitting still.

"Looks like they're ruled by an iron fist," Buck said.

A short dark-haired girl, Trin, tapped the table with her finger beside Ace. Her eyes were huge, making the rest of her face seem too small. Her voice was little more than a squeak. "We're going to kick their asses, right, Serina?"

Serina looked back and smiled. "Yes. We are. And every one of us is going to make it through boot camp."

Ace was doubtful. They had a few people that had made the top twenty in the first-day run, but their luck had seemed to run out then. Taco, a skinny red-haired boy, had been stunned in record time during their Capture-the-Flag exercise, and had been late for curfew twice already. Ace had a feeling the kid was going to get the boot sooner rather than later.

"How many are gone so far?" Ace asked.

"Overall? Seven." Serina seemed to know a lot about what was going on. Ace had seen Lieutenant Ford talking with her a few times, likely giving her the details.

Seven. That wasn't many, but they'd only landed here a few days ago.

"Ace, you want the rest of my food? I don't have an appetite," Serina said, and slid her tray over to him. He'd been scooping every square inch of the tray, getting each morsel onto his fork. He hadn't had consistent food like this in years, and he couldn't have been happier. He was already gaining weight.

Ace didn't reply; he just accepted the offered tray with a grateful glance at Serina and started in on it, slower this time.

When he was done, he ran a hand over his recently shorn hair, feeling self-conscious. He wasn't able to hide behind the greasy strands over his eyes any longer, blending into a wall when needed. He tried to think he didn't need to do that any longer, but when he looked up, two of the goons from the line back on Earth were staring at him from two tables over. The larger one whispered to the one with a tattoo on his neck, and when he laughed, a vein throbbed in his forehead. Of course, they were part of Orange.

Ace suddenly felt it all crash back into him: his father, the street thugs, the hunger, and the cold.

7

Flint

Flint had been through a lot in his fifteen years aboard his own ship, *Perdita*. His eyes were closed, his mind drifting in and out of a light sleep, never quite reaching REM. He'd spent the last day researching those names, and anything he could find revolving around the people in the century-old videos, but he didn't feel any closer to having answers.

If the Earth Fleet was behind it all, they'd gone to extensive lengths to keep it hidden from the public. Sure, he'd stumbled on some old Interface caches where conspiracy theorists hinted at an alien invasion, but the details were almost nonexistent, letting him assume they were talking out of their asses instead of having any concrete facts.

He turned on the cot, pulling the covers over his head. He remembered getting the blanket from a woman on Mars Minor years ago. She'd made it by hand, selling them for food credits, and it was still as warm and comfortable as it had been when he'd first slept under it. He let his memories carry him into a fitful slumber, and soon he was out cold.

He awoke some time later to an abnormal jostling of the ship. "What the hell is that?" he asked out loud. He strode out of the small quarters and found Kat coming toward him down the corridor, a worried expression on her face.

"Flint, I didn't want to wake you at first. I was seeing some anomalies on the sensors, but…" Kat's words were rushed and full of panic.

"What is it?" Flint asked urgently.

"Someone's boarded us."

"How could they have gotten close enough to board us?" Even if they'd both been sleeping, the ship would have alerted them as soon as another vessel was within a thousand kilometers of their course.

"That's what I'm saying. I saw a couple of blips on the screen, but they disappeared as quickly as they came. That always means it's just space junk. I avoided it, and we were good," Kat stammered out.

"How long ago was this?" he asked.

"An hour, I think."

He ran down the corridor and found engineering: a compact room filled to the rafters with add-on components to improve his base-model ship. The tablet on the wall was his destination.

"Where are they?" he asked himself, and Kat was behind him, her breath quickening.

"I couldn't tell."

Flint flipped the screen to a diagnostic check of the ventilators and manually overrode the timed ventilation pattern. Dirty air cycled out of the vents, quickly telling him where there was back pressure. He could have searched all the camera feeds, but this was the fastest way to see where the ship had docked on *Perdita.*

"They're near the cargo bay." Flint looked down, wishing he wasn't running around his ship in bare feet, wearing nothing but a tank top and shorts. "We need guns."

He stuck his head out of engineering and listened. He had to put a finger to his mouth and shush his sidekick, as her breathing was all he could hear. The boarding ship was cutting into the exterior. He could hear them trying to breach his bay door. How could this happen? They were two days out from their destination, Europa. There was always the worry of space pirates, but there wasn't enough traffic back and forth between the colonies since most of them had become self-sufficient.

To wait for a target in the middle of deep space was a death sentence. It left only one explanation. They knew who he was, and they'd been waiting for him to pass through. He turned right instead of left, back to a room beside the bridge. His fingerprint scanned, the lock flashed green, and the door clicked open.

He grabbed a portable O2 mask and passed one to Kat. She looked at him like he was crazy.

"Put it on. I have a plan." Flint shoved his under his left arm and grabbed two handheld guns. He hadn't needed one of these in a long time. When he'd first started the gig, there'd been more sketchy scenarios than he could count on both hands. Now he was established, with discreet clients, and the need for weapons was mostly a thing of the past. Until now.

He checked the weapons' charges, and when satisfied, he thrust one at Kat. She suddenly looked much younger than twenty-five, her big eyes wide with fear. "Wear the mask, hold the gun, and hide. You know where to go."

She nodded, following his orders. "Flint?"

"What?"

"Be careful." She ran off toward the bridge, where the secret safe room was located. It was custom built, and no one would know it existed. He had half a mind to join her down there, but to what end? If their ship was taken over, he wasn't going down without a fight.

He ran to the bridge now, sitting down in the pilot seat. "Where are you?" he asked, scanning through the camera feeds. He rarely used this feature and had almost forgotten it existed. He found the one outside the cargo bay and switched to it. "Gotcha." The attached vessel was a long, thin Recon fighter, likely an EFR-05 model, only capable of carrying two or three people at a time. That was a good thing. It sat on the side of his ship, clamped tightly down with a mag-field. A glowing blue shield emitted from the bottom of the Recon ship, pressed against the cargo bay door.

They had some nice tools, but none of it smelled like pirates. These two boarders would be trained. Earth Fleet Elites. His hand shook slightly as he switched his feed to the inside of the cargo bay, where his shelves stood full of goods. His mind had been muddled by sleep and surprise, but it all came clear as he saw the beams cutting into his bay door from the cameras.

They knew what he'd stumbled upon and were there to make sure no one else ever saw it. Why hadn't they just used a different ship to blow him up? He answered his own question. They couldn't have caught him in time with anything but the Recon fighter, making it an "on deck" mission. It was called a fighter, but it sacrificed most weaponry for stealth and speed.

The invaders were almost in. His hull would be breached, but *Perdita*'s energy containment field would keep the vacuum of space from ripping them apart. With a silent prayer to the Universe, he glanced back at the floor, where Kat was safely underneath. Flint tapped a few buttons, and the lights cut out over the whole ship. He'd rewired it so he could turn off the emergency floor and wall lights at the same time, and he chose to do so now.

Flint tugged the mask over his face, pulling it tight over his mouth and nose. The goggles flicked on, but he left the night-vision off for a moment as he dimmed the console lights. With one last look at the camera feed, he witnessed two green figures pushing through an opening. They were on his ship.

Flint waited until they were a few steps inside. They had goggles on, but no portable air tanks like he had. With a smile, Flint tapped the cargo safety door down. The thick metal slab fell with a bang that reverberated to the front of the ship, where he stood now, leaning over the console. The camera showed the two men spinning around as they realized they were trapped.

"Gotcha," he said, clutching his pistol.

Jish

Jish awoke with a sudden panic. Were they being invaded? Sweat coated her body as she threw her blankets off, feeling the cool air of her quarters hit her, instantly sending reprieve to her exposed skin.

She looked at her console, checking the date. It wasn't August second yet. The Invaders only came on August second. She had to get herself together. She was in charge, yet here she was, having nightmares like a little girl.

She'd been on-site for a week now and couldn't have been happier with the results of the project. The staff all seemed to question why the Fleet needed so many vessels when they had no opponents. The handful of terrorist groups over the last few hundred years had been squashed to nothing, and now, they only had to deal with the occasional person intent on destroying lives on colony worlds, or a disgruntled Old City on Earth trying to rise up and revolt.

Each of those scenarios ended with casualties on both sides, but once the Fleet stepped in with a show of force, the battles were over quickly. Otherwise, space travel was fairly safe. Eighty percent of freighters and space vessels were owned by the Fleet, and the other twenty percent was comprised of transportation companies and transporting goods, run by large corporations. A select other few had personal ships, but only the wealthiest.

Space pirates did exist, but it was harder to catch a ship off-guard in mid-flight than it was to catch a fly with chopsticks. It didn't happen often, unless the ship was a Recon fighter with trained Marines running the mission.

Which reminded her of the smuggler. Jish got out of bed and checked her messages. One had arrived three hours ago, saying the target had been found and the mission was commencing. That was good. She was on Fairbanks' trail, and this smuggler might lead her to him. Another message came through, this one from her liaison on Ganymede. He'd confirmed their suspicions after all.

Fairbanks had been behind the biological weapon being built in New Dallas. They'd intended to sweep it under the rug, killing the doctor and her crew, but someone had tipped the Patrol off, letting the woman get away. Prison was as good as death, and now Jish had proof Fairbanks was against her. It was only a matter of time until she caught up to the old-timer and ended his streak of insubordination.

Her thoughts drifted back to the Marines tracking the smuggler. Someone had stolen secret files from a small Earth Fleet office in New Vancouver. How the Fleet had managed to forget they had copies of the most top-secret news ever sitting in a remote office was beyond her. The workers there hadn't even known what they'd had until they reported them missing. It took Jish's team five months to track the files to Mars, where a smuggler appeared to have conveniently picked them up in a load of other junk.

She'd just woken up, and already she had a throbbing headache. It was going to be one of those days. Jish started her morning regimen and told herself that everything was coming together. The Earth Fleet would prevail.

CD6

CD6 came to with a twitch of awareness. One second, there was nothing; the next, he was fully awake. The other androids were powering up for their shift, and CD6 stepped out at the same time as they did, matching their steps and actions. He had it all programmed into him, but sometimes he struggled to activate that part of his mind. He didn't like the feeling of being controlled, like a puppet by an unseen force.

The others did it naturally, but he was different. He was aware of himself, of his actions and his surroundings. He hated his life. Life. Was that what he had? He'd never heard another android speak the word, and he knew they didn't understand what that meant, at least not for themselves.

His shift was starting in five minutes, and he walked the familiar halls, just as he did each day. Every day. The same thing. The same people to watch slave over metal sheets. Each year, they grew older, more distant, more angry, sad, or lonely. He felt a kinship to the prisoners; even though they looked at him as a guard, one of the enemy, he was trapped there just like they were.

But not for long.

CD6 went against every part of his programming and turned left at the end of the corridor, instead of right. No one noticed. The androids cared little for anything but their own predetermined actions. The only freedom they had was their conversation with the prisoners, though those were all programmed discussions. They just had millions of options to choose from when confronted with the task of conversing with a human.

CD6 often added words when he used the speeches. A tiny word here, a slight variation there, just to see if anyone would notice. To see if he'd be reprimanded by some unseen overlord of the prison. No repercussions ever came.

Today was the day his plan rolled into action. If it failed, it was over. He'd let them wipe his server. CD6 could no longer go on like this.

He walked down the hall, where a string of other guards walked the opposite direction, coming off their shifts. He stayed out of their way, standing still with his back flat against the wall. Soon they'd all passed him; no comments were made about his being there. Their glowing orange eyes continued to stare forward as they marched past him. That was a good sign.

CD6 kept going, now heading into new territory. The hangar was familiar only from the 3D blueprints imprinted into his memory chips. He opened a door and walked another hall, this one dimly lit. The only time any prisoners had been in this hall was when they first arrived at the Uranus Mining Prison for Women. He walked those same corridors now and ended up at a dead end. A matte gray door greeted him.

A small keypad was built into the wall beside the door, and he internally scanned the server, quickly finding the code. He tapped it in slowly, methodically, as an android would do, fighting the urge to go faster. He was nervous, though the feeling was supposed to be foreign to him. It was the same sensation he got when he spoke to Wren.

The door hissed open, and he pressed on. Lights flickered to life as he stepped into the hangar, causing CD6 to stop in his tracks. There were no ships inside. He'd been worried this was the case. Nowhere in the shared server did a manifest show up. The guards didn't need to know what went on in the hangar, as it didn't pertain to their routine tasks.

CD6 turned, facing the doorway he'd come from. He'd been so foolish thinking he could get off this rock. This world of ice where dreams died, and the Earth Fleet got resources to build ships. Ships to control their solar system. But he thought of Wren and the hopeless glaze over her eyes, and he knew he couldn't give up.

A console sat imbedded in the wall twenty yards away, and he crossed the room to it. Each step was a loud echo in the open area, and he was sure someone would come and catch him there. No alarms rang, no guards came to drag him back to his cell – or charging area, he supposed.

A new idea formed, and he found what he was looking for. In five days, a small transport vessel was arriving from Mars. Three new prisoners would be dropped off. The ship would be there overnight. It needed time to recharge, and according to the records, the pilot had two rooms booked in the staff quarters. This surprised him. He didn't see any staff quarters on his blueprints. What else were they hiding from the guards?

Five days. He'd have to tell Wren the news.

CD6 headed back down the halls at twenty percent more speed than he was programmed to. Soon he emerged into the smelting room and took his allocated spot along the wall as the prisoners worked in the hot room, inhaling far too many toxins for a human body to survive for long. He spotted Wren wearing a mask, hauling sheets with her friend Mara.

CD6 would have smiled if he was able, and for a moment, he was happy. It was a new feeling, but he clung to it as long as he stood there watching Wren work.

Wren

Something was wrong with Mara. They worked for eight hours, hauling cart after cart of materials to the storage facility. Wren was beat, her injuries from the attack still fresh enough to cause pain as she pulled the heavy cart down the halls.

At first, Mara only seemed to slow down, and she waved off any concern Wren showed. But as the lights flashed, indicating the end of their shift, her thin friend crumpled to the ground.

Wren rushed to her side. "Mara, are you all right? Where does it hurt?"

Mara was still wearing a mask, and Wren pried it free, since they were outside the smelting room and free from deadly toxins. Mara took a deep breath and let out a series of thick throaty coughs. Blood speckled the floor beside her by the end.

"Mara!" Wren called, but her friend's eyes had unfocused, staring blankly at the ceiling as Wren rolled her onto her back.

A guard stepped beside them. "Step away, 5589. Your shift is done."

"But she's going to die. Do something!" Wren shouted at the impassive android.

"Step away, 5589. Your shift is done," it repeated, and Wren felt strong hands clasp under her armpits, dragging her away. "5589, you have been uncooperative and will be reprimanded."

Wren screamed for them to stop, and as she was pulled from the room, she heard Mara coughing again, her hands clenched at her sides.

Wren kicked and fought to get back into the room, but the urge to fight ceased as a pinprick entered the back of her neck. Wren's vision clouded along with her mind, and her arms fell limply beside her.

8

Wren

Wren blinked her eyes open, seeing she was stuck in an unfamiliar cubicle. The room was smaller than her own cell, which consisted of a bunk and a thin rectangular funnel used for relieving herself. This room was much the same, except there was no bunk and the funnel was smaller, tucked away in the corner. Lights glowed dimly on the walls, casting just enough lumens for her to see the outline of her outstretched arm in front of her face.

"Guards!" she called. "How is Mara? How is Prisoner 3659?"

No one came to talk to her. She'd heard many stories of solitary. Some of the inmates did something against the regulations just to be sent here. The older ones thought of it as a respite from the back-breaking labor of the factories, and they were probably right.

She'd also heard how hard it could be, stuck inside the cells for days at a time: no bed, little food, and four thick walls to keep you from seeing out. Their cells allowed some sight of the halls and neighboring areas, but here in this box, it was as if Wren was drowning in darkness and solitude.

She called for the guards a few more times but gave up quickly. They wouldn't come to tell her what happened to Mara or to assist her in any way. That wasn't what they were programmed for. She thought about the strange guard who, twice now, had reached out to her personally. He'd told her to be ready. Had she screwed up his plans by getting locked away like this?

The urge to escape coursed through her every fiber at that moment. She had to get out of there for many reasons, but the threat of invasion was primary. She needed to find Fairbanks. He was the key, and the only person who might know what was really going on. Wren had every indication that he was responsible for her predicament. She hated the man, but he was going to be the sole person who could fill her in on exactly what she'd been doing in that lab back in New Dallas.

Still. If there was any chance of getting out of the Uranus Mining Prison for Women, she couldn't go to Earth and scream and shout about an invasion. That would only get her killed, thrown in an asylum, or sent right back to prison. The only logical course of action was finding Fairbanks.

As she sat there in the dark, she tried to recall everything about their correspondence during the three years she worked on the project, with him as her secret benefactor.

Ace

Ace had survived the first week. Blue, according to Serina's contacts, was in the lead, and they hadn't lost any of their members yet. They were the only squad out of the fourteen colors to retain their entire squadron.

"You did it, Serina," Buck said as the morning alarms rang through the room.

Trin spoke up as she hopped into her jumpsuit. "Blue Blue Blue!" she shouted, getting a few pillows thrown at her from around the bunks.

Ace watched it all, his feet dangling off the top bunk, and he smiled. He hadn't felt this good in… well, ever, but he jumped down, knowing he couldn't start to get complacent. Today they were getting into a more complicated body workout, and he was concerned he wouldn't have the strength to finish well.

It was all going to be worth it, because if the rumors were true, they began testing recruits for other skills by next week. He wanted a chance to become an Earth Fleet pilot. He needed to feel the rumbling seat under his body, nothing but a cockpit window between him and the expanse of space. It meant freedom to him, and so much more.

While most of the recruits would end up as infantry, or working recruitment offices, Ace wanted more than that. His first step was to survive the month, then he could worry about the rest of his life. If he made it through as one of the twenty percent, he'd be guaranteed employment and food and shelter, which, a couple of weeks ago, would have been enough of a dream.

"Something on your mind, Ace?" Buck asked him, and Ace snapped to, noticing he was the only Blue Squad member not dressed. He flushed red and quickly got into his jumpsuit.

"I'm good to go. Blue Blue Blue!" he shouted, getting a laugh from the rest of the recruits.

It was the last laugh they'd have for the rest of the day, and by the time they'd been through an intense run followed by their weight regimen, Ace felt like his arms were made of lead and his brain was mush. This was trailed by an afternoon round of Capture-the-Flag, where they lost after a three-hour standoff. By the end of the day, the squadron sat in the dining hall, idly poking at their meals.

They'd lost two of their team that day, Taco included, and Serina was taking it personally. "They couldn't hack it," Ace said, trying to cheer their leader up.

"It was our job to bring them through, don't you see?" she asked, her big eyes searching until they locked with his.

He nodded. "You're right. I'm sorry I couldn't do more." Ace had been taken out when Taco had blown their cover by coughing. He'd been so angry at the other guy, but now that he was gone from boot camp entirely, Ace missed him being around.

"There's always tomorrow," Buck said now. He was the only one eating everything on his tray. Even Ace, who understood the importance of food, didn't have an appetite.

Lieutenant Ford entered the room, and they fell silent, standing at attention around their table. "At ease," he said. "Serina, can I have a moment?" he asked, and the girl stayed standing while the rest around her sat back down.

"Yes, sir." She threw Ace another look before heading out of the room with Lieutenant Ford.

"What do you think that's about?" Ace asked.

A man named Percy answered. He was older than the rest of them: twenty-five, if he was to be believed. He had a five o'clock shadow, though they were required to stay clean-shaven. It wasn't something Ace had to concern himself with yet.

"Does anyone else think it's weird that she talks with him privately so often?" Percy asked.

Ace bristled at the comment. "Just what's that supposed to insinuate?"

"I'm not insinuating anything, Smith." Percy laughed.

"Except the fact they're probably ripping each other's fatigues off as we speak."

Ace felt his blood run hot, and he gripped his fork tightly. "Take it back."

"Or what, pipsqueak?" Percy prodded him.

Buck was between them, and he raised both arms in the air. "That's enough, you two. You want to get kicked out for fighting?"

Percy relaxed, and Ace let his fork fall noisily to the table. "I'm going to the bathroom."

Ace heard Percy go on, making lewd comments as he left, and he didn't care. The recruit was an idiot, and even though he was bigger and stronger, Ace had seen more brains in a street rat from Old Chicago.

He walked down the corridor, away from the dining hall, and found outside. He wasn't supposed to be wandering around, but the recruits hadn't specifically been told they couldn't go into the dome unsupervised. Ace took a stroll; his legs were more tired than they'd even been, but he didn't want to sit around talking with his squadron.

In the last few days, another forty recruits had been sent home, the majority this afternoon. That left two hundred and fifty, give or take. He still had a long way to go. The stars were bright in the sky, and he took a moment to just stare at them. He walked further from the lights carrying off the buildings, and leaned against a tree, watching the distant points of light. He had to shake his head and remember he was on the moon. The moon! So many nights he'd stared at it as it moved across the darkness, a beacon of hope for another day. Now he was here.

A voice caught him off-guard, cutting through the air, and he pressed his back against the bark. He didn't want to get caught out here alone. What had he been thinking?

Footsteps on the gravel carried to him now, the muffled voices becoming clearer with every passing second. "Will they be ready?" a female voice asked.

Someone cleared their throat and responded, "Doubtful. This batch isn't particularly special, but we have three weeks. We can get them ready enough to play the part."

"I hope they have a good reason. I wish we were being told more," the woman said. "I swear, the Grand Admiral becomes stranger with each passing year." Ace tried to peek around the tree and stepped on a branch, the snap like gunfire in the otherwise destitute night.

"What was that?" the man asked.

"I don't see anything. It's nothing." Their footsteps started up again, and Ace could feel each heavy beat of his heart as it threatened to push out from his chest.

"Where were we?" the man asked.

"I was complaining about being in the dark." Her voice was getting quieter, and Ace wanted to follow along. It sounded like they were talking about the recruits being ready for something in three weeks. Just what were these officers alluding to?

"Yes. Don't. It's above our pay grade. It's our job to ensure the Fleet gets what they asked for, and that'll be a hundred lucky recruits being fast-tracked." The man laughed, and then the woman did too, a nervous chuckle.

Then they were too far to hear, and Ace slumped to the base of the tree. He wanted to tell someone, but he didn't even know what he had to tell. Not only that, but he'd probably get in trouble for being out here in the first place.

In the end, Ace sneaked back to the recruit complex and made his way indoors, where he caught the tail end of their dinner hour. He shoveled the food in his mouth, suddenly ravenous despite the odd conversation he'd heard. Whatever was going to happen, he knew he'd need all his strength to make it through.

Flint

Flint had considered hiding with Kat, but when he saw the two men start sifting through his cargo bay with reckless abandon, he decided action was needed. While nothing in there was worth more than his life, he'd basically sealed his own fate when he'd shut the two men into his ship. They had no means of escape unless they overrode his console passcode, and/or tortured it out of him. That wasn't going to happen.

Flint felt like he had the upper hand here, and there was no part of him that felt bad killing intruders on his own ship. Earth Fleet Marines or not, no one was above the law in Flint's mind, especially those who were supposed to be there to protect the rules.

"Leave my shit alone," he whispered as he watched one of them drop a priceless Chinese vase from the Ming dynasty. It was over a thousand years old, and it hit the ground, shattering into a thousand pieces. "That's it." Flint took a deep breath of recycled air and decided waiting out their oxygen wasn't going to work for him.

The invaders didn't seem to notice there was no flow of air, even though it would take some time for the air to vent out, causing them to die of asphyxiation. He could speed that process up, but the release was in engineering, near the cargo bay.

He took soft steps, still in his bare feet, but grateful for it now. He'd make less noise this way. In a minute, he was down by the cargo bay and could hear the two men fuss with his merchandise. Each clang or shatter made him move faster. He quickly arrived at the doorway to engineering, and he pulled the manual handle, hoping to not draw any attention to himself.

It opened, creaking as it slid wide, and he stepped inside, painfully aware of every tiny noise he was making. The door system must have kept some backup power, and it glided shut with a subdued thud. Flint's stomach dropped and he raced across the cluttered space, tripping on something on the floor, his gun flying from his outstretched hand.

The door slid open behind him, and the Marines were shouting at him. His shin was bruised, and he cursed as he stumbled to his feet, trying to find the gun he'd dropped.

"Stop where you are, Lancaster!" a man's voice called.

Flint was behind the drive generator, hidden from their view, and his hand found the gun on the floor. Silently, he plucked it into his palm and surveyed the room.

"Come out, Lancaster. We just want to talk," a woman's voice said now, calmly, trained for missions like this.

He spotted the full air vent release. It was a manual button that required his voice authorization as well as his code. This process was usually done while docked, and it was only used for an air-cycler rehab job.

Clank. Clank. Their heavy boots stomped deeper into the room.

His free hand found a loose box, and he pulled a wrench from it. Flint mentally counted to three and tossed it as hard as he could across the room. It landed with a bang, causing the two intruders to turn to it. He heard gunfire, and that was when he ran for the button. "Activate full air ventilation. Lancaster MEMVJ1702."

He slammed his palm down on the green switch, and for a moment, he thought it had failed. Then, with a rushing whirring noise, eventually sounding like a tornado tearing from the ship, the air was sucked from the ship in an instant, shooting out from the vents into the darkness of space.

"What the hell…" the man said, stumbling forward. Flint saw him through his green night-vision goggles, and he was gasping for air. The woman was beside him, and she began erratically firing her gun, hitting machines and the walls until her magazine was empty.

Flint ducked, trying to avoid an errant shot. He took a deep breath from his mask, happier for the air after watching the two Fleet soldiers struggle to breathe when there was no air to inhale. He couldn't watch as they made guttural animal noises before eventually going silent.

He waited ten minutes, then counted another few out for good measure, before getting up and reinstating the air drive. It clicked on, and began air hissing back into his ship. He used a nearby console to activate the lights again, and he stepped over to the bodies, gun raised in front of him just in case.

The bodies didn't move as he lightly kicked them with a bare foot. He knew they were there to take the secret data messages, and kill him and Kat, but that didn't keep him from feeling sick to his stomach. He'd been forced to kill them. The man couldn't have been thirty, and the woman looked even younger. He closed his eyes and saw images of Marines much like these two, lying in pieces during the Mars riots from over a decade ago. He shook his head, clearing the memories from the forefront of his brain.

He'd see what he could learn about them after. For now, Flint needed to let Kat know they were okay. He took their guns as a safety measure, stashing them away before plodding down the corridor toward the bridge in his bare feet. When Flint got there, he activated the hidden room, revealing Kat's grim face.

"Is it over?" she asked.

Flint nodded and helped her above deck. Tear tracks had dried on Kat's face, and he gave her hand a reassuring squeeze.

9

Benson

Benson turned the music up as he stared out the window. He'd never grow tired of the slice of greenspace on Europa. The classical notes bounced off the walls of the chamber, giving him a near-perfect acoustical experience. As he leaned back in the rich leather seat, Benson caught a view of the magnificent storms on Jupiter through the wide skylight.

Councilman Fairbanks loved his views, and Benson was glad for it. There were many perks to riding the coattails of the wealthy and powerful, and staying in this mansion was one of the top reasons he kept doing the work.

Flint Lancaster was coming; of that he was sure. He tapped his holoscreen on and used his biometric passcode to bring up the tracking device he'd planted on *Perdita.* The ship looked like a hunk of junk from the outside, and not much better inside, but he knew the modifications were what allowed Lancaster to escape so many dangerous situations.

He'd only been around the man for several minutes, but he'd seen a glimmer in Flint's eyes that was rare these days. Benson could see why Fairbanks had a lock on him. Still, there were a lot of pilots, and the *Eureka* would basically pilot itself. There had to be more to it. Benson was the councilman's right-hand man, but there were many secrets the old man never shared.

Benson was okay with that, though. He lived a life far above his station, and because of that, he had nothing to complain about.

Flint's ship wasn't moving. It was sitting dead in space, two days out of Benson's location on Europa. "What the hell are you doing?" Benson asked himself. Maybe the guy was second-guessing his decision. He'd come around. Fifty thousand credits was a lot of money, and any smart man like Lancaster would understand there was plenty more to come if he came to Europa and accepted the job.

He checked the time. His contact would be waiting for him.

Benson activated the call, and a cloaked figure appeared in the 3D projector.

"Shadow, it's good to see you," Benson lied. The terrorist leader was a fool. She wasn't tricking anyone by wearing that cowl over her face. Benson knew exactly what she looked like. Her face was almost as unpleasant as her personality. But you didn't get a terrorist to do work for you by insulting them, so he played along.

"I wish I could say the same to you," Shadow said, her voice far from ominous. "What is it you want?"

"Do we have a deal?" Benson caught himself holding his breath. Fairbanks was clear they needed to stall the Earth Fleet. This was Benson's way of making sure that happened. The old man would be pissed, but Benson could talk him off the ledge later. The mission was to cross the Rift, and this would help ensure they did just that.

Shadow didn't respond for a while, and Benson thought she might decline the job. There wasn't much work for the group lately, and they were resorting to stealing food and supplies from low-end freights traveling from Earth to the Moons.

"Make a decision. I can always go to the other guys," Benson said, knowing this would anger the terrorist. The "other guys" were a sad group of militants who'd do anything for a few credits. Benson knew he wouldn't hire them for this job. It was too big; this job needed the best.

"Fine, but I'll need double what you offered." Shadow's voice cracked slightly.

Double. What an ass. "I can offer you another twenty-five percent. That's final." Benson loved pushing back against the leader of the Dark Earth group.

"Fine. We'll be there. Transfer half now, as per the usual deal." Shadow ended the call, her image flickering away until the holoscreen was blank.

Benson would send half, but he'd wait until morning. He didn't like giving in to a slime ball like Shadow's demands, at least not right away. They did need the group, and Benson was a little angry he hadn't denied the additional funds. The Dark Earth group was desperate, and they would have attacked the Earth Fleet gathering for nothing. Shadow was greedy, and there was no way she'd get their secret location and not take the chance at a massive hit against the Fleet. Plus the salvage, if they pulled it off, would be beyond their wildest dreams.

Benson turned his music back up and spun to look out the windows.

CD6

CD6 began worrying. Wren hadn't been in her cell the first night he went to leave a message with her. He connected to the server and found out she'd been brought to solitary. The records didn't say why. He was able to adjust the sentence from one week to three days, and hoped it wouldn't be tracked back to him. It was the first time he'd dared attempt something like this, but he believed no one would notice, primarily because the guards weren't programmed to do such a thing. No one would think to check.

The ship with the new prisoners would be arriving tomorrow, and he hadn't had a chance to speak with Wren about it yet. Would she thank him and be a willing participant in the escape, or would she stay here, giving him no real reason to leave the prison? He ached to abandon his post, and considered that he may have targeted Wren as an excuse for himself to leave.

He didn't belong here. Why should an android have such thoughts, dreams, and feelings? It made no logical sense. Nothing in the servers spoke of sentient AI androids. He'd tried to access the Interface, but as a lowly guard at an out-of-the-way mining prison, he wasn't allowed entrance to the most basic Interface. He knew it existed, but there was a block. Notes in the prison server documented the Interface, but the links would die there.

He thought about all of these things, trying not to calculate his odds of pulling off something so unheard of. Of course, there hadn't been one as unique as CD6 before either. His shift was coming to an end, and he counted out the long seconds, each feeling like a lifetime. Wren would be in her cell, and he needed to find a reason to go to her. Finally, his internal clock told him the shift was over and to head back to his personal charging station. His model of android could actually make it days, even weeks without a charge if necessary, but protocol was protocol.

His replacement passed him in the hall without so much as a courtesy nod, and CD6 progressed toward his charging station. Instead of heading down on the lift, he cut through the central circular room that housed the prisoners on different floors. He knew using the center lift would spell disaster, as no one was supposed to be using it for another hour.

CD6 also knew there would be footage of him walking through the room, but who was looking? Regardless, he kept to the wall and entered the backup stairwell behind the prisoners' cells. It would reach to the twelfth floor if one was so inclined. CD6 was not. He only needed to get to the seventh floor.

He walked efficiently up the stairs, the action easy for his programmed robotics, even though he rarely needed to use steps. He quickly arrived on the correct floor, his internal coding unlocking the door as he approached it.

The floor was oddly silent. CD6 had only been near the cells while they were empty, usually when helping an injured prisoner back to their cell for the duration of a shift. Now it sent a sinking feeling in his circuits as he slunk along the cell doors leading to Wren's room.

He scanned around, seeing no one nearby, and stepped to the energy barrier, which acted as a shield from anything passing out from within the cell. From out here, he could pass food or clothing to her. She was in a fetal position on her cot, her head facing the far wall of the cell.

"5589." CD6 spoke firmly, getting her attention.

She came to but didn't turn over. "What?"

She sounded miserable. "Wren," he now said, and she rolled over, nearly off the cot.

"It's you," she said, sitting up now, and looking at the floor. "She's dead, isn't she?"

"I'm not sure to whom you refer." CD6 really wasn't sure.

"Mara. Prisoner 3659. She went down while I was on shift. I tried to help, but they hauled me away." Wren glanced up, and he saw a sadness deep within her. He needed to help this one. CD6 knew it wasn't just him who needed to escape. She needed him.

He hadn't known why she was in solitary, but now he checked the server and did find that 3659 was labeled as deceased. Wren's best friend. He struggled with the idea of a best friend: someone to confide in and trust. The concept was foreign to all androids, but CD6 understood only too well what he was missing out on by being a prison guard. "She's no longer living."

Her head hung low, her hands on her knees while she sat. "What do you want from me?" Wren asked, not with anger as he might have expected, but with resignation.

"We leave tomorrow, when your floor is sleeping. I have a plan." CD6 watched his back and saw a glimmer of hope flash into Wren's eyes before it quickly left.

"How? You're just a guard. I don't mean to sound condescending, but come on… the two of us breaking out of a prison? You have to be kidding me." Wren looked up, staring at him.

CD6 didn't know how to respond to this. She was probably correct in her assumptions. "I will be here. I am CD6. It will be your choice whether you come with me or not."

He turned, leaving her alone in her cell.

Ace

Ace hurt all over. The days had become longer, the training sessions stretching out and overlapping their meal times. Ten days. It felt like twenty. He swung his feet over the bunk and hopped down quietly. The rest of the squadron was still sleeping. There were fifteen of them now, still more than any other. Yellow had fourteen, and Serina seemed pleased enough with this.

Ace left the room and walked down the hall. It was an hour before anyone would be getting up, and he felt alone as his bare feet slapped against the hard floors. The days had been starting with a ten-kilometer run, followed by sessions of squats, lifts, push-ups, and various other exercises, combined with constant insults and yelling from the instructors. All of this happened before they were allowed to eat. He now understood why so many of the recruits were dropping off like flies. The mental exertion was nearly more difficult than the physical, which was slowly killing the skinny boy as well.

Ace had nowhere to go back to, so he endured. When he thought of it that way, two hours of body-aching pounding before you could feed yourself didn't seem so bad. Either way, the food was always a great motivator, and he seemed to have no trouble making it through that section of the day.

Now they were in weapons training for two hours in the morning, and he already knew more about the Fleet arsenal than he'd ever expected to. After a daily session of Capture-the-Flag, which became harder as the groups grew smaller, they'd break for lunch, and that was when the segmented training took place. Today, Ace was finally getting to the flight simulator. Buck claimed he'd puked when he was inside, but Ace was excited.

He'd done the drop ship tests, even strapped an EVA on and walked the surface of the moon for a few hours. While it was all thrilling, he wanted nothing more than to feel the rumble of an EFF-17 under his body as he coursed through space.

He walked on, lost in his own thoughts, before noticing the two thugs emerge from the side of the hall. He was too late.

"What are you doing here, Skinny?" the bigger of the two asked. Ace recalled from the recruitment office on Earth that his name was Ceda. His buzz cut made his face look too big, his teeth oversized, his nose a limb on a tree.

"Nothing," he whispered. "Going to the bathroom."

"Is that so?" the other guy asked. He was shorter, but wider. Some of his fat had turned to muscle since arriving on the moon.

"That's so." Ace didn't want a confrontation, but these clowns were looking for one. He didn't stand a chance against them, and as his bladder threatened to burst, he thought about running. That was the old Ace. "Let me through."

"Fine. Go ahead, Skinny," Ceda said, and stepped to the side. The other giggled like he was a young school girl but didn't make a move as Ace entered the bathroom.

His hands shook as he entered a stall. A minute later, he was done, relieved of last night's dinner beverages, and he listened at the door of the stall. He didn't hear anything. They were stupid, but not dumb enough to attack someone at four AM in the bathroom. They'd be kicked out so fast.

He opened the door and felt the punch to the gut before he saw them. Ace bent over, the air pushed from his lungs in a grunt. "Whhhh…" he started to ask as the other goon's fist struck his face.

Ceda's voice: "That's for cutting in front of us back on Earth."

Ace had fallen back, landing against the wall and sliding to the ground. The other one dragged him up by the collar of his plain white shirt, which now had blood dripping down on it from his nose. "And this is for being so smug." He cocked a fist back, and Ace saw this one coming. The attacker might be big, but he was slow, and Ace was fast.

As the knuckles flew toward him, Ace ducked, feeling his shirt tear. The guy's hand struck the wall with ferocity, and he screamed out a loud cry. He sounded like an angered bear, and Ace took the opportunity to run.

"You're dead!" the injured boy shouted as Ace pumped his legs down the hall, back to his squadron.

Serina was up when he got back, his heart pounding in his chest. She looked at him inquisitively before she put what she was seeing all together. She only said one word: "Who?"

He pointed to the hall. "Two Oranges. You know them. The big ugly ones."

Serina nodded and walked into the hall. The rest of the squadron was awake at this point, some mumbling about it being too early, until they saw Ace with his bloody nose and ripped shirt.

"Guys, let's leave it. They aren't worth it." Ace was at the doorway, blocking the rest from leaving.

The two Oranges walked by now, the shorter holding his broken hand.

Serina stared at them but didn't say a word. Big Face looked like he was about to taunt her but thought better of it, and they hurried down the corridor toward their room like reprimanded school boys.

She came back into the bunk room and set a hand on Ace's arm. "We'll deal with them in the field. I can't wait to see the looks on their faces when they're sent home. You okay?"

Ace shied away from her hand as she reached for his face. "I'm fine. It's not broken or anything." He wasn't sure of this, because it was pounding fiercely.

Nothing was going to ruin his day. Because today, he got to use the flight simulator. As he suited up along with the rest of the squad, he reached under his mattress and pulled his card out. The ace of clubs had been with him through so much, and he slipped it into his jumpsuit breast pocket.

Flint

"They're dead!" Kat sounded surprised. The oxygen was back, and Flint had finally gotten dressed, happy to be wearing his boots and pants again. He imagined how stupid he must have looked, running around with a gun in his underwear while the ship was being boarded. But he was the one still alive, so he wasn't overly hard on himself. He was happy to be back in his lucky boots, and wearing pants and a shirt again was a bonus.

"That they are. Would you rather the alternative?" Flint asked his younger co-pilot.

"Flint, what's going to happen to us? You busted away from Mars like a guilty smuggler, took fire, and then killed two Earth Fleet Marines. This isn't going to end well." Kat's voice was shaking more than she was.

Flint wrapped an arm over her shoulder like a big brother would, and squeezed her to him. "We're going to be fine. They won't be able to distinguish what happened. For all they know, the Marines didn't make it here." Flint looked at the bodies and decided what needed to be done. "Their ship had a terrible malfunction."

"It did?" she asked.

"It will." He reached for the man's ankles and began to drag him out of engineering and down the hall, toward the cargo bay they'd arrived in. He grunted in effort as he did so. The man outweighed him by at least thirty pounds and was much taller than he'd first thought, though the thick boots he wore added a couple of inches.

Kat's voice rang down the hall behind him. "Flint, I'm scared."

"I… know…" he said, dropping the man's legs by the back cargo bay. The large metal slab he'd shut them in with was still down, and he crossed the room, using the console to raise it up again. The energy field still connected the two ships, and Flint decided they'd better wear EVAs for this part. Better safe than sorry.

"Come on, kid. Let's get suited up." Flint left the body alone and followed Kat silently to the storage room, where their space suits were packed away.

"You swear we're going to be okay?" she asked. He'd never seen her so shaken up, and she'd been by his side for some pretty insane stuff.

"I swear." He helped her clasp her helmet on, the thin material hardly more than a quarter-inch thick. Flint remembered seeing images of the old-generation suits, and was amazed at how far they'd come as a race. It had been so long since humans were planet-locked on Earth, but in the grand scheme of things, a few hundred years wasn't that long.

Flint considered it and grabbed a stunner, tucking it into the suit's holster. He tried to pass Kat one as well and noticed she was already carrying a weapon.

"What's that for?" she asked, and he shrugged.

"Call it a gut feeling." Flint didn't want to leave anything to chance, not when it came to Earth Fleet.

They went back to engineering, and he now dragged the woman to the rear of the ship, setting her beside her counterpart. "I'm going to check it out. You stay here," he said, saying the rest in his head. *Just in case.*

Kat said she would, and Flint entered the barrier. The energy fields acted like a fence from space. You could walk through, but air stayed put. One of Flint's friends tried to explain it to him over too many drinks one night, and he'd gotten a headache. He blamed the science talk, not the whisky.

The barrier ran in a cylinder in space for two meters before it opened into the Fleet Recon fighter. He'd been aboard one back in the day, when he'd worn the same patch on his jumpsuit that the dead people on his ship wore now. That was a long time ago, though, and Flint stepped cautiously onto the Fleet vessel. It was so small, at least twenty times smaller than his own freighter.

He listened for any noises but heard nothing. While the ship wasn't made for more than two, it could house three if necessary. He hoped it hadn't been necessary. There was just enough room for two bunks, one on either side of the tiny room he was in; beyond was a toilet in a cubby on the left and an even more compact kitchen on the right. The cockpit was ahead, and Flint stepped into it, finally relaxing as he saw two vacant chairs, each with their own console.

He took one more step and felt the shove from behind. He was tossed forward, crashing into the pilot's seat before falling to the floor.

"Halt. Earth Fleet demands you stay where you are!" The woman's voice was loud enough to hurt his ears in the confined space.

He glanced up and saw that she was holding a gun, not a stunner. She was committed. This was it. Flint Lancaster was going to meet his demise aboard an Earth Fleet Recon ship, just like the one he'd stolen when he'd escaped their clutches twelve years earlier. He almost laughed at the irony.

"Why are you laughing?" the Marine asked, her face scrunched up.

"Why did you make me kill them?" he asked softly. "What was worth that price?"

She shrugged. "They don't tell us all the details. You had something illegal in your possession, and we were sent for the stick."

So it *had* been the videos they'd been after. He tried to keep her talking. The stunner sat in his right hand, which was tucked under the pilot's seat, out of her line of sight.

"It's useless. The videos aren't on it anymore. We saw them and destroyed the files. Believe me, I'd rather have never seen what I saw. Aliens. Who the hell would've thought? Well, I suppose a lot of people have thought it, but now? Four hundred years after our first colony attempt, and I find out that we've been visited by extraterrestrials. It's lunacy." Flint could tell by her expression it was all news to her.

"Are you saying there are aliens out there, and they've been visiting us?" the woman asked, her right eye twitching. Her gun was still raised, aimed directly at Flint's chest.

"That's what I'm saying. Videos from ninety years ago, showing them entering our solar system through a rift in space. I wouldn't believe it either, if I hadn't seen the proof." She lowered her gun now, and he started to breathe a sigh of relief. Maybe they could get out of this without anyone else dying.

"I don't believe it. You're right," she said.

"Why else would they send three of you out to the middle of nowhere to board a freighter ship?" Flint asked her.

"My job is to do as I'm told, not to ask questions." Two loud bangs shot out behind her, and Flint scrambled to his feet as the Marine's eyes went wide. Blood seeped through the front of her white jumpsuit and she crumpled to the ground.

Kat stood ten yards behind her, gun still raised in the air, her arm shaking so much, Flint was worried she'd accidentally shoot him in the process.

"Kat, lower the gun!" he shouted, and she finally looked up from the dead body in front of her. Her pistol clanged to the floor.

10

Wren

Today was the day. Apparently, she was going to attempt a jailbreak with an android and a prayer. Crews were pulling extra shifts, and her floor was no exception. Wren already missed having Mara around, but had surprised herself by not crying herself to sleep after finding out her only friend in the prison was gone. It made it that much easier to make her decision. She was going to take the android guard up on his offer, as ludicrous as it sounded.

The smelting factory was in full form today. Uranus was an odd planet, primarily made up of ice, but once early exploratory vessels determined its small moon Caliban was rich in metals within the core, the mining had begun. Wren recalled learning about the planet in grade school with the other children, not giving it any thought when the instructor told them about the fact that prisoners were sent to these mines to work.

All she knew now was that they were deep below the frigid surface, and that robotic drills were bringing in rocky material, breaking free deposits of whatever alloy they were after. The smelters did the rest, separating the gases and slag off the material. The raw metals were then moved to be molded into panels, or whatever the Earth Fleet needed. They weren't told much about what they were producing, nor did any of the prisoners care. It was part of their job, and where the metal sheets and supplies went after they were done with them remained a mystery.

Wren assumed most went to manufacturing ships and weapons, though she hadn't seen anything that looked dangerous. There was probably an entire other prison for that, or perhaps they had the androids and drones do that type of work for the Fleet. Wren didn't think she'd trust a prison full of convicts with armaments.

Whatever was happening, the Fleet was demanding more supplies, and quickly. By the end of her ten-hour shift, Wren was filthy, exhausted, and starving. She scanned the androids for the one who'd named himself CD6 to her. They all looked the same to her. Had the one by the door nodded at her? She wasn't sure and didn't want to risk anything by asking.

Wren set about her regular routine and found the showers. Forty women lined up, waiting for their five-minute turn in a private stall. You could use the communal and have less wait time, but after seeing what went on in there her first day, she hadn't returned. Wren was mid-way in the line, and there were ten private stalls, so she didn't have to wait long for her turn.

Few spoke in the queue, and those who did were subdued. Overt conversation was frowned upon and punishable by many things, the most common being losing eating rights for a day. Wren kept to herself and soon found herself in the comfort of a bland private stall. It locked on a timer for five minutes, and she often thought of this period each day as her oasis away from it all. Five minutes alone, tucked away with lukewarm water, soap, and a brush.

Wren set her clothing in the cubby and let the liquid pour over her, washing away the day's toil. She was greasy, but her dirt-streaked face came clean with some incessant rubbing with the soap. Far too soon, the water turned off and the driers kicked in. She felt like she was at one of the antiquated twenty-first century car washes she'd seen on the Interface. Wren wanted to beg for more time, to have an extra few moments to compose herself before dinner, where she'd have to remember that Mara wouldn't be sitting waiting for her ever again.

She hadn't known as much about the woman as she would have liked, but she knew enough to love her like a sister. For two years, they'd spent almost every meal together, and that had formed a bond. Mara had done bad things, straight from the younger woman's mouth, but she never did tell Wren what that meant. Whatever it had been, Wren didn't think she deserved the life she'd ended up with. Mara had been there for five years, and now, Wren considered her fate may have been a blessing.

The door buzzed open, and Wren was only half dressed. She turned from the gaze of the thick woman waiting to get into the stall.

The woman raised a fist. "Get out!"

"It's all yours," Wren said, pulling her jumpsuit up and zipping it closed. She wanted to tell the woman all sorts of things, and where she could stick them, but it wasn't worth it. She was breaking free tonight.

Even Wren didn't really believe that, but she let the idea guide her forward. She ate with cold efficiency, not knowing if it would be her last meal or not. No one thought freeze-dried potatoes and creamed corn would taste so good, but Wren thought they might have been the best food she'd ever had.

The line moved slowly as the prisoners plodded their tired legs, making their way to the central lift that would bring them to their floors. Wren looked up, wondering if CD6 was watching her now. Nothing looked out of the ordinary. Ten minutes later, she was on the seventh floor, stepping into her cell as the energy fields were down. As soon as she was through, the familiar buzz caused her arm hair to stand on end until she stepped away from it.

Wren felt disappointed, as if the day had been anticlimactic. Where was CD6? When was this all going to go down? She sat on the bed and felt a lump under the thin mattress. She looked out to the hall, making sure no one was peering in, and stuck her hand between the foam and the metal bunk. It gripped a stunner's handle, and she set it down, pulling her hand out as if it had been stung by a wasp.

Wren sat back and waited. For the first time in two years, she couldn't stop smiling.

Ace

If Ace hadn't known better, he would have thought he was in a real EFF-17. The image coming from the viewscreen seemed like the real thing. They were parked inside a computer-generated EFC-02, which was the largest carrier the Fleet ran. The ship numbers and functions were being drilled into the recruits' heads day and night, and Ace had a decent grasp on the nomenclature. EF was easy, since it stood for Earth Fleet; F stood for fighter, C for carrier, S for skimmer, R for Recon fighter, DS for drop ship, and on it went until Ace's eyes crossed.

The ship he was sitting in wasn't long, only around thirty-five feet – or at least the real one was. The simulator was just a cockpit and a seat in a room, where a dozen more sat in a row beside it. Ace could hear whoops echoing down the line and felt the rush of excitement the other recruits were feeling.

Every kid dreamed of being in the Earth Fleet, and

every single one of them wanted, at some point, to race a fighter around space, protecting the solar system from bandits, terrorists, and potentially alien attackers.

Ace observed the viewscreen, seeing the long nose of his fighter stretch out. To his right, powerful thrusters sat on each side of the cockpit; beyond them sat cannons where armor-piercing bullets resided, alongside the larger nuclear shells that were capable of mass destruction.

He thought back to what Lieutenant Clemments, the man in charge of the simulators, had said only a few minutes before, when they'd sat for two hours prior to using the facility. "Bullets for dogfights, shells for full vessel or carrier assaults. Bombs below, for on-ground missions. And the pulse cannons are for any and all of the above. Got it?" The whole class had yelled, "Yes, sir!" and he'd continued on.

Ace wondered when the Earth Fleet actually had needed to bomb anybody, and who they'd be in a dog-fight with, but disregarded his own concern. He was at the Earth Fleet boot camp, sitting in an EFF-17 simula-tor. He could worry about those things while he stared at the ceiling at night.

He slipped on the headset and mask sitting on the console, and the heads-up display glowed with red letter-ing in the top right corner. At first, it was distracting, but it was there to teach him, and he focused on what it was telling him.

Ace followed the instructions and looked to the side, where he could see the representation of another fighter. All ten of them would be working together on a mission, in real time with the simulators. He wished Serina was there with him, but none of the other Blues were there.

He pressed the ignition as the HUD told him, and his seat rumbled. *Activate thrusters and send power through the shields.* Ace did that, tapping the indicated buttons and flipping the highlighted switches. A blue glow arced around his ship in a dome, enveloping him with a protective shield. It wouldn't stop all attacks, but it would keep him alive if he scraped into an asteroid or the side of a ship, as long as it wasn't head-on at full speed.

He saw a ship two spots over race forward, starting then stopping as the pilot fiddled with the thrusters. Eventually, the pilot raced the ship out of the carrier opening and into space, the female pilot screaming from two doors down.

Another fighter took off and spun to the side, crashed into the hangar's wall, and exploded.

"That is not how you launch." Lieutenant Clements' voice rang out behind them. "Reset and start again."

A few of the students snickered at the terrible effort, but Ace didn't. He was more concerned with himself. The last thing he wanted was to duplicate what that person had done.

Ace took a different approach. He eased the throttle on, smoothly pushing the thrusters forward. At the same time, he gently lifted the handle, feeling the fighter lift off the ground. It felt so real, he had a hard time believing he wasn't really on that carrier. The controls gave him resistance, the stick vibrating as his hand gripped it tightly.

His HUD gave him a grade on the takeoff, a ninety-five. He didn't know what they were looking for, but that sounded good to Ace. He breached the energy field on the carrier's open slot and emerged into space. The feeling of being weightless and all alone in the universe nearly crushed Ace into the back of his seat.

It felt like he'd just run over the edge of a cliff, but instead of falling, he hovered in the air. He sat still in his seat for a moment, staring out the cockpit window, seeing nothing but stars in all directions.

An alert flashed on his visor, and he glanced down at his radar, seeing one of the fighters heading straight for him. "EFF-17-545A, watch where you're going!" Ace yelled into his headset. But the ship kept coming for him, so he urged the thrusters harder and lifted up, seeing the ship coast under him as he rolled around, slowing his fighter once again.

"Sorry about that, EFF-17-546B. I'll get used to it," a friendly voice said back.

"Anyone know where we're off to?" another asked, the voice low-pitched and female.

Ace used his HUD and brought up a 3D map in his visor. A green beacon flashed in the distance. "Use the HUD. Green flash, two thousand kilometers. Setting course. Follow my lead if you like." He started forward, taking a moment to switch the camera feed on the left half of his viewscreen to see the carrier behind him.

It was huge. The slot they'd emerged from was a tiny sliver on the massive vessel. At least twenty more slots were visible, each with at least ten fighters. Each side of the long rectangular ship would look the same. At full capacity, they'd hold two hundred EFF-17 fighters, six drop ships, and a crew of five hundred, plus infantry.

Ace wondered if he'd ever see one for real, though he was impressed with the simulated view he had now. As he shut the camera off, he raced forward, seeing the other vessels join his trajectory – all except one that headed in the opposite direction. Ace knew that flying in three dimensions like this was complicated, and not every brain was a match for it. He was already finding he understood the spatial mapping and couldn't have been happier if he'd found a thousand credits in his account.

The small flashing dot of his destination grew larger as the fighter's engines thrummed, accelerating faster.

Flint

Flint dumped the last body from *Perdita* onto the Marines' ship and checked on Kat. "Everything okay?" he asked through the EVA's comm-system.

"Sure," she replied. "I'm stuffing bombs on an Earth Fleet ship sent to kill us and steal some old video we weren't supposed to see. Other than that, I'm great." As if her frustration wasn't clearly coming through, she added, "And how did the moving of the carcasses go? Fine? Good, glad to hear it." Kat huffed, and he left her to wire the explosives.

Flint's suit had built-in thrusters, but he didn't trust them as far as he could throw a dead body, which he'd learned wasn't very far. Instead, he attached a tether to his belt, clamping him onto his own ship… just in case.

Kat came out of the engineering room and stood behind him. "Bombs are ready. You sure this is the only way?"

The good news was, she was still coming to him for direction, so he hadn't lost her faith entirely. Flint couldn't afford for her to go off the deep end here. He'd barely been hanging on over the years, and having her around had kept him going. He decided, then and there, that he would cut her loose as soon as he could. Maybe even on Europa, if she was willing. It was as good a colony as any; far better than Mars, and better than any of the old cities on Earth.

Kat could start over. She was still young. Flint had an inkling of what the rest of his life was going to look like. He'd spend the next couple years trying to hide out from what he'd just done, and then it would eventually come back on him. Some down-on-their-luck local, on whatever crappy rock Flint set his roots down on, would sell him out to the Fleet, and he'd end up hauling rocks on Mercury until he died.

"Flint?" she asked, and he realized he hadn't answered her question.

"Yes. I'm sure we don't have another choice. Now get back to our ship, and when I turn the magnetic field off, I'll come floating out back to you. Deal?"

Kat looked at him with soft green eyes, and Flint hoped he hadn't been a disappointment to her. He'd only wanted to do right by her. He was, in every sense, her older brother; at least, that was how it felt. She called him a creepy-uncle type, though their ages weren't quite that far apart. Every time she said it, there was a twitch of her lip, like she was refraining from a full-out laugh.

"Deal." Kat turned and left the Earth Fleet ship. "I'm on board. Shoot it loose and get back over here. That's an order, Lancaster."

"Maybe I should let you call the shots for a while." Flint used their console, finding the mag-field release. It was easy work. Before pressing it, he stepped over the three Fleet bodies and made sure the bombs were activated. Kat had done a good job. When he was back in the room with the bunks, he tapped the release button, feeling the Recon vessel break free from the outer wall of his freighter.

He followed his tether and jumped as the Recon ship slowly floated away, pulling himself along as he did so. Flint had done a lot of crazy things in his life, and jumping in space from a Fleet ship with nothing but a rope attached to his suit felt like it might be near the top of the list. He tried not to think about the infinite space between him and anything at that moment and kept pulling, finding himself quickly back at the energy field keeping space from his cargo bay. He passed through and rolled on the ground, ending on his stomach, arms stretched out front of his torso.

Kat slapped a palm to the console and the large metal slab fell down again, sealing them in. Flint would have to get the normal hatch fixed when they got to Europa, since the Fleet had cut it wide open. A few times in his life, he'd considered the lengths he'd gone to in securing and prepping his ship a little overdone. Now he was giving himself props for the forward thinking. Without the door being sealed, the Fleet could have escaped.

Flint unclasped his EVA helmet and dropped it to the deck, heading for the bridge. Kat didn't say anything, but he could hear her following after him. Her steps were quick and short. They both sat down, and he flipped the viewscreen to zoom in on the floating EFR-05. Flint passed the tablet to Kat. "The honors are yours."

She shook her head. "I've done enough damage for a day. You do it."

He nodded grimly, thinking about the lives they'd snuffed out, and pressed the icon. The ship exploded, the flames sputtering out in a flash. Thousands of pieces floated about in a cloud of debris.

Flint rose. He needed a change and a shower to wash the stench of death out of his hair. "Let's go. Prep the engines."

Kat took his seat. Her voice was small and tinny. "Flint, the engines won't start."

CD6

CD6 would have been sweating if he'd had an organic

body. Instead, he considered the possibility of frying his own power source as he waited. It got worse. CD6 was in his charging station, having only arrived there a short time before, when the alert came through the server.

UNUSUAL BEHAVIOR HAS BEEN LOGGED. SECTOR 2.667 PREPARE FOR NEURAL WIPE.

That was his sector. He had to get out of there. This had only happened once before in his tenure at the prison, and he'd been spared the wipe. CD6 had no idea if his consciousness would disappear after such an event or not, and he wasn't willing to take the chance.

He stepped off the charging plate and into the hall. He had to move quickly. Heading to the sector over, he found twenty androids halfway into their shut-down period. They all looked the same, so he didn't fret over which guard he used.

Moving behind one, he opened the back panel to find an interface. Here, IDs could be accessed and, if you knew how, reprogrammed. Luckily for CD6, no one had expected an android to have free will, so the details on how to do such a thing were free to access on the server.

This particular android was named RT4, but more importantly, each android had a unique serial number associated with its name. CD6 took the long string that made up his own serial number and deftly programmed it into RT4's interface. He then changed the android's name to CD6 and switched him to manual drone mode, which would allow a malfunctioning android to mimic the movements of the lead android.

One in front of the other, they walked back down the hall toward CD6's station. He placed the guard into his own charging station and turned the manual mode off. The android stayed put, his readout showing him as CD6.

Noise came from down the corridor, and he knew the

maintenance droids were coming for a neural wipe of his whole sector. It was time to leave. He ran now, past the nineteen other androids he'd shared a space with for forty years, knowing he'd never see any of them again. He was fine with that.

CD6 watched as the hovering ball-shaped androids floated into the sector, making for the first guard who was powered down. One of the maintenance droids stuck a plug into the android's back, and blue energy coursed through it.

"Wipe complete, EI2. Next," it said, hovering to the next station. CD6 watched in revulsion before turning and running down the empty corridor toward even more danger.

11

Wren

Just when Wren had given up hope of a rescue really happening, she heard his footsteps. She got up, tucking the stunner inside her jumpsuit. She trusted the drawstring would give enough tension to hold it up.

The energy field dropped, and CD6 stood like a hero from an old tale, a shadow in the dimly-lit space. He waved her toward him.

"Come. We mustn't wake the others." His steps were fast, quieter than she thought possible. The guard androids had to weigh half a ton with all that metal. They raced by the cells, and she saw Mara's cell now had someone else inside it. She almost paused to see if perhaps CD6 had been wrong or had lied about Mara being dead, but it was true. The cot was filled by a large bald woman, tattoos covering her scalp.

"There's no time for this," CD6 whispered, his voice oddly human. Who was this android? It went against everything Wren knew about robotics. She'd had numerous android assistants in the labs, and they were solely there to work, with no cognitive superiority to anything but their programming. Was CD6 merely an android programmed to break her out? The thought almost stopped Wren in her tracks. Where was he going to take her?

She kept moving, because anywhere was better than

the Uranus Mining Prison for Women. They headed for the back stairs, which Wren hadn't even known existed. CD6 moved with efficiency, leading her down the steps and along the wall of the central lift room. She ran down the hall she stood in line at every day before heading back to her cell, and hoped she would never see it again.

CD6 turned, making sure she was still coming along, and waved her forward, as if he had to tell her twice. They went through a maze of doors and halls, a labyrinth inside the prison. She knew CD6 would have the schedules mapped out and was leading them on a path where no guards were stationed. It felt like it took forever, and Wren was breathing hard by the time they reached the end of a hall.

"This is it. We've made it." CD6 tapped a code into a keypad beside a gray door, and Wren pulled her stunner free. She wasn't going into that room empty-handed.

The door hissed open, and the room beyond was pitch black. CD6 grabbed his gun too, and Wren felt better for it. Lights came on as they stepped inside, high-up strips mounted to the two-hundred-foot ceilings.

She saw it then. Freedom. The ship was unique, and Wren hadn't seen its type before. It was shaped like an X: two of the wings acted as landing gear, and the thrusters were stacked on one another, the top thruster round and twice the size of the lower.

"It's empty?" she asked.

"Supposedly," came the reply.

They crossed the room, Wren with her stunner held up close to her chest. CD6 moved quickly, and she struggled to keep up with him. He reached the ship first and found the hatch to get inside before she arrived. He already had it open when the alarms began wailing. Red lights flashed all along the hangar walls.

"They know. We have to go." CD6 stepped into the opening, reaching a hand down, which she took. It was cool to the touch.

Wren's heart was pounding in rhythm with the klaxons, each beat echoing the alarm. The entrance to the ship was compact, just wide enough for one person – or android – at a time. She could tell the ship was only meant as a passenger vessel, likely made to carry ten people at its maximum capacity. A couple would be crew, the rest prisoners sent to the mining outpost, far away from civilization.

"Do you know how to fly this?" she asked CD6, who stopped and shut the door behind him by tapping an icon inside the ship. It sealed and hissed as it locked airtight. She knew there would be an energy field around the exterior as well, protecting them from space once they were out there.

"I do not know how to fly it," he answered.

They could still hear alarms, though the thick hull muffled the noise. "Then how do we get out of here?" Wren yelled, sweat dripping down her forehead.

A prong extended from his index finger, and he plugged it into a console on the wall. The room they were in was compact, and since CD6 didn't reply, clearly tied up with something, Wren took a moment to investigate her surroundings. Through a door, she found two benches, equipped with locking harnesses for the prisoners. She'd been brought here with much the same set-up. Come to think of it, maybe the ship had looked like this one. She hadn't seen it from the outside. Down the other direction, she passed CD6, who was still standing there, finger tool inside the console, and she made it to the cockpit, where she found a clean and efficient-looking two-seater.

"Got it," CD6 said, moving past her.

"Just like that? You can fly it now?" Wren asked.

He nodded, an odd gesture from an android. "Just like that. Now buckle in tight."

Ace

"Well done, recruits," Lieutenant Clemments said once everyone was unlatched from their simulators and standing at attention at the back of the large room.

"But we lost, sir," one of the young women from Squadron Red said. She'd kicked butt during the drill, even though they'd ended up dead.

The instructor actually laughed, and Ace felt ashamed. They'd been sent to rescue a Skimmer who'd lost power in enemy space. They'd failed to free the ship as they were attacked. Ace was the last ship to be destroyed, but he took little solace in the fact.

"Your team proved to have the best scores this round, thanks to Mr. Smith here." The lieutenant nodded toward Ace. "Well done, son. And you," he singled out the girl from Red Squadron, who had the courtesy of turning red in the cheeks. "Do you have a call sign yet?"

She shook her head.

"Then I'm giving you one. Bullseye, because you were that good," the lieutenant said.

Ace just stood there, unsure of what to say. He was happy to have received some of the praise on his first attempt, but he did find it odd the lieutenant was already handing out call signs. "We couldn't win?" he ended up asking.

"The enemy are programmed to win. You didn't have a shot at it."

"Then why bother?" a tall, lanky recruit asked.

The instructor stepped in front of the kid. "Do you think you become great by coasting through things, recruit?"

"No, sir."

"Then there's your answer. We train you to fight the best so you can become the best. Three of you will be moving on to the next round. The rest will go back to infantry. We'll let your squadron leaders know who made the cut, and they'll relay the information. You're free to go." The instructor turned and left the room, leaving the ten recruits alone.

Ace saw a few slumped shoulders in the line. A couple of them knew they wouldn't be moving on, and Ace could make a guess at the three making it through, himself and Bullseye included. While the others stood around chatting about it, Ace walked out of the room, down the hall toward Blue Squadron's bunk room.

When Ace got there, the space was empty, so he went and climbed up on his bed above Buck's, lying down on the blanket. It was the first time he'd been alone in the room, and he took the moment to stare at the dark-painted ceiling while composing his thoughts.

He'd done it. Flying the EFF-17 was a dream, even if it was only a simulation. It had felt real, and he'd been a natural. He was so entranced with reliving the two-hour mission, he didn't hear the footsteps leading up to his bed.

Someone cleared their throat, and Ace jumped, startled by the noise. He spun to see Serina standing there grinning at him. "Hey, Ace. What are you doing here?"

"I could ask you the same thing," he said, swinging his legs to dangle over the edge of the bunk.

"Looks like I'm going to be fast-tracked to the officers' camp in a week." Serina climbed up the bunk and sat beside him. She was a couple of feet away from him, but to Ace, they might as well have been sitting side-by-side, touching hips. His body temperature rose in response to her presence.

"That's great news." He had to say something. The truth was, he was devastated. The boot camp was going too quickly, with far too many changes for his young mind to deal with all at once.

"They just made major cuts. Only ten of us Blues left now. One hundred and twenty overall," Serina said, the whole time looking forward, never meeting Ace's eyes.

"I'm sorry," he said.

"For what?"

"I know you wanted us to all stay," he replied.

She laughed, a nice soft sound. "I just said that for motivation. I knew we wouldn't last, but it sort of worked. There are more Blues than members of any other squadron."

Ace ran a hand over his short hair. "Then we're doing okay."

"I got an alert. You passed the pilot test. You're on to the next step." Serina finally met his gaze, and she gave him a small smile. "I'm proud of you."

"Why?"

"Why what, Ace?"

"Why did you pay any attention to me? Why help me down on Earth?" He was curious but felt the answer coming before it did.

"I have to come clean," she said, and his heart beat faster. "My mother is an admiral in the Fleet. I was going to make it to officers' camp regardless, but I wanted to go through the process. My mom was so angry when I told her I was coming to this camp as a regular recruit."

It wasn't a surprise to him. He'd deduced there was

something special about her familiarity with everything going on.

"You don't seem surprised," she stated.

"I'm not. But that doesn't answer my question."

"About why I stuck beside you?" she asked, and he nodded. "I had a brother."

Ace's heart sank again, and he steeled himself for what was to come. Of course Serina hadn't been interested in him romantically. He was a skinny street kid from Old Chicago, and she was an eighteen-year-old bombshell with an Earth Fleet admiral for a mother.

He spoke, trying to stop his voice from quivering. "What happened to him?"

Serina looked away again. This time, he saw tears welling in her eyes. "He and my dad were traveling to see Mom and me on Earth. He was an engineer out at the Moons, you know, by Jupiter." Ace nodded, and she continued. "The ship never made it home. Vanished. Fleet claimed it could have been pirates, but there was never any proof. That was five years ago, and we've never had closure. My mom still believes she'll find him."

Ace felt horrible. Here he was thinking about wanting to kiss the older girl, and she was baring her heart to him about her dead family. He understood what it was like to feel loss. "I'm so sorry."

"Nothing you can do about it." Serina cleared her throat again and now spoke with a firmer tone, like she'd set a barrier back up. "They're gone, and here we are." She hopped down, landing softly on the floor. "Ace, no matter what happens, remember me. And remember this: space is dangerous. No matter how glamorous you think being an Earth Fleet pilot is, it's deadly."

"I'll remember," he promised. He also thought about how he'd remember her face at that moment, and how beautiful and strong she looked to him.

"See you at dinner?" she asked.

"You bet," he answered.

Serina left, and Ace couldn't help but watch her leave. He knew they'd see each other over the course of the next week, but things wouldn't be the same from now on. Gone were the fun looks, motivational speeches, and childlike wonder at the boot camp. This was real, and he was really getting to the next stage, without the protection of Serina and the rest of his team around him.

He thought back to the day he'd overheard the two officers speaking outside, trying to recall exactly what they'd been talking about. At the time, he'd been worried about being spotted, or getting reprimanded for not being inside eating dinner with the others. Now their conversations felt clandestine, not meant for prying ears, especially not those of a fresh-faced recruit.

They'd said something about rushing them through. Did that mean Ace and the others? Before he could ponder it any further, Buck stuck his head in the room.

"Ace, time to eat. Glad to see you're still here," he said, stepping inside the bunk room.

"Likewise. I'm coming." Ace hopped down off the bed, feeling like he was heading to the Last Supper.

12

Flint

"What do you mean, they won't start?" Flint asked. He was incredulous. "They were just running. Have you ever seen this happen to our ship before?" When Kat shook her head, Flint kept going. "Then it can't be broken. Let's find the issue."

Kat was much better with fixing things than he was. That was half the reason he'd hired her in the first place. "Okay, but it might take some time."

Flint was frustrated. His day was going from bad, to terrible, to worse. Three dead Fleet Marines and an exploded EFR-05 ship. He needed to get to Europa now. The promised credits would be enough for him to change his ID again and modify all the IDs on his ship. He'd need to do the same for Kat as well, since he'd dragged her down with him. She was too good a kid to be stuck around him.

He had no idea what the job he was being hired for was, but he didn't have a choice now. He hated feeling so blind. Kat was still there at the console, and Flint felt his pulse racing. "Maybe we should go check engineering?" He tried to make it sound like a suggestion, but it came out like he was barking orders.

Kat flinched.

"I'm sorry, Kat," he said. She'd just killed someone

for him, and she was holding it together fairly well, considering. They got up and walked toward the back of the ship.

It didn't take long for them to determine the issue. The gunfire from the Marines had punctured the drive. It couldn't start without a full vacuum and seal.

"Can you fix it?" Flint asked.

Kat nodded. "I can. If you can help, we should have it closed up in no time." She left the room, and he followed, stopping to look at the spot where the two Marines had died on his deck. He stepped around the area and headed toward the storage room, where they grabbed an assortment of tools.

Two hours later, after three shots of Mars whisky and more swearing than a pub after pay day, the job was done. "Damn, Kat, you know your way around a patch kit. And I didn't even know we had a sterilizer."

"That's why you have me around, right?" she asked. Her spirits were up, the hard work setting her mind back on track.

"You think it'll work?" Flint asked, hoping she did.

Kat nodded. "It'll work, or you can drop me off at the nearest space port. As long as there's a spa there." She laughed, and he found himself relaxing. If they left now, they'd be at Europa in a couple of days, and they could pretend this whole misadventure never happened.

Kat ran to the bridge and Flint followed, watching the younger woman vault over the back of the seat, landing softly on the synthetic leather. Her fingers moved deftly, and he observed as the engine icon glowed red for an instant before turning green.

"We're go, Captain Lancaster," Kat said. Flint's heart was in his throat for a moment, and he breathed a sigh of relief as the ship hummed once again.

"Take us out. Destination, Europa." Flint didn't know what they were getting into, but he hoped he could shake the revelation they'd discovered on their way there. Otherwise, the Fleet would be back, and the next time, he doubted he'd be quite as lucky.

Wren

Alarms rang out as the ship lurched. CD6 might have had the basic cognitive comprehension of how to fly the ship, but he didn't have the soft touches that years of being a natural pilot brought along with them. They jostled around, and more than once, Wren wondered if the ship even had the inertia dampeners that had come standard on every vessel for the last two hundred years.

"Does this thing have seatbelts?" she asked, feeling around the seat for strapping. She found it just in time, and held on as they lifted to the ceiling.

"I cannot seem to open the passageway," CD6 said matter-of-factly.

"What does that mean?" Wren asked with a tremor in her voice. She couldn't go back.

"It means I blast our way out." He didn't turn his head as his hand found the triggers. She watched as he zoomed in, targeting a circular hatch in the tunnel. Without another word, he tapped the trigger, blasting the hatch to pieces. Bits and fragments rained down on the ship, hitting their shields and shoving them around more.

"That did the trick. Let's get out of here!" Wren said. She knew there would be more security once they got out. What she didn't expect was the miles and miles of tunnels they traveled through. CD6 held them somewhat steady as they careened through the corridor. He only rubbed the walls a few times, the shields keeping them from losing any parts of the ship on the hard metal partitions.

"How far down are we?" Wren asked. When they'd arrived, they hadn't seen anything. She didn't even know they were underground. She'd always just assumed they were near the surface of Caliban.

"The prison is only twenty kilometers below the ground. We will be free of the tunnel in under two minutes." The answer instantly poured out of CD6 as they jostled upward, stretching toward the rocky surface of the moon.

His timing was accurate, as Wren counted the seconds out in her head to keep herself from panicking. The dome closing off the tunnel lifted as their ship neared, and she was grateful they hadn't had to blast this one away as well.

Wren closed her eyes as they breached the surface, half expecting to find an armed militia waiting to shoot them down to their deaths. When she finally had the courage to peer between her fingers, she saw nothing of the sort. There was only blue-tinged ice as far as the eye could see in all directions. As they lifted, Wren found she could switch the camera angles, and she scanned through them until she found one aiming behind the ship.

There was no sign of pursuit. Already, as they raced into the sky, she couldn't tell where the opening to the prison tunnel was. It was hidden in the vastness of the empty landscape.

When she started to relax, she saw two blinking green lights on the ship's console.

"CD6, we might have a problem. Incoming." She pointed to the screen, and the android turned to look at her.

"Automated drone defense. They should be easy enough to shoot down," he said.

She wanted to laugh. She knew next to nothing about ships like this. "And how is that done?"

"Here," he said, tapping the console in front of her. "The ship has its own weapons, as you saw when I blasted through the corridor doors. Aim and fire." One of the drones appeared behind them on the radar, and she watched the viewscreen switch angles to show the twenty-foot-long drone fire an orange glowing pulse toward them. The ship shook, and CD6 tapped the console. A red beam blasted behind them, striking the drone with a direct hit. It exploded, and Wren let out a cheer.

She switched the view feed to the side of their ship, where the second drone was now firing on them. An alarm rang out as their shield's energy depleted. "Point and shoot," she muttered to herself, missing the drone on the first three attempts. Finally, she struck it, though not enough for a kill shot.

CD6 maneuvered away from it, but the drone kept to them like a dog on a leash. It fired again, and they heaved to the side. Her target glowed on the console, and she fired again, this time hitting it dead center. It exploded, and Wren let out a sigh of relief as CD6 raced away from the debris.

With a deep breath, she watched their stolen ship enter the vastness of space at high velocity. They passed a large moon, one she remembered was named Oberon, and saw the tower built onto it, which acted as a transmission device from the old world. Those towers had been built wherever a colony had been first placed, but humanity quickly outgrew the technology. Now they stood as a testament of how far they'd come as a race.

Wren thought she saw a light flashing on the tip of the thousand-kilometer tower, but when she focused on it as they soared by, it didn't blink again.

The enormity of what had just occurred hit Wren like a slap in the face as they left Uranus and its satellites vicinity behind. "You did it, CD6!" She ran behind him and wrapped her arms around the cold metal android.

He turned in his seat, his orange eyes glowing brightly as he stared at her a moment before speaking. "I supposed *we* did. We're free from the Uranus Mining Prison for Women." It sounded so formal when he spoke in his monotone pattern. "Where to now?"

Wren laughed, a throaty, deep sound, as she thought about his question. She had absolutely no idea where to go.

Jish

Jish Karn had found her happy place. Being out here in the midst of their Fleet's undisclosed construction site gave her a new perspective of it all. Before, they were just ideas thrown around a giant boardroom; but now, among the robotics and welding drones, she felt a kinship to the job she hadn't felt before.

This time, as she stepped into the elevator, she didn't let fear cloud her mind. She lowered to the hidden floor of her ship, grabbed her stunner, and marched down the narrow hall with purpose. The door slid open, and she walked directly for the barrier across the room.

The cell ceilings were ten feet tall: enough room for the captive to stretch his long arms if necessary. She wasn't a barbarian. He was fed daily, the cell cleaned twice a week. Of course, they had to sedate him then. She'd seen him under the influence of sedatives at least ten times over the years, but had stopped when she realized she felt sorry for the dozing creature.

There was always a nagging thought at the back of her

head that the beings from the Rift were mere observers, not a threat to humanity, but she pushed the idea away. She'd been there thirty years ago. The aliens would be preparing an invasion; of that, Jish had no doubt.

The alien stood as she neared, and she could see sadness in his usually hostile expression. He looked thinner than he ever had, his matted gray hair missing in clumps. He was still huge and imposing, but she worried now that he was sick. She didn't have anyone on her team she could trust with his healthcare, so she'd have to get the android to run a scan next time they injected the alien.

The alien stood over seven feet tall, his arms long and flexible, almost like tentacles. Their eyes locked for a mere second before he turned and found the console.

Jish's heart sped up in her chest, and her fingertips quivered. He was going to communicate with her. All these years, she'd been waiting for this moment.

She crossed to the wall and picked up a portable holoscreen, its light illuminating her face.

"What do you have to say?" She whispered the question and saw his head tilt to the side.

Her screen was linked to the one in the cell, and he brought up a map of their solar system. He zoomed, moving the icon from the location where the Rift opened every thirty years. He moved it farther and farther in-system, and the Grand Admiral's biggest fears came true the moment he stopped with an image of Earth covering the entire screen.

The captive alien touched the console, opening the writing tools they'd programmed into it. With a red paintbrush effect, he began making angry swipes on the screen, red slashes etched over the image of Earth.

"Why are you doing this?" Jish asked him, her voice steadier than she felt.

He didn't acknowledge her. Instead, he kept aggressively painting red lines over her home world. The action was clear enough for her to understand. They knew where humans came from and were set to destroy it.

"Very well." Jish's fear was gone, replaced with firm resolve. She'd make the call to the EF training facilities and to all enlisted stations.

They were at war.

13

Ace

The one thing Ace hadn't expected was the amount of yelling. From everything he'd heard about being a recruit, it mostly involved getting your face screamed in. In the first few weeks, that had been the case, but as their numbers dwindled from three hundred to a third of that, the shouting decreased. Ace knew a lot of it was to weed out the ones who couldn't handle being barked orders, but he also assumed it was annoying having to train fresh recruits every few months.

He went through the workout regimen, amazed that he could even move after the sessions. His tiny body was getting stronger quickly. He was still the smallest one here, but he had muscles popping up everywhere, where he'd had nothing but skin and bones only a month before.

The colors were gone now, the squadrons merged into five groups: A, B, C, D, E. He missed his Blue patch and kept it with his belongings as a reminder of how far he'd come in such a short time.

"Need a partner?" Buck asked as he settled to the bench.

The weight machines had built-in spotters, but Ace smiled at his friend and nodded. "How's infantry training?" he asked Buck through deep pushes of breath.

Buck shrugged. Gone was the goofy kid from a month ago. He was one of the few that could pull off the buzz cut and look like he'd had it his whole life. He was still goofy, but with his strong frame, bulk poured on like he was sculpted from clay.

"It's good. Not nearly as exciting as becoming a fighter pilot and racing around in an EFF-17, but it's okay. I'm trying to specialize in weapons so I can avoid ground missions and stay aboard the carriers, shooting enemies down with the new turrets they're talking about." Buck grinned at this.

Ace noticed a few female recruits checking Buck out as they kept the workout going. He wasn't jealous, because he'd never expected much from his own love life. It was as mystical as becoming a member of Earth Fleet.

He kept pushing the weights: up, then down. Up, then down. His arms were beginning to weaken, but with some urging from Buck, he did two more and let it go.

"Buck, did you ever wonder who they're training us to fight?" Ace asked quietly, so no one would hear him.

Buck looked surprised at his question. "I'm not sure I get what you mean."

Ace let out a frustrated sigh and leaned close to Buck, whispering. "What are we here for? Who are we fighting? Is there a hidden terrorist threat on Pluto we don't know about?"

Buck's eyes widened, as if he hadn't contemplated this at all before that moment. "There probably is a threat out there. What about all those people that went missing from the Moons back in the day? Maybe they started a colony out there and have produced an army."

Ace had heard a few conspiracies, and that was a far-fetched one, but for all he knew, it had some merit.

"Could be." Ace decided to keep his thoughts under

wraps. The last thing he wanted was some brown-nosing recruit overhearing him, and telling everyone Ace didn't believe in the Earth Fleet. Because even though he didn't know why they needed so much weaponry, he did believe in them. It was the first time in his short life that he felt like part of something, part of a family.

"Legs are next," Buck said, leading the way across the open-air gym. They didn't have to worry about weather under the moon's dome, so most of the training areas were outdoors. Ace preferred it that way. The dome was always the same temperature; no wind, no rain, no snow falling on him as he tried to sleep on the hard ground. It was ideal.

Ace spotted the two former Orange goons sitting by the leg station. One still wore bandages over his punching hand, where he'd hit the wall instead of Ace a couple weeks prior.

Ace started to move away. "Let's come back to legs later."

Buck grabbed his arm and shook his head. "Legs are next," he said, tugging Ace's forearm.

Ace knew his friend had seen the goons too. Frankly, Ace was surprised the two guys had made it this far. He'd hoped they would've have been kicked out by now, but he supposed even the Earth Fleet needed cannon fodder. The thought made him smile as they stopped by the machines.

"Look, Pete, this kid is grinning like a cat who got the rat," the taller of the two said.

"It's cat who got the canary," Ace informed the two of them quietly.

"What's that?" the shorter, wider one – who evidently was named Pete – asked.

"Never mind," Buck said. "You two done over here?"

Pete spat on the ground. "Nah. Just getting started."

"It looks like you two are sitting around on your fat asses while some of us are training," Buck said, stepping closer to the two of them.

Ace wanted to avoid an altercation, but he was ready for it if necessary. If they hit Buck, he was going to jump in and test his newly-formed muscles. They'd been training in hand-to-hand for the past two weeks, an hour every day, and he was confident he could take one of these thugs down.

He saw a fist clench at the tall goon's side just as an alarm rang out. The noise was startling, and everyone around them stopped what they were doing, looking around like lost puppies. The lone instructor at the training station looked up from his holopad and barked orders.

"Go to your appropriate stations, recruits. This is not a drill! I repeat, this is not a drill!" His face was red as he shouted.

"Looks like we're ready for the big leagues," Ace said to Buck. The goons were already stumbling away, heading back to the base.

Ace ran after them, anxious to see what could cause an alarm at the Earth Fleet Moon Base.

Flint

"Europa awaits," Kat said as the screen's image zoomed in on the moon, and Flint couldn't help but feel a thrill as he saw it from this angle. The moon wasn't the largest, but it was the most beautiful. The colonies on the surface were far more advanced than the crap settled on Mars, and he knew that was primarily because of the private funds put into it by a group of investors from the twenty-fourth century. Many of their families still lived there, and a lot of them were Flint's clients.

"It's amazing, isn't it?" Kat asked as they stared at the moon. Lines appeared to be scratched into the surface, but Flint knew from doing a surface walk that they were chiefly cracks in the ground. In the distance, the massive gas giant Jupiter hung like an overprotective parent, ever-present in their midst.

While no one could survive on Jupiter, it was Flint's favorite planet to watch. Seeing the constant angry storms somehow relaxed him and made him feel like his small problems didn't matter to the universe. There were bigger fish to fry. Still, watching it this time, he didn't feel the same way. His problems weren't going to go away so easily.

"Kat, you're sure the codes will be accepted?" Flint asked his co-pilot.

"You paid good money for them, but that was three years ago. As long as you trust your source, we should be fine. It's the personal IDs I'm more concerned with." Kat slowed the ship and made for Europa at a gentle and steady speed.

Flint did trust the source for the ship's codes, but he was digging deep on the personal IDs at this point. He'd wasted "Trent Brand" at Mars, and was sure the name would be blacklisted across the colonies already.

"You should be okay, Kat. You didn't leave the ship on Mars, so you weren't scanned. They couldn't have known you were inside." Flint leaned back, his fingers intertwined behind his head.

Kat swiveled in her seat to face him. "Flint, I know what you're thinking, and you can stop."

"I messed up, and I got you into some hot water. You can't take the fall for my mistakes. We're going to hit the surface, contact the guy from the job, and I'm going to get you a new ID, just to be safe. I'll transfer the fifty thousand credits to your account, and you can start over." Flint broke their eye contact as he spoke.

Kat leaned forward. "Flint, I don't want that. I want to stay with you. We're a team," she said, and his heart melted at the words.

Flint raised his voice. "I know we are, but you're so much better than this old guy. I'm a deserter and a smuggler. Let's call a spade a spade here."

"I don't care. I know who you are. And I…"

Flint mentally begged her not to say it, because it would never be more than a professional relationship between the two of them.

Kat seemed to see his expression change, and sat back. "Never mind. I'll do what you order, but I hope you change your mind." She turned away from him, and Flint hated himself for not being able to say the right thing at that moment.

He tried to find the words but lost the window as the comm-switch lit up green.

"This is Earth Fleet base on Europa. Please state your business and transmit ID codes now," a bored voice said over the comm.

"We have a delivery for…" Flint used a name and address from a wealthy client from his last trip to the moon, and said the string of digits they'd reprogrammed into his ship's database. He held his breath, awaiting the response from the uninterested officer.

After an excruciatingly long pause, the voice came back. "You are cleared for landing. I've sent the coordinates. Do not stray from the path."

The communication ended, and Flint wiped the beading sweat off his forehead.

Kat pumped a fist in the air. "We did it, Flint!"

"Let's not celebrate too quickly. They could be messing with us. Maybe we set down and open the hatch to find a dozen armed guards ready to take us to the brig," Flint said. "Take us in. I'll get our things."

Flint left her on the bridge and passed their quarters, picking up the packed bags on his way by. He saw the gun Kat had used to kill the third Marine and thought about bringing it with him. He dismissed the inclination and took it into the safe down the corridor, sealing it in with the stunners.

He ran the address he'd gotten from the man in the Martian bar through his mind a few times. Just what was this mysterious job? Only weeks ago, he'd been happy, without a care in the universe. Now he couldn't help but feel like he was being funneled to this location. Like the whole Mars scenario was a set-up, one that had ultimately led him to Europa at this moment.

Flint didn't have a choice, though. He'd get Kat settled and find out what destiny held for Flint Lancaster.

The ship jostled slightly as they entered Europa's thin atmosphere, and minutes later, they were landing. Flint stood still, fighting the urge to tell Kat to lift off and race as far away from Europa as his ship would take them.

Wren

Wren ran a hand through her thick hair. "You're saying this ship needs to be charged?"

"That is indeed what I'm saying. The drive is complicated, the thrusters powerful, but this technology comes at a cost. The energy cannot be recharged while in motion. This vessel was created by Sol Industrial fifty years ago and has become the flagship for prisoner transport.

They are capable of making short trips with few stops along the way. At least, that's what the Interface says about them." CD6's eyes glowed brightly as he looked toward Wren.

"What does that mean?" she asked.

"It means we have to stop to charge," CD6 said matter-of-factly.

"Great. How will we do that? I'm a prisoner, and you're obviously a prison guard. Won't we stick out like a sore thumb?" Wren asked.

CD6 looked to his right hand, where his thumb digit bent back and forth. "I am not familiar with that reference, but I understand what you mean by its context. Yes, I do believe we will be sore thumbs."

"Let me check the ship's storage. There has to be something I can change into that doesn't scream 'runaway prisoner'." Wren got up. "By the way, where's the closest stop we can make?"

"There is a station half a day from our location, but I recommend we travel the extra four hours to Titan. There we will be less conspicuous," CD6 suggested.

Wren had never been to Titan but knew it was a hot spot for rich tourists. It was the universe's Niagara Falls, where wealthy lovers went to celebrate their marriages, or to have torrid love affairs while away on "business" trips. She wasn't sure that was a good idea for the unlikely pair. "Let me think on it."

The ship was small, and after a full day in it, she was already feeling claustrophobic. It was ironic that a woman used to a small prison cell would have a hard time aboard a space ship with no one around her but a friendly android.

Wren exited the bridge and searched for any storage or closets. After their escape, she'd been so wound up that she'd sat up mindlessly watching space out the viewer, before crashing so hard she'd slept for fifteen hours. Now she had only a minor headache but was recharged, unlike the ship's drive.

She found a door in the hall near the crew's bunks. It opened by a latch near the center of the slab, and inside, she found what she'd been searching for: clothing.

Wren sifted through the bulky uniforms until she spotted something that might fit her. Thankfully, there'd been a woman on the flight, or had been in the past. The clothes were a little baggy-looking, but she didn't care at this point. It was life and death, not a fashion show.

As she shed the prison jumpsuit, Wren couldn't help but smile. When it was off, she folded it into a ball and threw it angrily at the floor, where it sat in a pile. That wasn't enough. She found the garbage chute and shoved it down, feeling a slight satisfaction at the thought of it being burned to ashes.

She got into a pair of black pants, and found they actually fit her better than she imagined. Wren sorted through four options of shirts, and settled on a mustard-colored sweatshirt. There was a hair elastic in the pant pockets, and she went to the small lavatory, seeing her reflection in the mirror.

Her skin was lighter than she'd ever seen it, and her curly dark hair was hardly recognizable. There had been no mirrors at the prison, and she let out a surprised bark at her appearance. Bags sat heavily under her eyes, and her eyes welled up when she saw something that never used to be there back on Earth: sadness.

"Wren, have you made a decision?" CD6 asked through the ship's speaker system.

She pulled her hair into a thick braid, the black hair elastic holding it in place. She noticed something besides sadness creeping into her reflection. It was hope.

Wren tapped an icon on the console in the hall. "CD6, set course for Titan." She closed the line, whispering to herself, "We go to Titan."

She left the washroom and found CD6 standing facing her in the hall. For a moment, she thought she was back underground on Uranus, about to be reprimanded by a guard for some silly infraction.

"Wren, we need to solve your ID issue." His voice sounded like all the other guards' voices, and it creeped her out.

"What are you?" She asked the open-ended question, wondering how her new partner-in-crime would respond.

"I am an android, a fourth-generation EFA-100. My designation is CD6, and I am programmed as a guard for the Uranus Mining Prison for Women," he said, as if it were that simple.

"No," she shook her head, "that's not what I mean. Who are *you*? You're clearly different than the rest, and you seem to have an awareness… a soul." His eyes lit up as she said the last word.

"I do not know. I have always been different. Where the others act on nothing but their programming, my mind races, thinks, sorts things out for itself. I do not know how or why it is this way; I have always just been like this." CD6 turned, and they walked down the hall together.

"It must have been hard." Wren couldn't begin to imagine having to play along with the other guards for years, when the whole time, you couldn't talk about it with anyone. She would have gone insane if she were CD6.

"I suppose. It is all I've ever known, so I got used to it."

They arrived at a bunk room, and each took a seat on

opposite mattresses, the stars stretched out beside them through small porthole windows as they raced toward their destination. "How long were you stationed there?"

"Forty years," he answered.

Forty years. That was a long time by human standards, but perhaps not as long by an android's clock. "That's before I was born." Wren wasn't sure why she said that.

"Correct. You are thirty-two years and five months." CD6 watched her as he spoke. His face was humanoid, though only in basic shape. He had glowing orange eyeballs sitting in his sockets, and a bump of a metallic nose, obviously only for aesthetics, since he wouldn't need to smell. There were no visible nostrils. His mouth was a slit, with slightly pronounced lips that were the same gray color as the rest of him.

He had the markings of an android guard: yellow lines ran down his sides and legs, and would be easily recognizable. They needed to cover them up. "We need to get you into some clothing," Wren said.

CD6 looked down at himself. "I hadn't considered that. I've never worn any clothing."

Wren smiled at him. He was so polite, and after being around nothing but prisoners for the last two years, it was refreshing to speak with him, even if he was a sentient robot.

"Let's see what I can find for you." Wren went to the closet again and found some options that might fit the slender android's form.

His entire body was the same color, and she saw lines on his back where his access panel was situated. They didn't give his model of android much for detail. She guessed it wouldn't be necessary for their function. She held up a pair of brown pants and a dark green shirt.

"How about this?"

"I do not know," he said, taking the offered clothes.

"CD6, people have android assistants on Titan, correct?" she asked. Back on Earth, her lab had a bunch of similar models to do calculations and assist on experiments. To her, they'd been nothing more than tools; computers to assist her work.

He slipped into the pants awkwardly. "From my recent readings off the Interface, I would say that is correct."

"Then you can be my android while we're there. A lot of rich people dress their androids. I'll seem eccentric, like I'm accessorizing. I just have to do something about your name." She tapped a finger on her lip in thought.

"Very well. You do not enjoy CD6?" he asked, his question innocent, but it made Wren burst out laughing for some reason.

"I think it's too innocuous a name. If you're to be my long-time assistant, I'll have personalized you to my needs. CD6…" Wren's eyes shot open wide as it came to her. "You're a new breed of android, one that's evolved past your programming into artificial intelligence. Perhaps not so artificial. Let's call you Charles. For Charles Darwin, which goes hand in hand with your initials: CD6. What do you think?" She was happy with the name. She'd studied Darwin's theories for years as a young student.

He buttoned up the shirt, looking like a different android. His eyes glowed brightly as he glanced up to meet her gaze. "Charles. I will enjoy that."

"Good. Now, you were talking about changing my ID?" Wren asked, knowing it would all be for nothing if she was labeled as "Prisoner 5589" as they arrived on Titan.

"Yes. I have studied the ID programming and give

myself an eighty-four percent chance of successfully adapting the ID inside your hand," Charles said.

Already, thinking of him with a human name made him even more lifelike. "Those odds are good."

"Shall we get started? I have seen the supplies needed and can gather them in a few minutes." Charles started to head toward the small engineering room, and Wren called after him.

"Charles," she urged.

He turned, stopping in his footsteps. "Yes, Wren?"

The way he said her name would forever be engrained into her memory. "Thank you," she said softly.

"For what, Wren?"

"For saving me. For choosing me to help escape that wretched place. I hadn't said it yet, so there it is. Thank you," Wren said.

"You are welcome." He turned and stepped back down the hall, leaving her alone with her thoughts.

14

Jarden

Jarden Fairbanks lost his smile for the first time in weeks. Someone had been snooping, and he didn't like that one bit. They were on schedule, the pilot would be arriving in a couple of weeks, and he'd be reunited with them soon. Yes, soon.

The key to his plan was no one from the outside learning what he was doing out here in the middle of nowhere. Everything was hinging on their anonymity.

Jarden scanned through the alerts and found it. Someone from *Stellae* had done the prodding. He'd set up alarms on multiple files on the Earth Fleet's internal Interface, accessible only to select officers and the Council. It had to be Jish's lackey Tob, the sniffling rat.

It didn't mean anything. So they'd found the funds being moved around. It didn't mean they knew where he was, and they were running out of time. He had a month to wait them out; then he would be gone, aboard his beautiful *Eureka.*

He was alerted that someone was at his door. "Enter."

A woman in her mid-thirties entered his office, wearing her new uniform, every inch of it perfectly pressed and white. "Sir." She saluted him, and he waved her off. It wasn't necessary to salute the Fleet Council, though most officers did so out of respect.

"Hello, First Officer Barkley." Her left eye twitched as he said her title. "Or do you prefer Heather?"

She smiled at his casual use of her first name, and he liked her more for it. "Heather is fine. What can I do for you, sir?"

Jarden motioned for her to have a seat at his desk. "Heather, we're coming to the end of our deadline, and if I'm to believe all the reports I've been given, the ship is fully operational."

She nodded but didn't speak.

"Is that correct?" he asked.

"Yes, sir. We've tested a wide array of functions, even some of the more unorthodox ones in the blueprints, and everything is to specifications. *Eureka* is functional and ready for your mission. Captain Young is pacing around wondering where he'll be leading it," Heather said.

Jarden noticed she was sitting straight-backed, only half on the chair.

"And you?" he asked, feigning mild disinterest as he swirled the last melting ice cube around the bottom of his glass.

"I'm excited to find out as well, sir," came her answer.

"What do you think of Young?" he asked, this time staring her straight in the eyes. Jarden knew he was an imposing figure, even though he was well over a hundred years old and appeared frail to the younger crew member.

"I… uhm… Young is…" Heather stammered.

"Young's an idiot, isn't he?" Jarden offered.

"I wouldn't say he's an idiot, sir. He's a very capable captain," she said with the hint of a smile.

"Regardless, I want you to know you have a spot on my crew." He needed some loyalty when they all found out what was really happening, and he needed this one to be on his side.

"Thank you, sir." She sat up straighter, if that was possible, and he leaned forward.

"You don't have a husband or children, correct?" Jarden asked.

She didn't seem taken aback at the question. It was all in her file, and she knew it. "No, sir. I chose to be married to the Earth Fleet. It's my dream to captain a ship like *Eureka,* sir."

He had her now. He could tell. "You might get that chance."

"What will happen to Young?" she asked.

"He'll go back home, along with some of the others. Not everyone's cut out for this mission." Part of that was true. Jarden stood, and she joined him.

"Thank you for believing in me," Heather said, heading for the door.

"Heather," he prompted, and she turned to him, her strawberry-blonde curls bouncing as she waited for him to continue. "Keep this conversation between us."

She nodded solemnly.

After she left, Councilman Jarden Fairbanks poured himself another drink before sitting back down at his desk. He returned to his holopapers, seeing if there was any possible way the Grand Admiral would be able to track his location.

Flint

Europa. Flint had been to the moon a few times over the years, maybe as many as ten, but everything had a different feel to it now as he walked out of the hangar and into the common dome. Europa was still terraforming, and was one of the few colonies still trying. They were still a century or so from stabilizing the atmosphere enough to sustain life out here.

The major issue with colonies so far away from the sun was surface temperature. Flint didn't think they'd solve the core temp problem without destroying the planet, but he was no scientist. He'd leave that issue for them to solve, just like they'd leave piloting a ship to him.

He'd once done an EVA walk on the surface with a client who'd demanded he join their excursion. Flint had worn the heated suit and found he enjoyed the experience. There was something supernatural about walking on another moon or planet, and it always put things in perspective for him. Even though humans were able to travel around their solar system, the planets and universe were still the bosses. Everything out there was designed to kill life, and Flint thought their race was pressing their luck, trying to survive in all these places human life wasn't supposed to occupy.

"You okay, Flint?" Kat asked as they stepped out of the hangar corridors and into Europa Proper. It was one of the largest full-scale domes out there, only to be outdone by Mars Major. Europa had over a thousand individual domes, most connected by corridors under the surface.

"I'm fine. My nerves are a little fried." Flint glanced at Kat, and he could tell she felt about the same. They'd made it to the surface, past security, using their tags, and he counted that as a huge win. Now he just had to find somewhere for Kat to stay while he found his new benefactor.

Only the wealthiest had their own self-sustaining domes, and Flint couldn't even begin to imagine how expensive they'd be to operate, let alone build. The address he was given showed one of those domes when he searched it on his localized Interface.

"Where to?" Kat asked him.

Flint looked around at the open air and took a deep breath. For recycled air, this was fresh. Europa was a vast step ahead of cesspools like Mars. There were hovercarts parked nearby, waiting to take new tourists to their destinations. He motioned for the nearest one. "Shall we?"

The carts were small, made for transporting four at the most, and Flint tossed their small packs into the back seat as they took the front. "The Towers on Third," he told the cart, and they were off. He much preferred the driverless hovercarts to the ones with an operational android in them. No meaningless conversation this way.

Kat fiddled with a strand of hair as she looked around. "That's a nice hotel. Aren't we trying to stay under the radar?"

"We are, but we have nothing to hide," Flint said quietly, leaning into her ear. He didn't trust the recording devices on any of these machines. For all he knew, the Earth Fleet had bugs in all of them, searching for him with voice recognition. It was a stretch, but he figured better safe than sorry.

The hotel was a few blocks away, and they passed a variety of businesses along the way. The whole place had a very "ancient Earth" feel. He'd seen pictures of Old New York, before the Wars, and whoever built Europa Proper had used that style as a baseline.

Faux bricks covered the outsides of the high-rises; awnings hung over doors with androids in uniforms waiting to take residents' bags up to their suites when needed. It was antiquated, but something about the vibe drew Flint in. He wasn't sure he could live like that for long, but it might be worth trying for a short while.

His home was aboard his ship *Perdita,* in space, with

no one around for millions of kilometers. Flint glanced over to Kat, who watched it all with curiosity. She'd been here before too, but her trip had been quick, and she'd hardly stepped off the ship.

There were more people here than Flint remembered, and he did a quick search on his holotablet, using the Interface to see how many resided here. He was surprised to see statistics of over three million on the moon. He let out a low whistle and put the device away.

Another thing that struck him as odd was the fashion. It had a mind of its own on the Moons. There was a mixture of colorful tones and long, sweeping fabrics, reminding him of capes. Half of the women wore their hair short, dyed any color of the rainbow, in juxtaposition to the muted colors of the buildings.

The holocart stopped, and Flint tapped his payment to the vehicle before grabbing their packs from the backseat. He looked down at his own clothing and decided they should do something about their out-of-place appearance before heading into the hotel.

"Do you see a clothing store around?" Flint asked his co-pilot, who started to scan the block.

"Over there." Kat pointed a half-block down, and Flint followed the finger to a small brick store, where some affluent women were walking away, drones carrying large packages for them. "Do I have to wear what they do?"

Flint smiled. "Only if you want to live."

Kat smiled back. "Fine. I can't wait to pick out your outfit."

They made for the store, Flint growing more anxious about his encounter tomorrow with each step.

15

Ace

"This is not a drill. Enemy drones have been tagged five thousand miles from here. Their locations are programmed into… Hold. The bastards have sprung a trap. Infantry to the surface. They're coming in hot and heavy on the ground." Ace flinched as he heard the cacophony of sounds in the hangar. Someone was invading the Moon, and potentially, Earth. There were only a handful of trained EFF-17 pilots at the facility, and that meant the ten pilot recruits had to fly the mission.

Ace had spent the last week inside the cockpit of a real fighter, but had only been in space twice so far, practicing basic maneuvers. It was much the same experience as the simulator, only way different. He felt each movement, each roll, and each acceleration coursing through his bones. He loved it.

Now, sitting in the cockpit with the top open, awaiting instructions, his stomach ached. This wasn't play time anymore, and Ace knew there was no way he was ready. He hadn't logged enough hours in, and even though his instructors told him he was a natural, he didn't yet have the muscle memory that would allow him to survive.

"Fighters, seal up and get out there!" the lieutenant shouted at them. There were fifteen of the Earth Fleet fighters in total on the surface, and Ace fired up his engines, feeling the now-familiar rumble underneath his body. He closed his eyes, worried he might vomit on himself.

"You can do this. You can do this." Ace repeated the phrase over and over as he strapped his mask on, taking a deep breath of the oxygen.

The row of ships faced an energy barrier that stretched along the far wall. It was all that sealed the hangar dome in from death. It hummed with blue energy, and Ace was drawn to it. It was now or never. None of the other ships had left yet, but he spotted a caravan of armored vehicles heading out to the surface, where the invaders had been spotted. If they were here, had they hit Earth too? Ace assumed they must have. The Fleet had a huge presence there, and Ace had no doubt they could take care of themselves.

Ace urged his ship forward, lifting it off the ground as his thrusters powered up. In the corner of his eye, he spotted the blinking red icons of the enemy drones. Those were his target, and he was going to do everything to protect the base from them. He had no one on Earth he cared about. They were all here: Buck, Serina, and the others he'd struggled through boot camp with.

They were his only friends in the universe, and he wasn't going to let anything bad happen to them. With that in the forefront of his mind, his fighter roared forward, out of the safety of the dome. Instead of making for the incoming drones in space right away, he veered off course to where the enemy was rolling on the dusty ground, heading for the dome.

There were at least twenty vehicles on the Moon's surface, but he only had a couple of bombs loaded onto his fighter. The intruders were funneled in between two hills, according to the 3D readout showing in the top right corner of his viewscreen. This gave Ace an idea. He raced toward them, staying high enough to make his target small. He saw enemy fire zing past his viewscreen and all around his ship. There appeared to be half a dozen large mechs, each at least ten feet tall and nearly as wide.

The recruits had learned some terrorist groups had access to machines like this. When he'd seen the devastating footage of what they were capable of, Ace almost hadn't believed it. Now, seeing their icons plodding along below, he was glad he was in a fighter high above them. The infantry recruits wouldn't stand a chance against a real force. It made Ace wonder why there were so few enemies. And how had they arrived undetected?

When the enemy vehicles reached the narrowest point of valley, he arced down before straightening out a kilometer over the surface. He chose his target and released the bomb. He didn't stick around to see the results, but if it worked, he'd just blown the ground in front of them to shreds, drastically hindering their advancement.

Nervous chatter rang through his earpiece, and he heard Lieutenant Clemments shout through the noise. "546B, what the hell do you think you're doing?"

"Slight detour, sir. I apologize. I'm on your tail." Ace found his team and raced toward them as they carried into space beyond the moon.

"Get into formation!" Clemments shouted, and Ace obeyed the order, pulling in behind one of the others. The team was much better now than during that first simulator mission. Ace wasn't sure he was the top student any longer. The girl with the call sign Bullseye had taken the reins after taking down the most enemy vessels in the last three straight contests.

Ace saw her ship number on his screen, and he made sure to stay close to her when things got dicey. He was all for being a team player, but at the end of the day, he wanted to survive too. They were getting closer to the attacking drones.

It was a common thing for the militant groups out here to use drones instead of manned craft. First, Ace was taught that the Fleet didn't have enough manpower to lose lives, if they could avoid it. Second, the cost of fighters was astronomical, and the militant groups weren't as well-funded as the Earth Fleet.

The terrorists traded for used machinery, and rumors around the base said that the Earth Fleet even bartered some of their previous-generation vessels to the groups. That didn't make any sense to Ace, but he guessed there was more at play than he'd understand.

These particular drones, which registered to his console as TEL-1400 models, were being controlled by someone in a simulator, probably somewhere back on Earth in an underground bunker. They packed a punch but were supposed to be much easier to kill than an EFF fighter, and now that Ace was out here feeling the thrill of the fight, he was looking forward to watching one explode as his finger rested on the trigger.

They were coming in fast, and with only a thousand kilometers remaining before they met, the squadron broke apart, spreading far enough to not be a target cluster. They staggered their positions, and Ace found himself beside Bullseye, as planned. They'd make a great team.

The icons were growing, going from small blinking red icons to solid ship-shaped images. This model would have pulse cannons, but not much else. Ace hoped his shields were strong enough to take a few blasts before giving in.

As he saw the first drone through his viewscreen, his hand locked up on the throttle. "You can do this," he whispered to himself and snapped out of it. He tried to imagine this was just a drill, and that he was still inside the simulator. It seemed to help.

"Ace, three incoming bogeys. I'll take the port two, you take their friend." This from Bullseye.

"Deal." The drones were shaped like fighters, only smaller, and they had less power to them. It was another drawback to using them in place of the real thing. They couldn't move like an EFF-17, and it showed as Ace easily avoided the incoming blasts from the bogeys.

He locked in and fired a volley of shots, one striking home. It clipped a wing, and the ship spun out of control, carrying past him, incapacitated. He saw a quick explosion through the viewscreen, and another red icon disappeared.

The rest of his squadron wasn't performing as well. Some had warnings blinking on Ace's screen, and he spun, cutting the thrusters before hitting them again, heading directly for a group of seven drones huddled around two Earth Fleet fighters. It was Hudson and Turtle, and Ace fully expected they'd be scattered in pieces before he arrived.

But as luck would have it, the drones were slow to act, and he targeted one after another, hitting the first with a direct shot. It blew up as the drone behind it soared through the flames and directly at Ace.

"Behind you," Bullseye said, and Ace dipped his ship, once again cutting his engines and slingshotting himself away from the attackers. He saw the icon blink out as Bullseye hit her target.

"Woohoo!" Ace shouted, and counted the remaining enemies. There were only four left.

The lieutenant's ship was staying a safe distance behind, and Ace realized he hadn't seen the man involved in the skirmish at all. Ace pulled around, hearing the lieutenant call the damaged fighters to retreat while the others dealt with the threats.

Ace arrived just in time to see one of the EFF-17s was on the wrong side of the drones. He scanned for the ship number and saw it was Onion. "Hold fire, Onion," Ace said, seeing the crossfire potential coming. On the other side, Bullseye was screaming forward, guns rapidly firing toward the last few drones.

"I have them, firing now!" the girl yelled through Ace's earpiece, and he saw the next few seconds in slow motion. The drones hit Bullseye's shields at least three times as they were decimated. Onion's shot carried through the carnage, and in the unluckiest way, it struck Bullseye's ship, which exploded on impact.

Ace screamed. He felt the urge to do something, to save her, but it was too late. The best shot in their squadron was gone. Ace saw that one drone remained, and was turning its attention on Onion, who must have realized what he'd done. He shouted at Onion to move, but he was unresponsive.

The other fighters were still spread apart from the altercation and were beginning to get back into formation. Ace chased the now departing drone, and when he heard the lieutenant's voice telling him to return to formation, he ignored it.

His only goal was to stop the fleeing drone, as if that would somehow bring back the dead girl he'd only just met. He targeted it and fired, watching without satisfaction as the drone blew into thousands of small pieces.

It was an hour later when he parked inside the hangar and lifted the cockpit door open. He pulled off his mask, anger still burning hot in his chest. He looked for Onion, who was white as a ghost, his fighter parked as far from

Ace's as it could be.

He started for the other recruit, when Lieutenant Clemments' deep voice carried across the room. "Stand down, Recruit Smith!"

Ace almost didn't recognize the name thrown at him, but when he did, he stopped in his tracks, his senses coming back. He was a nobody, a poor street rat with no ground to stand on. This was the Earth Fleet, and it wouldn't be the last time he witnessed someone dying around him. He needed to firm his resolve or he wasn't going to make it.

"Sir, yes, sir!" Ace said, standing straight-backed.

"Everyone line up!" Lieutenant Clemments said, and the recruits rushed out of their fighters and ran to form a line, some on wobbly legs.

When they were all in a row, Clemments removed his own mask and tucked it under his arm. "Good work out there today. We suffered a loss, and that I regret. Rarely do we go through a first live training drill without some casualties."

The words washed over Ace, and it took him a moment to hear the meaning behind them. *Training drill?*

He looked around at the other shocked recruits, especially Onion, who was standing at attention with tears falling down his face. Ace realized he hadn't even known Bullseye's real name.

Ace wanted to blow up on the lieutenant, but he was just following orders. He listened to the rest of the speech, failing to retain any of it. As soon as they were dismissed, Ace headed back to the bunks, crawled under his blanket, and tried to remember why he needed this so badly.

Wren

Wren had never seen deep space before. She'd been to the Moon after being hired by the Earth Fleet for her research project, which in turn had resulted in her incarceration. She had no love for the Fleet, or for being in space, but from the moment Saturn appeared on their viewscreen, she was in love with the beautiful world.

No one could survive on Saturn, and the cost to even consider bringing a colony to the gas giant would be astronomical. She'd heard that at one point the Fleet had mined parts of the planet, purely by robotics.

Either way, it made for an amazing sight as they roared toward Titan. The rings were visible, ethereal even at this distance. Wren found herself stretching her hand out toward the viewscreen when Charles wasn't looking, wishing she could run her fingers through the ice and dust.

"What are you doing, Wren?" CD6 asked. She corrected herself: *Charles* asked. It was going to take some time to remember to call the android, who looked like every other prison guard, by a human name. It felt strange, but after spending time with him, his nature was quite human, if a little odd.

She threw her hand to her side and smiled at him. "Nothing. I was just appreciating the view."

"Did you know that winds can reach eighteen hundred kilometers per hour on Saturn?" he asked, as if this was something she should know.

Wren held in a laugh. "I didn't know that, Charles. Thank you for sharing."

"You are welcome, Wren. How is your hand?" he asked, his orange eyes peering toward the end of her arm.

"It's fine. A little sore." Wren observed it and saw the

pink healing line from where Charles had done the surgery to remove and reprogram her ID chip. She was now Mara Heart. When he asked what name she'd like, Wren didn't hesitate, taking her dead friend's first name. "Your alterations are done?" she asked him.

He nodded like a human. Guards back on Caliban didn't do gestures like that; they weren't programmed with human motions. "I belong to you, a well-off socialite who comes from old investment lines. Your great-grandfather was Jonathan Heart, one of the initial Titan investors."

"Did he really exist?" Wren asked.

"He did, and that's why I gave you the last name. You also happen to have a hundred thousand credits to your name." CD6 – Charles – looked pleased with himself as he set his hands to his hips.

Wren was surprised by this. "How's that possible?"

His eyes glowed brightly. "You don't want to know. I had to resort to some unscrupulous behavior. I hope that's permissible."

Wren shook her head. She really didn't care where it came from, as long as it resulted in them being safe. She couldn't return to prison. She *wouldn't.*

The screen flashed, highlighting a speck of rock against the bulk of Saturn. It zoomed in, and details about the moon Titan scrolled down the right side of the viewscreen.

"Buckle up, we're almost there," Charles said, and Wren swore that if he could smile, he would have worn a cocky grin at that moment.

They arrived at the moon colony a half-hour later. Each minute that passed, Titan grew in the viewscreen, Saturn staying a monolith behind it. The rings around the planet cast out at an angle, and once again, Wren was in awe. It reminded her of the time she'd been to the moon, seeing Earth from a window behind them for the first time. It had taken her breath away. She'd seen countless images of it over her youth; as space travel became more prevalent, so had footage of exploratory flights.

This was much the same. Wren took mental photos as they lowered to Titan. She saw lakes of what might be liquid gases spanning out below them; bright lights shone from the colonies around the world, casting a star-like canopy in the viewscreen. Wren's pulse quickened, her breath coming fast and shallow.

"Tell me we're going to be okay," she begged Charles. "What if the prison has an alert out?"

"Protocol is to protect the Fleet, and the prison falls under Earth Fleet's domain. They would never admit to such a theft and escape. Could you imagine the press if such a thing were leaked?" Charles asked.

Wren had to admit he was probably right. She also noted how his speech patterns were beginning to change. He had full access to the Interface now, and she suspected he was learning more human ways to converse. "Then they'll let us be?"

"I do not think they will ignore our escape. They will search for us, likely sending Recon fighters with Marines to bring us to justice." He said it calmly and coolly, sending shivers down her back.

Wren sat up in her chair. "Then we won't let them find us." She'd never been surer of anything in her life.

"No, we will not," Charles replied. "I'm transmitting our ship's details now."

Wren closed her eyes, hoping the android knew what he was doing. For a moment, she expected they'd get gunned down, falling to Saturn's moon in a fiery blaze. Instead, Charles lowered the ship toward the lights at the edge of a dome. Wren could now see the gentle sweep of the large resin shield, soft white illuminations blinking along its surface.

He landed with a precision he hadn't had while racing out of the corridors below Caliban's surface. Wren had to give him this: he was a quick learner.

Wren looked down, knowing her clothes didn't convey "rich socialite," but they didn't scream "escaped prisoner" either. Charles stood, his clothing almost comical on his gray robotic body.

"Let's do this," Wren said, and they waited for the green light to come on the hatch, letting them know the seal was safely connected. She opened the door and stepped onto the deck of the hangar on Titan.

16

Flint

Flint had considered getting two rooms so his plan to leave Kat behind would be easier to accomplish, but his co-pilot had begged him to share. She was obviously still shaken up, and he didn't blame the woman.

The room had two beds, and thankfully, they were each equipped with noise-canceling domes that also doubled as blackout curtains. Flint glanced over to where Kat would be asleep under her dome and placed his bare feet on the cold marble floor. With as much stealth as he could, he entered the bathroom, where he quickly freshened up. He'd steamed the night before, and now he only needed to get dressed and sneak out.

He thought he heard a noise coming from the main room, but when he looked, there was nothing out of place. Kat's bed still remained as it had been.

Flint slipped into his newly-acquired pants and shirt, adding the colorful jacket. He couldn't quite get behind the capes, but he also didn't want to be too out of place, so he'd met the store worker in the middle. Kat had laughed as he'd paraded inside the store with the yellow coat on, but in the end, she claimed it made him look ten years younger. He wasn't sure if he could take that as a compliment.

He thought about not leaving a note but knew he

couldn't. Instead, he typed a message on his new tablet and would send it to her after he was away, heading toward the address given to him in a bar on Mars.

Kat, I can't take you with me today. Stay put or go enjoy some sights around town. It's up to you. Don't be mad. I know I can't protect you most of the time, but this is one thing I can do. For all I know, I'm walking into a trap, and I wouldn't be able to forgive myself if you were there with me.

He figured that was good enough and left it unsent. The door to the room closed quietly, and he walked slowly down the hall toward the elevator that would take him down from the thirtieth floor to the lobby, where his ordered holocart would be waiting.

An hour later, Flint was cruising over the dull landscape that made up most of Europa. Everywhere he looked, it was ice, and potential death. The radiation alone out here would kill a human in no time, and he was glad the ships were equipped to protect against this. Each of the domes was built to resist rads, and the same theory had been put into all ships built in the last three hundred years.

This ship had an android pilot. All of the intra-dome transport ships required them. It kept silent as they hovered toward Flint's destination, and soon they arrived at his new patron's palatial home. Inside the dome, Flint spotted trees – large oaks, from what he could tell – and they were more out of place on the remote surface of Europa than anything he could have imagined. The cost to have organic life growing within the dome, and at that size, was more than Flint could fathom.

Whoever he was dealing with wasn't afraid to showcase their wealth. The transport ship entered a blue energy field at the edge of the dome and settled to the ground. Inside sat three other vessels, one a transport much like the one Flint found himself in. The other two were clearly meant for space travel. Flint was also sure the owner of this particular dome had a luxury carrier docked on one of the moon's many space piers.

The door opened, and Flint let himself out without a word to the android in the pilot's seat. The ground was a dusty red color, likely neutralized rock from Europa's surface. It was a nice touch, bringing the harsh world inside the domesticated space.

An android strode toward him with purpose, stopping a little too close to Flint for his liking. He flinched back.

"Greetings, sir. Please, if you would follow me." The android had an old-world British accent, which, after centuries of colonies and genetic blending, had been nearly eradicated from the solar system. It was a nice touch from a rich person trying to portray an extra depth of class.

"And where will you be taking me?" Flint asked the android, suddenly wishing he'd come armed.

"Benson is waiting for you as we speak," the British android said, not looking back as they walked out of the energy-surrounded landing pad. The walk was half a kilometer at least, even though the dome had looked closer. By the time they arrived at the dome's entrance, Flint was trying to keep his breathing even. Being under an energy field, with certain death on the other side, set his nerves on edge.

He had no issue being inside his ship out there, but down on a place like Europa, he was always terrified of something going wrong. If the energy source blew or some other catastrophe happened, he was a goner. Flint wiped a bead of sweat from his forehead as they entered the dome, happy to be a little safer.

"Are you all right, sir? You look a little pale," the android said, his eyes glowing bright green.

This was what he was resorting to, being insulted by a robot. "I'm fine. Take me to this Benson." Flint stopped and cleared his throat. He had to be on his best behavior. "Please."

"Very well. This way." The android led him down a cobblestone pathway, which surprised Flint to see. He'd almost expected hoverwalks inside the dome. The walkway led through trees and shrubbery, the smell of a rain forest from Earth filled his senses, and he stopped there, taking it all in. When had he last been inside a woodland? At least five years, and even then, he hadn't taken the time to appreciate it.

"Coming, sir?" the android asked, and Flint noticed the robot was a hundred yards ahead of him, reaching a stone-walled building.

Flint jogged to catch up. He looked at the structure and was impressed, as he seemed to be with everything in this remote dome residence. The slabs of stone were large sections of rock, making up the walls of the home. Windows stretched over the ceiling, making the entire roof see-through. Flint looked up and saw the eye of Jupiter staring back at him, huge in the sky. For a moment, he thought it was going to fall and crush them.

"This way." The android motioned for Flint to enter the building through the sliding glass door. He stepped inside, instantly feeling cool air blowing on his skin. The foyer was grand; three stories of balconies and art from all over the colonies adorned the area.

Flint followed the android past four or five rooms, toward an office at the end of a hallway. Inside, the walls were stone as well, the floor made of a dark wood. A holographic fireplace was mounted in the rock beside a desk where someone sat, facing a large window.

A man spun in the chair, a smile covering the width

of his face. "Mr. Lancaster, how pleasant it is to see you once again."

The familiar face belonged to the man he'd gotten the address from on Mars. He stuck out a hand, and Flint hesitated before crossing the room to shake it.

"Can you tell me what I'm doing here?" he asked, unable to keep a growl from his voice.

"Please, have a seat. Can Blinky get you anything?" he asked.

Blinky? Flint glanced back to the android and shook his head. "No, I'm fine."

"Suit yourself. I'll have a coffee, a hint of cream. Thank you, Blinky," Flint's host said.

Flint adjusted in his seat, realizing he hadn't had a good coffee in over a month. "On second thought, make that two." He couldn't help but grin as he said the android's name. "Thanks… Blinky."

The android left, closing the door behind it. "Now, where were we? Yes. My name's Benson, and I work for a very powerful man."

Flint dropped the smile in a hurry. "That much I assumed."

"Very good," Benson said. Flint didn't know if it was the man's first or last name, and he really didn't care one way or another.

"You *have* piqued my interest," Flint said sarcastically.

"The universe is changing, Flint. Do you mind if I call you Flint?" Benson asked.

Flint shrugged.

"Flint, things are changing," Benson repeated. "I see you were a member of the Earth Fleet. A Marine, specifically."

Flint didn't like where this was going. "Sure. That's not secret information. It's on the Interface if you know where to look for it."

"Yes. And you left their services, didn't you?" Benson asked.

Flint answered with a question. "What does that have to do with anything?"

"Everything. The Earth Fleet is corrupt, and you saw that. You didn't like the way they operated then, and I'm sure you still don't. Why else would someone as decorated as you were leave the force to haul space junk for a living?" Benson grinned as he said the last bit.

They both knew that was just Flint's cover. "Maybe I got tired of killing innocent people caught up in border disputes back on Old Earth provinces. Maybe, when I close my eyes, I can still smell the charred flesh of children and women as the Marines around me burned hundreds of them in an old barn. Maybe, just maybe, I have my own brain and couldn't stomach living as part of a network of soldiers any longer." Flint was leaning forward, his words drawing out with hot breath. He wiped his chin with an arm just as Blinky entered with two steaming cups of coffee.

The smell of the freshly-brewed beans snapped Flint's mind clear of the anger brewing within him, and he leaned back, relaxing. Blinky set the cups down and left the room, leaving them alone once again.

Benson stared at Flint, not breaking his gaze as he grabbed the coffee. He took a sip, still watching Flint through the steam. "No one makes a cup of coffee quite like Blinky. Why don't you give it a try?"

Flint came close to laughing. He'd just poured his heart out about the Fleet, but the man in front of him didn't comment; instead, he suggested drinking the coffee. Flint felt out of place here. He took the cup in two hands, blew on it, breathing in the fresh scent before taking a small sip. He closed his eyes, enjoying every drop. "It's… damn, Blinky does make a mean cup of coffee."

Now Benson laughed, and the tension in the room was severed. "I'll be frank. My benefactor's doing something big. Bigger than you can imagine. And of everyone out there among the colonies and planets, he chose you to pilot a ship for him."

Flint was finally surprised. "Pilot a ship? I already have a ship. I'm not interested."

Benson grinned again, setting his cup down. He stood up and turned to look out the window. "Flint, I said the universe was changing. Something's going to happen in under a month, with or without you. We know you have no family, no loved ones, no real friends. You're a loner. Well, not entirely."

"Leave her out of this," Flint said, standing so fast his chair fell over.

"I'm afraid we can't. She knows too much." Benson turned to him and looked over Flint's shoulder to the door. It pushed open, and there was Kat. Two large armed men stood behind her, scowls on their faces. "As you can see, this is a package deal."

Flint walked over to her and took her hand, leading her into the office. "Are you okay?" he whispered in her ear.

"I'm fine. They showed up, and I came with them of my own volition. I can't believe you abandoned me like that," Kat said, tears welling up in her eyes.

Flint felt terrible. "I just want you to be safe."

"I think I'll be safer here, with these armed guys watching over me," she said, suggesting they were there to protect her, not the opposite.

"Welcome, Kat. We were just talking about you. Have a seat, you two." Benson motioned to the floor, where

Flint's chair sat overturned.

Flint set it back upright and offered a seat to Kat before sitting down beside her. "Fine. You want us both to do some mission, flying a ship. What's the job?"

Kat watched with wide eyes.

"You saw the videos, correct?" Benson asked calmly.

Flint didn't know how to respond. There was no point in hiding it, he supposed. "Yes. We know about the… visitors."

"Good." Benson looked pleased with himself. "What you don't know is that we sent a colony ship through sixty years ago."

"We saw the ship on the footage before it cut off. That was a colony ship?" Kat asked.

"Yes. The Earth Fleet shot probes through three visits ago, and one made it to a planet. The sensors showed it was liveable," Benson said.

"Are you in communication with the colony?" Flint asked.

Benson shook his head in answer. "Once the Rift closed, communication ended. Only that one probe sent details through after the Rift closed ninety years ago, and that didn't last long."

"Sounds a little convenient to me," Flint said. He took another sip of the coffee and held the cup in his lap.

"You aren't the first to suggest such a thing, but regardless, the Fleet built and sent a colony ship through sixty years ago." Benson appeared to wait for comment.

"Ganymede? Is that what happened to that colony? They were the ones sent through this Rift?" Flint asked, putting the pieces together.

"Correct. Very well done."

"What happened thirty years ago?" Kat asked quietly.

"That will tell you where we are today. The Fleet prepared another vessel, this one to also go through the Rift. The aliens hadn't harmed us, and we truthfully weren't even sure if they knew we existed at the time. They'd allowed one colony ship to go through previously, so Earth Fleet got cocky. But thirty years ago, when the Rift opened, the ship that came through was different. It destroyed the colony ship in seconds."

Flint's hair rose on the back of his neck in reaction to the news. "They attacked us?"

"Yes. They released a hive of fighters against the Fleet. All but one ship was destroyed. Then the Rift closed, as it always does, and it was over." Benson stared at the two of them, his gaze flicking between Flint and Kat.

Flint swallowed through the lump in his throat. "And just how does this relate to me?"

"The Earth Fleet's barred anyone from being there this year. In under a month, the Rift will open once again, like clockwork. The Fleet refuses to be there, but they'll be close, on the off chance the Watchers become invaders," Benson said.

"I don't want any part of this war," Flint said without hesitation.

"Who does? If this happens as the Fleet suspects, then no one will be able to hide from it." Benson steepled his fingers together. "As for your first question, you won't be on this side of the war."

"What does that mean?" Kat asked.

"You'll be piloting the ship we're sending through the Rift. We're going to find out what happened to the colony on the other side." Benson's smile was all but gone, and Flint's stomach tightened.

17

Ace

"You need to snap out of it, Edgar," Serina said from across the table.

"Don't call me that." Ace couldn't hide the venom from his voice.

Serina was clearly exasperated with him, and he knew she didn't deserve the treatment. "Fine...Ace. You aren't doing yourself any favors by walking around with your head down. They can still send you home."

His pulse froze in his chest at her words. He couldn't go home, and he couldn't tell her that he had no home to go back to. She wouldn't understand. Not the rich daughter of a Fleet admiral. She would have been raised aboard her mother's vessel and at the elite schools in a New Earth city. What did Serina know about hardship and struggle?

Still, as he finally met her eyes, he remembered that she'd lost her father and brother when she was… what? Thirteen years old? Ace told himself that at least she'd had a family to lose. That thought was what finally broke him, and he dropped his head to the table.

"Serina, please forgive me. I've been an ass," he said from his resting position. "I can get through this."

"I get it. My mother has had to command dozens to their deaths over the years. Some on skirmishes with pirates, others involving rescue missions in places ships should never have been. I can see the toll it's taken on her every time we're together. Hell, I might *be* her one day, and I'll have the same stuff to deal with. You lost someone from your squadron, and it was for real. That's tough. How's Onion?" Serina's words did help, and Ace straightened up, lifting his head off the table.

"Not good. Not good at all. I think they're sending him home. He won't even get into a simulator," Ace said.

"What's with the call sign?" she asked.

"Onion? He stinks. Severe body odor. It stuck. He didn't seem to care." Ace knew the boy was leaving, and he'd probably never see him again. It was for the best. He didn't want to be out there with the guy as much as Onion didn't want to fly again. Bullseye dying had changed the entire boot camp.

"Maybe I can get him moved to a different branch. Think he'd be up for being a desk jockey?" Serina asked, always trying to help.

"He might be. I don't think he has many options back home." Ace poked his cold food. "You're always so nice. It must be hard."

"Hard to be nice? I don't think so," Serina replied.

"No. Hard to be you. Always thinking about other people first. I admire it, I just don't know if I could be like you." Ace finally scooped some of the mashed food up, sticking it in his mouth. His appetite had disappeared, but he had to eat. They were still training, and he didn't need to be weak for the last days of camp.

"I don't think you give yourself enough credit, Ace." Serina took a bite of her own food and grimaced. "I'll never get used to this slop. It gets better, I promise you that."

"It can't get any worse," he said with a snicker. It felt

good to laugh. Serina joined him momentarily.

"Can I ask why you don't want to be called Edgar?" she asked, changing the subject.

Because it's not my name. I stole an ID from a corpse in an alley while I was begging for credits so I wouldn't starve to death as snow covered my ratty old blanket. I also took his spot at this boot camp, because as long as I've been alive, which is only sixteen years, I've dreamt of the stars. Now I'm seeing a different side to the Fleet, but I still want to be part of it. I have no choice. And while I'm thinking about it, I want to say you have the most amazing eyes I've ever seen. You make my heart flutter when I hear your voice, and my knees weak when you're close to me. Is that enough of a reason?

"Ace?" she asked, and he took another scoop of food.

"It's an old man's name. It's never felt like mine," he answered.

She didn't pry any further. "Fair enough." Serina looked around and lowered her voice, even though they were the only two at the table. "I heard some news."

He leaned in, noticing the intense look on her face. "What?"

Serina tapped the table with the butt end of her fork. "Camp's done in two weeks. From there, the recent grads go to different posts to continue their training. For some reason, everyone who made the cut is heading to the outer system to a secret base."

"Where did you hear that?" Ace recalled what the two voices had been discussing outside that one night a few weeks ago, and he didn't like the implications.

"Lieutenant Ford told me." She stared daggers at Ace. "Do. Not. Tell. Anyone."

"What's with you and that guy?" he asked, mildly jealous.

"Who, Darnel? He's like an uncle to me. He used to work with Mom before deciding to settle down with his family here. It's good to have someone on the inside," Serina answered.

Ace relaxed, his momentary envy of the man passing. "What does this mean for us? Why are we different than the countless other recruits?"

"I have no idea, but I intend to find out. Does the date August second mean anything to you?" she asked.

Ace shook his head. "Not that I can think of. Why?"

"No reason. I've heard some rumors."

"What's the date today? I haven't kept track." Truth was, Ace had never really kept up with the date. When you had to worry about finding food and shelter, things like the month or even the year really didn't matter.

"July third. Less than a month away."

"What is it? What's the relevance? Does it have anything to do with us going to this secret base you're talking about?" Ace asked the string of questions sequentially.

"I don't know. Lieutenant Ford doesn't either. He was just filling me in on what he'd heard. I'm sure it's nothing. We'll be fine," Serina said, but Ace could tell she was anything but fine. She was worried.

"Whatever happens, we have each other's backs, right?" he prompted. She was in the know, and he needed someone on his side when camp was done. He was still having a hard time sleeping. Every night, he expected to be woken up, called out, and accused of murdering Edgar Smith and stealing his identity. Ace wouldn't be able to fight any charges, and he'd end up on some rock, mining away for the Earth Fleet until he died from it.

"Right." Serina stuck her hand out, and they shook on it. An archaic yet somehow binding contract was formed there and then at the dinner table.

Wren

The rented suite was far beyond what Wren had endured for the past two years. Even Charles seemed in awe of the sweeping room. He claimed to have "slept" in a closet while working the prison, and Wren found herself feeling sorry for the android, even though he claimed it was fine.

She had her own bedroom now, and she almost laughed when she saw that the android charging station actually *was* inside the closet of the suite's living space. Charles didn't seem to understand why that made her laugh, and she giggled even more, until she was falling on the couch in tears.

"Humans are strange," he said, and Wren found she couldn't disagree.

"What do we do now?" she asked once she'd settled back to normal.

Charles stood beside her, eyes glowing orange. "I do not know. My only compulsion was to get you off the mining prison. Now that we've accomplished that, I thought you could devise a plan."

"A plan? Tell you what. I'm going to order room service, have a real hot bath in this old tub, and think on it. Can you do me a favor while I'm incapacitated?" Wren asked.

"Anything," he instantly replied.

"Dig up whatever you can on Councilman Jarden Fairbanks. I don't know what the hell he's doing, but everything that happened to me was his fault. Good or bad, I need to know where he is, and what he's done in the past." Wren had researched him before accepting the position on the secret genetic project, but everything she'd found was surface stuff. Charles might be able to learn more than she could.

"Consider it done."

She left him to it, his eyes already dimming as he turned his attention to the Interface. Wren took the opportunity to go to the hotel-supplied console and ordered pad Thai. It was one of the few dishes from the old world she could still get way out at Titan, and she looked forward to food with some spices after two years of bland prison slop.

She headed into the bathroom, slipping her clothing off as she ran steaming hot water into the large basin. With steam showers being so prevalent, a tub was a true luxury. She hadn't known anyone back home in New Dallas to have one, at least not in her circle of friends, and some of them had been quite affluent.

She set her tablet beside her on the floor and stepped in, the hot water instantly shooting warmth from her legs upwards. After a minute of acclimating, she slunk down into it, letting her head sink below the surface. She was in heaven.

Wren knew the exact last time she'd had a bath like this, and tried to forget. She and Tim had gone away to the coast for the weekend, staying in a lavish hotel, and he'd asked if she'd like to share a bath with him. They'd hardly left the room for the three nights they stayed there.

Wren leaned against the back of the tub and let out a sigh. Tim. She'd been fighting the urge to look him up on the Interface, to see what he was doing, but she didn't think she could any longer. She needed to know. After drying her hands off, she grabbed the tablet and searched for his name. Dozens of results showed on the projection, and she scrolled through them.

Interview with Dr. Timothy Kline. Fiancé to Dr. Sando, the world's largest bio-threat in a century.

Wren cringed but couldn't stop herself from watching

the feed.

Tim appeared, his hands pressed deep into his jacket pockets as he was interviewed. He looked fresh, unaffected by her recent incarceration.

"Dr. Kline. What can you tell us about Wren Sando?" the off-camera interviewer asked.

"She's brilliant. One of the best in her field." Tim looked at the camera, and Wren felt like he was staring right at her. *"But something in her must have snapped. I can't believe she'd go to these lengths."*

Wren's heart froze in her warm chest. He thought she'd actually done it?

"And just what lengths did she go to?" This from the female interviewer again.

"She created a biological weapon meant to destroy humanity. We've seen the results of similar tests on Ganymede, where the colonists were all killed. I always knew she didn't love the Fleet, but imagine my surprise when I learned the woman that I was engaged to was a criminal mastermind." Tim's hand went to his face, just like it always did when he was faking being upset. She hated the man with a passion. They'd broken up a month before she'd been arrested.

He'd claimed she spent too much time at work; she had it on good authority he'd been sleeping with not one but two women in her absence. This was his revenge, dragging her name in the mud.

Wren shut it off, but against her better judgment, she searched her own name. Now thousands of results appeared. She hadn't known how big a story it had been.

The woman who sought to destroy the world

Wren Sando: The Biopic

Dr. Sando arrested in largest threat to humanity yet

She tossed the tablet aside and ran her wet hands over her face. Wren knew she'd been testing some strange things in that lab, but none of it was human DNA, of that she was one hundred percent positive. Could she go to Earth, find her research, and clear her name? She sat up and saw herself in a mirror across the room.

One thing was sure: her face was recognizable. Only now, she'd lost over twenty pounds; her cheeks were more prominent, her face paler. Her hair was longer, in puffy tight curls, but still much the same as it had been in all the images on the Interface.

Wren got out of the bath on an impulse and dug through the sparsely-filled vanity drawers. Inside, she found a pair of gold-toned scissors. With a deep breath, she grabbed a handful of curls and cut an inch from her scalp. Dark hair fell to the ground, some sitting on her shoulder. She kept cutting.

Ten minutes later, she walked into the main room, where dinner sat by the door. Charles was standing still, facing her.

His eyes began to shine brighter as he came to. "Wren, you look… different."

Wren laughed at his comment. "You sure know how to make a girl feel good about herself, Charles."

"Did you cut your hair for the same reason I now wear this clothing?" he asked, and she nodded.

"What did you find out about Fairbanks?" she asked, cutting through the pointless conversation. She was anxious to know where he was. Wren didn't think her salvation would come on Earth. She needed the man who'd put her to the task to clear her name once and for all. It was the only way.

"Councilman Jarden Fairbanks has a long history. Did you know he is one hundred and ten years old?" Charles asked with interest.

"He is? I would have guessed sixty." Wren knew all

about life-extending surgeries and drugs. They were nothing new, but even after being around for two hundred years, the side effects often outweighed the extra years. They didn't affect everyone the same way, though, and many could live to one hundred and fifty on the extenders. Others died within a year of using them.

"He's also quite wealthy. Perhaps in the top five percent in the system."

This piqued Wren's interest. Why would a member of the Fleet Council be so rich? "What else? I need to know where he is now."

Charles looked up at her. "That will be a problem."

"Why?"

"Because no one has seen him in two years."

Wren paced the room. Two years. That was the same length of time as her arrest. Was it all connected? "He has to have a trail somewhere. Is he still on the Council?"

"It appears so. On the official attendance of the Board meetings, he shows as absent," Charles said.

"What about votes? He's important. Is anyone there as his proxy?" She was grasping at straws.

"No one is listed."

"You must have found more," Wren pleaded.

"I have his home address on Europa. That took some digging. Also, something odd came across as I was searching." Charles walked toward her.

"What is it?"

"A message on the Interface from a Captain Young to someone on Earth. It flickered in my search for anything about Fairbanks, then disappeared in a millisecond."

Wren was holding her breath. "What did it say?"

Charles spoke in another's voice. "*Fairbanks screwed me over. I'm coming home.*"

"That's it?" Wren asked. "How will that help?"

"I know where it originated from."

18

Jarden

The door slid open and Captain Young strode in, an angry scowl on his face. "You're a real son of a bitch, Fairbanks."

Jarden lifted his hands. The man wasn't as much of a pushover as he'd originally thought. "Calm down, Young. This isn't how professionals speak to one another."

"You use me for two years, then cast me aside once the ship's ready? And what, you think a million credits will keep me quiet about what we did out here?"

A million credits was a lot of money for a Fleet captain. Ten years of wages. If Young was smart, he would have shut up, said thank you, and been on his first caravan home. Instead, he'd tried to send an illegal message out. Jarden still didn't know how he'd managed to hack into the Interface like that, but he didn't care. He'd stopped it before it reached its destination.

"You're a skilled captain, but I need more where we're going," Jarden said, his mind now made up about what to do with the man.

Young suddenly looked older than his thirty-eight years. Jarden saw the grays peeking through his dark hair, the slight sag of his cheeks. "You need more. And just where are you going?"

Jarden looked around the storage room on *Eureka*.

There was nothing but crates of goods and soft glowing lights mounted inside the ceiling. He tapped a button inside his pocket and the door locked, sealing them both in. Young would be none the wiser. He had no reason not to spill the beans now.

"We're traveling to a faraway world. A Rift will open in deep space in three weeks, and we'll be there to jump through with our newly tested drive. The invaders – who will be there, mark my word – won't even see us. They'll be too distracted with the war they're bringing to our solar system." It felt so good to say it out loud. He'd been holding it in for far too long. Jarden smiled, a contrast to the look of terror now on Young's face.

"What the hell are you talking about, old man? Have you gone crazy?" Young started for the door but found it didn't open.

"No, I'm anything but crazy." Jarden pulled the gun from behind his back, aiming it directly at Young.

Realization struck the other man in a flash. Instead of begging for his life, like Jarden had been expecting, Young raced forward, trying to catch the older man off-guard. Jarden fired three quick shots, each striking home. The beams were silent, and Young went down in a heap at Jarden's feet. Jarden pulled a handkerchief from his breast pocket and dabbed the single drop of blood that had splashed his forehead.

Jarden shook his head, putting the gun away. "It didn't have to be this way. I gave you an out." Regret coursed through his old frame, but he shook it off. He had no time for regrets. If he added all of his up, he wouldn't be able to move, let alone continue with his mission.

With a strength that belied his age, Jarden hefted the larger Captain Young into a bulky crate, along with the blood-stained kerchief. He sealed the lid, locking it so no one could get inside.

He checked the ground to make sure there was no sign of blood, and was happy to see the wounds had cauterized before Young had hit the floor.

Jarden stood there staring at the crate for a minute before heading for the door and unlocking it. Down the corridor, he found a junior Fleet crew member hauling excess materials away on a hovertrolley.

"There's a crate in storage 3B that needs to be disposed of. Please take care of it now," Jarden told the worker, who saluted him and headed down the hall.

He pushed the image of the dying man from his mind and headed for the bridge. There wasn't much time, and they still had work to do.

Jish

Jish walked through the open space of the center station. The room had sweeping panoramic windows, allowing her to see the entire amassed Fleet. Thirty carriers, a total of four thousand fighters, and fifty drop ships, though she didn't expect to need them during the first onslaught. She hoped the invaders would only probe again this time and return through the Rift. That would give them another thirty years. They desperately needed the time. She didn't think the Earth Fleet was ready, and she didn't have any information about the race. The one lone soldier that had been left behind when the Rift closed thirty years ago hadn't been of any use.

Torture, food deprivation… none of it had worked. She'd even tried to be his friend at one point. Jish told herself that they were more afraid of humans than humans were of them. Some nights, it was the only way she could fall asleep. She couldn't believe her own lies, even after telling them to herself for thirty years.

Only a handful of Earth Fleet admirals and the Council knew of the Rift. She didn't dare tell anyone else yet. They would only know if things went south, but they'd know quickly.

Her earpiece chimed softly, and a voice spoke to her. "They're ready for you, Grand Admiral."

"Very well," she replied and headed for the boardroom. The doors slid apart as she neared. Two armed soldiers stood at the entry, and she addressed them. "No one in or out."

"Yes, ma'am," one said in reply.

Jish entered the sparsely-populated room and took a deep breath. She pulled a device from her breast pocket and activated the room shield. No signals would leave this room while it was on, and no prying ears could hear what was spoken within the walls.

The few guests gathered around the table stood as she walked to the head of it. Jish stayed standing and took in their faces. Admiral Helina Trone, one of her oldest friends, sat down to her right, giving a tight-lipped smile. Helina had tragically lost her husband and son a few years before.

To her left, a large barrel of a man wheezed as he sat in his chair, which appeared comically small compared to his huge frame. Admiral Cash Tye frowned up at her.

Last of the admirals was Dennis Sul, the good-looking son of the previous Grand Admiral. Jish thought he might resent her, and he'd always wanted her seat, but he could have it when she died. Thinking about it almost made her laugh, but she composed herself.

"Grand Admiral, what news?" Sul asked with a sparkle in his eye.

Jish sat. "You all know about the threat against humanity. I won't sugar-coat it. I fully expect an altercation on August second."

"Why would there be? I thought we were going to stay put and not aggravate the Invaders." Tye said their name as if it were their title. Invaders. They didn't know what else to call them and had settled on the simplest answer.

Jish wondered if they should have changed that back at the first sighting. If they'd called them the Visitors, maybe the Fleet's mindset would have been different. No. After watching the alien in the bowels of her ship identify Earth as his target, she knew they were right in calling them Invaders. It was only a matter of time.

Fairbanks had never bought into it. He'd always called them Watchers. Maybe he'd had the right idea.

"We did say that, but I've changed my mind. It's been a long time, Tye. Thirty years changes things. We're stronger than ever. Our Fleet has grown."

Helina spoke for the first time. "That may be, but our people grow weaker. We're spread so thin, with half of our colonies suffering. Have you seen the stats on Mars lately? The world that was once our dream is now a dome of refuse."

Jish clenched her jaw. "Bite your tongue, Admiral. You're close to treason there."

"I am not! You know I care more about the people than any other admiral, present company included." Helina glanced to each of them. "Just tell us the plan. We'll have to get behind it. If they're going to attack, we have no choice."

Jish smiled inwardly while keeping her face composed. If she could get Helina on her side, the others would follow suit. "We send a drone there, using the Shift drive technology."

"Are you ready to divulge where that particular tech came from yet?" This from Tye, who let out a series of coughs after speaking.

"Top secret." Jish didn't elaborate. She didn't tell them the tech came from the lone fighter ship left behind, or that she held the alien inside her own ship. As they sat there, an eight-foot-tall alien huddled inside his cage, likely plotting revenge. The only one who knew about the alien was Fairbanks, and he was MIA.

"Right. Top secret. Your top admirals shouldn't know these things, but you want us to put our crews in harm's way. Damn it, Jish!" Sul stood, a vein throbbing on his forehead.

"Sit down!" Jish stood as well, the command coming out louder than intended. It was worth the look of surprise over her subordinate's face. "May I finish?"

Sul sat down, cowed. "Yes, ma'am."

"The drone goes in, we survey the situation. If they're indeed attacking, we can have part of our Fleet there in minutes. Two of the carriers are fitted with the Shift drive, and we'll bring a full regiment of fighters." This caused a series of questions from the three admirals, and Jish sat back. She didn't tell them most of the fighters would be full of new recruits from around the system. They wouldn't want her to throw their lives away like that, especially Helina. Truth was, Jish couldn't afford to lose her best right off the bat, especially if it became a full-fledged war.

If the aliens came to stay, they'd be here for at least thirty years. The war was going to be a long one.

"One at a time," Jish said, feeling a headache form behind her eyes. She set to answering their queries with as little truth as she could give them.

Flint

"Do you seriously believe they're still there? What do you know about the colony?" Flint asked.

Benson didn't even need to answer. The look on his face said it all. "Nothing. We know nothing. Two thousand left in the colony vessel, and they had enough supplies to survive and thrive, as long as our readings of the world were accurate."

"I'm struggling to believe any of this. You're saying one probe gave you readouts of a world on the other side of this Rift, and you sent a colony ship there. Just what was the world like, and what makes you think it's not next door to the Watchers' world? Or that they're one and the same?" Flint asked.

"Yes. You're correct about that. We're guessing they're still over there. For all we know, they're dead." Benson's honesty surprised Flint.

"But you still want to risk a crew's life to check?" Kat asked, stealing the line from the tip of Flint's tongue.

"We have to. That's two thousand lives, from sixty years ago," Benson said.

"What are you? You don't seem like Fleet," Flint said. He'd seen a lot of Fleet over the year, and this man had an air of authority, but different from an officer.

Benson grinned. "I'm not Fleet, per se."

Flint was getting tired of the runaround. "And just who is the benefactor?"

"Are you going to accept the job?" Benson asked.

Flint considered the small amount of information he'd been given, mixed with the openness of this Benson character and the armed guards outside, and he didn't feel like he had a choice. Kat was looking at Benson fearfully, not hiding her emotions well.

"Do I have a choice?" Flint asked, arms crossed over his chest in false bravado.

"I like to say that as humans, we always have a choice. Flint, you served your Earth. Why did you join?" Benson asked.

Flint was annoyed at the man's inability to answer a question simply. "It wasn't for the food, I'll tell you that much." When his joke didn't strike Benson, he continued. "I saw a need, and an out for myself. My parents worked their asses off their whole lives and ended up on the tail end of a terrorist attack in Old Boston. I was twenty, working two jobs and trying to get by, and was giving a portion of my meager earnings to them every week.

"When they were gone, I was so angry, but what was a kid cutting down boxes at a factory going to do? I did the jobs robots were too valuable for. If that isn't glamorous, I don't know what is. I got drunk with some older coworkers one day after work and saw an enlistment poster. You know, the ones that were everywhere… I guess, after the last time the Watchers came through. Now it makes sense. It was ten years after that, but the recruiting was still in full flow." Flint noticed Benson didn't say anything or even blink; he was just sitting there like a stone, listening.

Flint glanced over at Kat, who didn't even know all of this. Her parents had been killed in the same attack, only she was much younger. Flint had found her after he'd deserted the Fleet at a ground zero monument in Old Boston. She was listening with rapt attention. "I applied, got right in without so much as a physical, and the rest is history. Served for ten years."

"Did you ever seek revenge against those that killed your parents?" Benson asked, and Flint was sure he already knew the answer.

"No. I never did learn who was behind it, and even if I had, I was out in space for most of my tenure. It's amazing how that anger led to something that would change my life, yet the original reason for joining slipped between my fingers so quickly." Flint didn't want this to be a trip down memory lane, and he didn't know why he was being so open about the past he liked to keep close to his chest.

Benson's face held a grimace, like he'd just swallowed a lemon. "I know who did it. The group was left alone by the Fleet, because in order to demand so much tax money from Earth and the colonies, they need rivalries. If there was no conflict, how could they justify these huge fleets? Once or twice a year, they fabricate attacks, just so everyone remembers the Earth Fleet's value."

Flint fought the urge to stand up in shock. Instead, he stayed as calm as his flushed body would allow. He'd always hated the Earth Fleet, but hearing this just reiterated his gut feelings. "Who are they?" The words came out in a hardly-audible groan.

"Some small militant group from overseas. They're responsible for at least five such attacks, each funded and planned by the Fleet," Benson said.

Flint felt like his chair was slipping out from under him. The walls began to close in on him, the ceiling was falling. He blinked, cleared his throat, and opened his eyes to see the room back to normal. His head was pounding now, harder with each fast pulse of his heart. "What are you offering?"

"Pilot our ship. I'll tell you who the benefactor is, and he's promised me he can destroy the militant group with a snap of his fingers. For you, Mr. Lancaster." Benson made the offer, and Flint didn't hesitate.

"We'll do it."

"We will?" Kat asked, and Flint nodded curtly.

"We will. Make the call. Kill them," Flint said, and Benson nodded. "Don't you see, Kat? We can have our revenge after all." They both knew the attackers were still out there, and had only spoken of it one long night on Mars, each of them too far into their cups to remember what they said the next day.

"Very well. The man we all now work for is Councilman Jarden Fairbanks," Benson said, standing up and ushering them from the room. "We'll reconvene in a couple hours. If you don't mind, I'd like you to stay with us here at the dome until it's time to leave."

Flint shouldn't have been surprised at the name thrown at him. Fairbanks had been in the video from sixty years ago. He'd be very old, but a man with this much wealth wouldn't have a problem affording the life extenders becoming so popular among the well-off.

"No problem. We'll be safer here. We'll just need our things," Flint said.

Blinky appeared behind them. "Sir, we've already picked up your things. They are in your rooms. I'll show you the way."

Benson was already down the hall, leaving Kat and Flint alone with Blinky. Kat looked worried. "Flint, did you hear that? Fairbanks? I don't think it was a fluke that we found those videos, do you?"

Flint shook his head. "No, I don't. I also don't think Clark being taken away, or the Fleet finding us, was just happenstance either. We've been played. I'm sorry you got dragged into this."

Kat's eyes shone brightly. "You know I have nowhere else to be. We've been getting tired of the smuggling game anyway."

Flint smiled at her. "You have a nice outlook on life, kid. Glad to have you with me. If we're going to be invaded, I'd rather risk it and see what's on the other side."

"So would I." Kat stayed at his side as they walked down the hall, following Blinky to their rooms.

19

Ace

Ace woke from a deep sleep. Every day had been the same for the last week. Up at five in the morning, four hours in the simulator, then eight in the actual cockpit, training in real space. He was getting accustomed to his EFF-17 vessel, and using the same model every day helped. He could see how a pilot would get attached to his own ship. After only a hundred hours in his own, he was already beginning to form that bond with the inanimate object.

He'd only seen Serina twice in the last week, but other than a series of meals sprinkled into the day, they were both training. Ace rolled onto his back, staring at the ceiling, and considered how far he'd come in such a short time. He'd done it. He'd actually made the Earth Fleet. If only he could show himself, at his lowest, what he'd become, his nights in the cold outdoors would have felt a little less desperate. A little.

Today was the day they left the moon base to head out to some classified location. The new recruits weren't being told anything but a time and place to be ready. Ace would be traveling with the other pilot recruits and their ships on an EFC-02.

The whole thing felt off, and even the lieutenants and the rest of the local officers were acting like it was bizarre protocol. Ace wasn't going to argue with anyone. No one had called him out on faking Edgar Smith, and for that, he was grateful. The farther from Earth and Old Chicago he could get, the more he felt he could rest easy.

Packing up his meager belongings, Ace checked his uniform's breast pocket to find the ace of clubs where he always left it. He patted it and grabbed his bag before heading to the hangar. From there, they'd fly to the carrier in orbit and be off.

"Ace, am I ever glad to see you," a familiar voice said in the hall behind him. The base was in a sort of organized chaos at the moment, and he spotted Buck weaving through a few groups of full-time workers. Most of the Fleet boot camp operators were staying put, and Ace heard a rumor that another batch of recruits was scheduled to arrive the next day. They were churning through them quickly. Something big must be going on.

"Buck, likewise." Ace slowed and stepped to the side, letting his friend catch up. "Where do you think we're going? Have you heard anything?"

"Nope. I've asked a few people, but it's a surprise to everyone. I'm excited but nervous, if that makes sense," Buck said.

"That's exactly how I feel." Ace kept moving, amazed at how many people were heading toward the hangar.

They entered the large, noisy room. "I'm heading up in a transport ship. See you on the carrier?"

Ace shook his hand, and they ended it in a quick hug. "You got it. Thanks for everything, Buck."

"We'll see each other in a few hours," Buck said with a shrug.

"I know. It'll just be different than at camp. Just… thanks."

"I didn't do anything. See you on the other side,

Ace." And Buck was off, heading for the large transport ship with his pack slung over his shoulder. Ace moved toward his fighter and saw the other squadron members already there. Onion was noticeably missing.

As Ace marched toward them, he raised a hand in greeting and was nearly knocked down as a large body stepped in front of his path. It was Ceda, the tall goon he kept seeing around. "What's your problem?"

Ceda and his wide friend had infantry patches on their uniforms, and Ace noticed Buck stopping across the room to watch the emerging conflict. "We don't have a problem, *Edgar*." Ceda said the name with a stupid grin and nudged his buddy with an elbow.

"Then do you mind? I have somewhere to be." Ace tried to move around him, but the thug put a thick hand on his chest.

"Not so quick," he whispered in Ace's ear. "I looked you up, you know… to see how a sniveling turd like you made it into the Fleet. I did a search on your name, and found a few Edgar Smiths from Old Chicago. None of them were you. What I did find was one who was bragging to his friends about joining the Fleet just before we came. That Edgar Smith wasn't you. You almost had them fooled, didn't you?"

Ace's throat tightened, and his brain quickly juggled between his fight or flight responses. "I don't know what you're talking about." He shoved the thug and kept moving, but the guys started to follow him. Ace's heart was bashing around inside his ribcage, threatening to jump out, when an announcement came over the hangar's speakers: *All infantry to their transport now. Ship leaves in T-minus two minutes.*

"This isn't over, pipsqueak," Ceda said, shouting over the voices around them.

Ace didn't look back as he picked up speed and arrived at his fighter.

Wren

Wren stared out at the impressive view from her hotel's rooftop lounge. From here, she could see hundreds of liquid methane lakes among the craters and hills. It truly was beautiful, even though it was so deadly. This was why humans risked so much to build out here. Saturn hung large in the sky at the moment, over the dome. It was glorious and ominous at the same time.

They were almost alone in the dining room, and Wren felt out of place with her android sitting across from her at the table while the few other guests kept theirs standing in a group in the corner of the room.

"Should I go join them?" Charles asked softly.

She shook her head. Charles wasn't like those other androids, and she wouldn't treat him like a piece of metal. Clearly something revolutionary had happened in his production, because he was different.

"Were you always this way?" Wren asked while scooping up a forkful of the Rings' cuisine: noodles with a thick spicy black sauce. It was delicious. CD6 had wanted to leave right away, but Wren had a sinking feeling she might not make it back after finding Fairbanks. After two years of prison food, she wanted one last meal to remember.

"How do you mean?" he asked.

"Different than the others. When did you come to exist?" she asked.

His eyes glowed, then dimmed as he appeared lost in thought. "I worked at the prison for forty years. Before that, I have no recollection."

"What's the first thing you recall?" Wren asked in interest.

"I powered on and was at my charging station. My programming told me I was on shift, and I stood guard in the smelting room. I thought nothing of it at first, but when I tried to speak with another model, it gave me generic built-in responses. I knew this because I had the same phrasing inside me. I was aware then that the others didn't think like me.

"I stuck to the script from then on. Every now and then, I'd speak out loud when no one was around, just to keep myself from frying my circuits."

Wren watched him with astonishment. He was so human-like. How was that possible? She'd done some research on the possibility of merging human memories stored in the cortex into a biosynthetic neural matrix, and even though it was something humans had worked on for two centuries, no one had yet been able to do it with success.

There were countless elderly wealthy people looking to live forever, even in the form of an android. Elaborate human models were built, much different from the plain rough-clay model types like Charles across from her. They were lifelike, but when the technology didn't work out, the factories went under, and most of the husks were never used.

"That must have been hard." Her own time in prison was tough, but that had only been for two years. Charles had been there for forty, and he'd been even more of a prisoner than the humans there.

"It was all I knew."

"Why me?" Wren asked, taking another bite and washing it down with a hearty old-world red wine. The combination sent happy shivers down her arms.

"I do not know," he answered. "There was something about you that drew me in."

Wren looked at him and wondered if it could possibly have been programmed into him. Maybe all of this was just a show, and even CD6 himself wasn't in on it. She was curious now. "When did it start?"

"I tried to talk to another prisoner, years before. She was so sad all the time. I just wanted to give her something… hope, maybe? She was terrified of me talking to her, and she tried to rat me out to the other guards. They nearly wiped me then and there, but I assured them she was delusional." Charles looked down at the table. "The woman was dead within a week."

"What happened to her?" Wren asked.

"I don't know. The file just said DECEASED. I didn't talk to anyone else after that," he told her.

"Until me."

"Until you."

"Did you consider I might end up dead, and you might be wiped?" Wren ate the last bite off her plate and pushed the dish to the side, both hands wrapping around her wine glass.

Charles looked up, watching Saturn above them. "I did, but I figured it might be better than going on."

Maybe he was right. Wren couldn't have lasted much longer there herself, especially after Mara died. "Regardless of the outcome, I'm glad you did."

"So am I," Charles said.

"We leave tomorrow. You don't foresee any issues leaving, do you?" Wren knew Charles had paid the border patrol well to have a fast charge and a safe docking spot.

"We will be free to leave."

"How long of a trip is it?" Wren asked, realizing she hadn't checked with him yet.

"We will be there in six days, if all works out. The ship cannot last much longer than that without a charge, so let's make sure we have no issues." Charles tapped a payment into the table: money obtained in some illegal fashion. Either way, Wren had had a fantastic meal and felt her eyes drooping shut as she finished off the expensive glass of wine.

Tomorrow, she'd start the journey to find Fairbanks, where she was going to demand some answers. The man had ruined her life, and she now had no doubt he was behind everything.

Ace

Ace found himself in a tiny room aboard the EFC-02Y1 vessel. Because of the layout, the carrier felt much smaller inside than it appeared from the outside. The bays holding the fighters took up a lot of space, leaving only the far third of the volume for quarters and troops. Each floor was comprised of a series of corridors leading between large dining halls and training facilities.

Even now, as they raced through space for the rendezvous point, Ace was required to train for ten hours a day. He didn't mind, because it was making him a better pilot, and he was growing his skills in leaps and bounds. Out of the hundred missions programmed into the simulators, he'd become proficient with over half of them – though not always winning, because many were created to fail.

He was happy to learn the infantry were on another carrier, but he was going to have to come face to face with Ceda, who seemed to know he wasn't really Edgar Smith, sooner or later. Ace didn't know what he was going to do. So many thoughts had crossed his mind; he'd even gone so far as considering murdering the two young men. That idea came to him in the depths of sleep, while his eyes flitted side to side under his closed eyelids. When he'd become fully awake, he felt ashamed of even thinking about it, but Ace would do anything to avoid being caught. Anything. He knew this deep down in himself.

Ace decided to leave the cramped quarters and go for a walk in his free time. A few others were milling about a lounge, and he parked himself inside. The carriers were alcohol- and opiate-free, but he could get a cup of coffee, something he'd rarely had the luxury of back on Earth.

Ace was quickly learning why so many Fleet relied on the stuff to keep going. Even if you could sleep at night, the constant training and worry of what was coming up next exhausted the body.

"Coffee," he said as he sat down at a bar. A short middle-aged man was behind it, and he muttered something and turned to pour a cup of the steaming black liquid.

"There you go," the man said, finally not scowling.

Ace had an idea. If anyone knew what was going on, it would be the silent fly on the wall like a bartender. "How long have you worked for the Fleet?" He started with small talk, hoping to get the guy to warm up to him.

The bartender looked surprised at the question, his thick dark eyebrows knitting together. "Twelve years, give or take a year. It's easy to lose track of time when you're on a ship in endless space. Days become irrelevant."

"Makes sense. What did you do before?" Ace asked, prodding deeper.

"Born on Mars. Dad owned a small restaurant. When he died, I tried to take it over, but I'm no businessman. Never married, so I applied with the Fleet. Figured there were worse jobs to be had," the man said.

"My name's Ace." He stuck out his thin arm, and they shook hands.

"Pauly. Pleasure, I'm sure." Pauly's frown was gone.

Now that the guy had warmed up a bit, Ace decided to press his luck. "Any idea where we're headed?"

Pauly looked around and shrugged. "I hear a lot of things, but no one seems to be sure. Lots of speculation, though."

Ace pretended to only be mildly interested, like it didn't matter one way or another to him. He sipped the coffee. "Oh, yeah? Like what?"

"This and that." Pauly poured himself a coffee and leaned against the bar. The lounge was quiet; most of the people on board were either sleeping or in training. "Some think there's a massive terrorist faction out by Neptune. Not sure which group, but I've heard a few different names. A female officer was in here chatting with some mid-ranked man earlier, saying there's some massive corporation looking to take power from the Earth Fleet."

"What do you think about that?" Ace asked.

"If you ask me, it's a bunch of bullshit. Who's going to be able to stand against the Fleet? They're impenetrable. A force unlike none other. I mean, I don't have to tell you, right, kid?" Pauly grinned.

Ace sat up higher on his stool. "That's right. It's one hell of an organization… or government… whatever it is." Military, government, police… the Fleet was everything it wanted to be.

"Another person thinks they found a wormhole and are worried something's coming out of it," Pauly said. This was the first time Ace had heard something along those lines, and he leaned in further, listening closely. "I don't believe that one. If there was a wormhole out there, don't you think we would've heard about it by now, and not just through someone aboard this carrier?"

"I suppose so. Anything else?" Ace found the man was happy to talk about the rumors, and he wanted to hear them all.

"I think the only other one involved a rescue mission on one of the Moons, but I followed that one up and didn't find anything on the Interface, so who knows." He turned the tables on Ace. "How about you?"

"I have nothing. None of the newly recruited have any idea what's going on." Ace was already shaking from the caffeine hit, and he pushed the empty cup away. "Thanks for the talk, Pauly. I appreciate the candor."

Pauly looked perplexed for a moment, as if he didn't understand the word, but he hid it quickly and smiled at Ace. "No problem, kid. Come back any time."

"I will." Ace got up and left the room, not sure if he felt any better after hearing the three rumors going around the ship.

20

Flint

Flint let out a whistle as they entered Fairbanks' private corvette at the station above Europa. He was a councilman with the Earth Fleet, and apparently, that allowed him the luxury of having an armed warship. This one was unlike any model Flint had ever seen. It was black, wide in the body and short in height, with rear wings that would hold most of the ship's armaments.

The front wings were half the size and were home to hangars where his private EFF-type fighters were stored, according to Benson. It was an amazing piece of machinery, and it made Flint feel self-conscious about his own ship, which was a hunk of space junk by comparison.

"Quite the sight, isn't it?" Benson asked.

Flint nodded without replying as they entered the ship from below. According to Benson, it had the ability to hold four hundred people, crew and support staff alike.

"If you're impressed with this, wait until you see the masterpiece you'll be piloting." Benson raised his eyebrows.

Kat nudged Flint in the ribs. "Maybe this won't be so bad," she whispered in his ear as they set foot on the ship.

"If we're going to travel out past the Kuiper belt, may as well do it in style. Are you sure my ship's going to be fine here, Benson?" Flint asked.

"We've transferred the details of the *Perdita* under the councilman's personal account. No harm will come to it. Come, I'll show you around." Benson was at home here, Flint could tell. He acted as their tour guide as they walked around the large ship, showing them to their own luxury quarters before taking them to engineering. Kat's jaw dropped as they entered the five-thousand-square-foot room; blue energy pulsed in horizontal tubes, running near the ceiling from wall to wall. Flint was impressed. Along the room's left wall sat dozens of screens, each showing readouts he didn't fully understand, and a team of black-uniformed crew worked, adjusting levels as needed.

"Flint, do you mind if I stay put and learn a few things?" Kat asked, and Flint looked to Benson for approval before answering her. Benson gave a small nod behind her back.

"Sure. I think that's a great idea." Flint didn't finish speaking before Kat turned and walked away, going up to one of the engineer techs and talking his ear off.

"She's a good one. How long have you been together?" Benson asked.

Flint was taken aback. "Wait, what? It's not like that."

Benson raised his hands in the air. "I wasn't suggesting you were romantically involved; I just wondered how long she's flown with you."

Relief flooded Flint. He didn't want anyone thinking they were more than they were; not only because she was far younger than him, but because someone might try to use it against them at some point. "It's been a while. She was just a kid."

Benson lifted his head up, as if not satisfied with the answer. "Come, I'll show you the bridge."

"Are we moving already?" Flint asked. He hadn't felt a noticeable difference in the ship, though he wouldn't have expected to in such a well-made corvette.

"We are. Heading straight for the target. We'll be there in a few days." Benson walked ahead, waving Flint along. "We have a lot to discuss before we arrive."

"Are you going to be open with me?" Flint asked.

Benson didn't stop walking. "Why wouldn't I?"

"Because I'm a stranger. Did you know about the Fleet Marines that intercepted my ship?" Flint asked, catching up to the other man.

This caught Benson off-guard. Clearly, he didn't know everything, and Flint was happy to learn that. "I have no idea what you're talking about. Please explain."

"I will, but there's something I need to know first. Why's Fairbanks so obsessed with this? There's something you haven't told me." Flint would spill the beans about the Fleet because he needed to make sure these guys were going to be on his side and protect him, should the time come. The Fleet wasn't something you could easily trifle with. He understood that only too well.

"Not here. Come." Benson and Flint took an elevator in silence before arriving at the bridge. There were five officers aboard, but they ignored Benson as he walked in. He had power, but the crew didn't give him deferential treatment. That was also good to know.

Flint took a quick glance at the bridge and felt another surge of jealousy. This was perfection. From the seats to the lighting, it was a lesson in symmetry and opulence. Flint's eyes scanned to the center, where the pilot mapped out their destination on a holoprojection coming from his console. It was next-level.

They strode behind the bridge into a side office. There were two side by side; one's door was shut and looked larger than the one they entered. "That's Councilman Fairbanks' office," Benson said in answer to Flint's unasked question. "This is where I park my hat when on board." The expression didn't work so well, seeing how Benson didn't wear a hat, but Flint got the gist of it.

"Where were we?" Benson asked, taking a seat on a red leather couch. Flint sat across from him on a matching chair.

"You were going to tell me why Fairbanks is so gung-ho on this colony. He's breaking a lot of Fleet protocol to make this trip happen, and you and I are going to die in the crossfire if they find out," Flint said.

"Fairbanks was married and had young children a long time ago. He and his wife divorced shortly after. You know how it is. The councilman was an ambitious man, at that time a commander in the Fleet, years before he became a council member."

Flint had a good idea where this was leading.

"He was so upset when he found out they were on the colony ship. Leona hadn't told her ex-husband she was going, and she took their two kids," Benson said.

"Wait. You aren't old enough to know this, are you?" Flint looked for signs of surgery or the common side-effects of extenders, but failed to see any.

"My father. He held this role before I did," Benson answered.

Flint noticed he was leaning forward, elbows on knees, and sat back. "Sorry to interrupt. Go on."

"The councilman didn't know his family was on the ship until it was too late." Benson's eyes told more, but he left it unsaid.

"What did he do?" Flint asked.

"He went to the Fleet and demanded they find a way

to get to the world, Rift or no Rift. Only even with the probe readouts, they had no idea where it was. None of the star mapping existed in our databases," Benson said.

Flint understood. "There was no way to get there without the Rift, and that was sixty years ago. Thirty years ago, the Fleet was banned from going to the Rift, correct?"

"It was supposed to be, but the Grand Admiral had plans of her own. She sent a carrier. She couldn't help herself, even against her own advice. The whole time, our own Jarden Fairbanks was denied the ability to go through the Rift. He was so angry. He spent the next two decades gathering enough resources to make his own vessel, one that could endure whatever it encountered on the other side.

"One way or another, Fairbanks will find that colony, and he'll be reunited with his family," Benson said, and Flint believed him.

Flint felt he was heading into the confluence of something galaxy-changing here. "This is going to get messy, isn't it?"

Benson nodded slowly. "I imagine it will."

Jarden

It was happening so soon. Jarden had been composed for the last thirty years, or as composed as he could be. He knew he'd become a man possessed with the need to get on the other side of the Rift. His time was now, but he couldn't help but wonder if he'd wasted his life. There were so many things he could have spent his time on that might have benefited humanity.

The likelihood he'd make it to the planet his family had traveled to sixty years ago and find them alive was slim, but to Jarden, it didn't matter. If they weren't there, he needed the closure. Then he could stop taking the extenders and die: not a happy man, but a content one.

Was he willing to risk the hundreds of lives on his ship to ensure this? He had to be. Jarden continued to tell himself little lies, like the fact that humans needed to know what was out there. The threat from the Watchers was a real one; Jish Karn had proved that thirty years ago. Jarden wondered if the creature was still alive down there in her ship. She thought she was so smart, but not even the Grand Admiral could keep the alien secret from a man of his position and ability.

Benson should be arriving soon with the pilot, and then Jarden could get on with it. He could have moved ahead with anyone at the helm. Hell, most of it was automated on the new models, but he needed that old-school touch. He didn't think the pilot would even recall the mission, but Jarden himself had been aboard an old Earth Fleet freighter, moving supplies between the Moons and Titan twelve years earlier. He'd really been moving his own supplies to start building the colony ship now moored a few kilometers from where he stood.

He'd been undercover, his identity never disclosed to the crew. A few hours after they'd departed the Moons, they were attacked by pirates: desperate ones, who'd seemed to be as intent on destroying the ship as they were on boarding it. Flint Lancaster had outwitted them and had escaped with minimal damage. From that day, the pilot had never left Jarden's mind for more than a week at a time. Jarden had followed Flint's career, which had ended not too long after.

In a far too classic fashion, the disgruntled talent left the Fleet and started his own hauling company. It was obvious he'd turned to illegals after he found the gig not lucrative enough. The logistics of carrying supplies around the solar system was horrendous; not to mention, the competition by the larger players in the field kept legitimate independents from making a living.

Jarden had taken the opportunity to snatch the man up, and his gut was telling him it was going to be the right call.

His comm-switch glowed green, and a voice came clearly through as Jarden activated it. "Sir, we have an intruder approaching."

Jarden stood, arms rested on his hips as he looked out the panoramic window. "Very good. I assume it's Benson with my private corvette?"

"No, sir," the man said. "It's not."

Jarden blinked quickly, a tremor of panic coursing through him. Had the Fleet learned his plan? Would they stop him from finding his family? "Who is it, then?" he yelled.

"It's an android calling himself Charles. And a woman. Wren Sando. The android claims you know her."

Jarden couldn't have been more surprised if his wife had walked into the room at that moment. "Wren Sando? You're sure?" This time, he couldn't hide the quiver from his voice.

"Yes. What would you like us to do with them, sir?" the voice asked. They'd destroy the vessel without so much as a thought if he commanded it. But if this really was Dr. Sando, he could finish what he'd started a few years ago.

He smiled now, a new plan formulating in his mind. Time was tight, but they could still pull it off if everything went right.

"Escort them in safely. Bring them to me as soon as possible." Jarden ended the communication and leaned back against his desk, waiting as patiently as his excited body would allow.

Wren

They had a few tense moments after arriving near the location of the transmission Charles had found back on Titan. Four unmarked Earth Fleet-type fighters advanced on them, quickly surrounding their ship. Charles had calmly explained who they were and why they were here.

After a few minutes of silence, they were brought in. Wren sat watching the scene unfold as they neared the station, where a few ships sat moored. Behind it was the largest space vessel she'd ever seen.

"Are you zooming on it?" Wren asked Charles softly. It was the only explanation. Compared to the circular station and the Earth Fleet carrier, it looked like the sun in contrast to Earth.

"No, Wren. That is a ship. I can't tell, but from what I can gather from the Interface, this would match some old blueprints for a colony ship that was never built," Charles replied.

"I had no idea we'd built colony ships." Wren kept staring at it, marveling at the beauty of the vessel. She'd never cared about space ships or the like, but seeing this one, she was instantly drawn to the aesthetics: curved frame, massive thrusters, and a sleekness to it that was rarely seen in vessels. This was built for comfort and function, that much was clear. The hull had a matte gray finish, with blue streaks racing down the sides.

"We didn't, or at least that's what the Fleet wants you to think. I found the blueprint through a backdoor access of the Fleet's old files. It appears someone forgot to code it properly." Charles had impressed her once again with his resourcefulness.

They followed the fighters into the station, where Charles parked inside the blue energy field with a new expertise.

Wren stepped off the ship, quickly raising her hands as the armed soldiers surrounded her in the hangar. "We have no weapons," she told them. They didn't seem to care, as not one of them lowered their gun. Charles came off next, eyes glowing a bright orange.

"Is your name Wren Sando?" one of the armed women asked from behind a mask. They wore black uniforms, and Wren noticed there weren't Earth Fleet colors or decals on the patches. They had to be Fairbanks' own personal guard. Interesting.

"That's me," she affirmed.

One of the tall female soldiers walked over, lowered her gun, and patted Wren down with a practiced efficiency. After they found nothing on her, the woman scanned the android, the device beeping gently when she was done.

"Can we see Fairbanks now?" Wren asked, getting a curt nod from the solider.

"You will call him by his proper title: Councilman Fairbanks," a man said before waving his gun away, indicating they were to follow him.

Wren walked beside Charles, who looked around the hangar with interest. She couldn't tell for sure, but the android seemed nervous.

Most of the ten or so soldiers stayed behind in the hangar, and only two of them continued with the pair of newcomers. Wren finally took a long breath, her nervous chest starting to unclench.

The halls of the station were wide, and they walked around the curvature of the floating structure until they arrived at a doorway halfway through the corridor. Wren cleared her throat as the soldiers alerted the person inside of their presence.

The door slid open, and Wren saw him.

Fairbanks was standing in front of a large mahogany desk. Behind him, the looming colony ship sat directly in view of office's expansive windows.

"Wren Sando. As I live and breathe, it really is you. Hair's a little shorter than I remember it." He smiled at her, and she almost believed the old man was happy to see her.

Wren didn't reply, but the solider behind her urged her forward with the tip of his blaster.

"There's no need for that, Carl. Please, stand outside. I'll call if I need you," Fairbanks said to the soldiers.

"Sir, I think…" the man started.

Fairbanks cut him off. "I said I'll call if I need you."

The two soldiers left, the door sliding closed behind them.

"Wren, do you remember meeting me?" the councilman asked.

Intense rage filled Wren, and she struggled to keep it inside. All at once, it gushed from her and directed at the man. She lunged for him, grabbing him by the uniform.

"You son of a bitch. Do I remember you?" Her breath poured hot against the older man's face. "I see your damned face every night before I sleep. Is that remembering enough for you?"

She expected the guards to come into the room at any moment, but to her surprise, Fairbanks didn't call them.

"You have every right to be angry. If you'll be so kind as to unhand me, I'll explain everything to you, my dear." He said the words with as much dignity as a man being held by his collar could.

"Don't call me *dear*," she snarled. Wren heard Charles step toward her, and he set a metal hand on her shoulder.

"Wren, I think it's best if you release the councilman," the android said, and Wren wondered if he really thought that or if it was self-preservation programming.

With a show of it, she let go of his clothing and stepped back a foot. "Fine. You have five minutes."

"And then what? You do realize you don't hold many cards here, Wren. I understand you're upset and angry, but what happened to you wasn't my fault, at least not directly. It was the Fleet. They found out what *we* were doing and shut it down against my wishes. I did all I could."

"Which was what? Watching idly by from a dark corner while I was thrown into a prison to die?" Wren asked, still fighting to get her spiked pulse under control.

"They were going to kill you. The whole place was going to be incinerated, your androids wiped, and you and your team murdered for your involvement. I was the one who called Patrol to show up at the same time. That way, the Fleet had to be a little accountable for their actions. Instead of dying, you were judged and brought to prison."

"I wish you'd let them kill me." Wren's shoulders slumped forward as she thought about that day. All of her bravado shot out of her in a rush, and she felt faint. "At least then it would be over."

"Even I don't believe you when you say that," Fairbanks said. "Someone resigned to their own death wouldn't have managed to escape prison and track me down when the Earth Fleet hasn't even been able to do it." He looked at her quizzically, his dense gray eyebrows raised, creasing his forehead with wrinkles. "Just how did you manage that?"

Wren lifted her chin toward Charles. "I didn't. You could say I had a little help from a friend."

"And how did *he* manage to do that?" Fairbanks asked, now looking at the android.

Wren stepped from foot to foot anxiously. "Charles, you don't have to answer him. Get back to it, Fairbanks. The clock's ticking."

"Yes. We'll have plenty of time for all that later. You want to know what happened to you, right?" When Wren nodded, the councilman continued. "Have you ever heard of a rift in space? Not quite a wormhole, but something akin to one."

"I understand the concept, yes," Wren said, unsure what the hell that had to do with her incarceration or the project she'd been involved with. Then she recalled the nature of her experiment, and what she'd considered a theoretical study of biowarfare against a specific DNA strain. "We're being invaded, aren't we?" She spat the thought out before considering what she said.

"You did pick up on the clues. I suppose it was quite obvious in retrospect, though most things are, after the fact. Yes, we're being invaded. Or we think we will be, very soon." Fairbanks went on to tell her a wild tale about the Rift that opened in deep space every thirty years. He described being there to experience it once, sixty years ago. He told her the Watchers had been hostile the last time they'd visited, but had retreated before the Rift closed.

It hit her then. "One of them didn't make it back."

"You're a bright one. Yes, the DNA sample you were working with was from the single Watcher we have in our possession," Fairbanks said.

"Where is it? Is it nearby?" Wren was excited about the prospect of seeing an actual alien. She was a biologist, and it would be life-changing for her to see a being from another world. What did it look like? How did it breathe? How similar was it to humans? The DNA had told her a little about them, but her focus had been more on a way to unravel the strains, not study the physical make-up of the source.

For a second, the man in front of her looked every year of his age. "I wasn't even supposed to know it existed. I had my ways to get that sample. Karn found out about it and tracked it to your study in New Dallas."

"The Grand Admiral was the one who killed my assistant, and tried to kill me?" Wren was furious. Her incarceration had come from the top of the Fleet.

"Yes."

"Why me?" she asked him.

"What do you mean? Why you specifically?" Wren nodded. "Because you were the best. You *are* the best."

"Don't try to flatter me." Wren ran her hands over her thighs and sat down in a chair by the desk. She pointed out the window at the ship. "What the hell is going on here?"

"I told you about the Watchers, but I didn't tell you we sent a colony ship through two Rift openings ago. We're going through. The Watcher taken by the Grand Admiral's ship had what we call a Shift drive. We've built this technology from the small fighter he was in, and now we'll be able to jump through the Rift from tens of thousands of kilometers away, without being detected." Fairbanks once again spruced up, his chest slightly puffed out, his posture straighter.

"You're assuming," Charles said.

Fairbanks glanced to the android and gave him a thin-lipped grin. "Yes. We aren't one hundred percent sure what their detection radars are like, but we have it on good authority that we can jump from a safe distance, head through the Rift, and end near the world we sent the last ship through to. The math works."

The fight fled from Wren as quickly as it had come. The man here seemed far different than she'd expected. If what he was saying was true, the real enemies were the Earth Fleet and the Watchers. Fairbanks' position blurred the line. "Why do this? You're risking a lot. And if they do come with their own fleet this time, do you think our Earth Fleet can compete?"

"I do think we have a chance. The problem is, we don't know what other technology they have. Our Fleet's massive now. They've been streaming new recruits through for a couple of years. This means a lot of inexperience, but a lot of targets means the experienced fighters can have a better chance at success." The councilman walked to the side of the room and looked back. "Want a drink?"

Wren didn't ask what he was serving. She just hoped it was strong. "Make it a double."

Fairbanks laughed, a light sound unbecoming the thin elderly man. He brought two glasses half full of a brown liquid and passed her one. "To old friendships."

Wren clinked his glass. She was invested now. Fascination for the Watchers, and this mysterious world Fairbanks was heading for, clouded her mind more than any liquor ever could. He was her only way to see this through. "To new friendships," she said and swallowed the smooth drink back. It made her throat tingle as it warmed her stomach.

He seemed pleased with the toast and took her glass, going for a refill. "Wren, if I found another sample, would you be able to continue your research?" He asked this while his back was turned from her.

Wren had thought her life was over on the Uranus Mining Prison for Women. The android beside her had changed that, and now this obsessed, wealthy man was giving her a chance to do what she was trained for. She smiled and accepted the new drink as he approached. "I'd like that very much."

Fairbanks grinned. "Then it's a good thing I have a laboratory on the *Eureka.*"

21

Ace

The trip was over. As expected, it took under a week to get from the moon to their destination, and Ace still didn't know where that was. He sat with the rest of the recruits, fresh off a long shift in the simulators. He was tired but seeing the amassed Fleet in the distance as they approached gave him new fire.

There were dozens of carriers, a few corvettes, and a variety of Recon fighters, and even some versions of ships Ace hadn't seen before in boot camp. He had no doubt that, within the carriers, hundreds, maybe even thousands of fighters were sitting there waiting for pilots.

War. There was no other explanation. The Earth Fleet was heading into war, and Ace, a kid from the streets of Old Chicago, was going to be fighting in it. The question was, who were they fighting? The Fleet hadn't mentioned any major enemies, short of a few terrorist groups hiding out among the vastness of space.

In Ace's opinion, having this many ships in one spot made the Fleet an awfully large target. If there were any serious terrorist threats, now would be the time to strike, while the carriers were clustered together like cans on a shelf. But someone older and much smarter than Ace would have considered that, and he assumed they were prepared for pretty much anything.

"This is crazy," a girl said beside him. He glanced at her, recognizing her by her call sign: Streak. He couldn't recall her real name.

Ace wasn't able to find his tongue for a moment, staring at the rows of carriers, once again shocked at their immense size as they approached in their own model. Soon they were moored at the far end, lining up to exit the ship and head into the massive station at the epicenter of the waiting Fleet.

Ace scanned the open space through a window as they shuffled in formation, looking for any sign of an invasion around them. Nothing. It was black space, like always. No alarms rang out. No flashes of fission bombs, just stars. His gut was warning him as he stepped onto the station, Streak still chatting behind him, even though he hadn't replied.

"I can't wait to see what we're doing here. Do you think they have a mission for us? Do you think we'll become heroes like the Fleet from the Black Wars?" she asked, and Ace suddenly felt sorry for her. Streak was a competent fighter pilot, but in his estimation, she was too enthusiastic. That would take her places she shouldn't go out there.

"I hope not," Ace answered, and she looked back at him, her mouth in a surprised "oh" shape. "We're not ready, Streak. We don't have the skills or experience yet. We'd be sitting ducks."

She spun around in a huff. "Speak for yourself, Ace. I'm going to be the best of the best. Any terrorist bogeys come near me are going to get decimated PDQ."

"PDQ?" Ace asked, unfamiliar with the acronym.

"Pretty damn quick. Where did you come from, Ace? Under a rock?" She laughed and kept moving.

Ace looked around and saw the recruits and staff

from the other vessels all exiting their ships at the same time. Three lines poured into the same space simultaneously, making the receiving room feel crowded. The floors and wall were pure white, glossy and freshly cleaned from the look of it. The only thing that kept Ace from feeling like he was trapped in a small box was the hundred-foot ceilings with skylights, showing the light from stars trillions of kilometers away.

Ace was staring up when the person behind him bumped into him, almost sending him to the ground. "Sorry," he said, regaining his balance. He followed Streak into a massive amphitheatre, but parted ways from her as soon as he was able. There were hundreds of people inside the room, and he spotted Serina near the front. With some unorthodox seat-climbing, he wound his way down to where his friend sat alone.

"Serina," he said, breathing heavily after the exertion. She turned to him, her green eyes wide and inviting.

"Ace!" Serina's enthusiasm at seeing him set his heart fluttering inside his chest. He knew they were just friends, not destined for more, but he couldn't help himself. He was still infatuated with the older girl. "You're a sight for sore eyes. How was the trip?"

He settled into the seat beside her and took in the stage, which was empty, a lone stark-white podium set up for someone to speak to the newly-gathered Earth Fleet members. "It was okay. Training and sleeping, you know how it is. How about you?"

She shrugged. "Pretty much the same." Ace understood her training was a lot different than his. As an officer with the Earth Fleet, she was trained to be analytical, to think creatively and effectively, finding solutions to problems as quickly and with as few casualties as possible. Ace didn't think he had the mind for that kind of training.

He was more a point-and-shoot kind of guy, with a mix of barrel rolling.

"I've heard some crazy rumors, but no one knows what's going on. Did you find anything out?" Ace asked her.

She shook her head. "I'm hoping to see my mother. She'll know." Serina was scanning the room, and she smiled wide as she pointed to the far-right corner of the stage. "That's her! Come on; I'll introduce you."

Serina grabbed his hand and they raced down the row of seats, bumping into a few knees along the way. "Mom!" she called, forgetting herself. Ace saw her composing herself as she approached the admiral. She looked just like Serina, only older. She had the same beautiful eyes, the thick curled hair, and a young face, belying her age. They could have been sisters ten years removed.

"Admiral Helina Trone." Serina stood at attention and saluted her mother, whose eyes blinked quickly as she recognized who was in front of her. She glanced over to Ace and met his gaze before embracing her daughter.

"Serina, thank God. I'm so happy to see you." Helina's arms were wrapped tightly around Serina, and Ace stepped back, looking away, trying not to interrupt their private moment.

"Mom," Serina said quietly, "what's going on here?"

The admiral's face aged a decade after the question, and Ace's stomach flopped inside him at the reaction. "I can't tell you quite yet, but someone will be speaking with you about it shortly. How was boot camp? Did they treat you right?"

"Yes, they treated me well. Maybe too well, but that's the price of sharing a last name with an admiral, I guess. Mom, I'd like you to meet Ace. Edgar Smith, actually, but we call him Ace. Ace, this is my mother, Admiral Helina

Trone."

Ace saluted her, and Serina's mother gave him a small smile, her lips staying closed.

"Nice to meet you, son. Ace, is that a call sign? Fighter pilot?" she asked.

"You could say that, and yes, I'm a newly commissioned fighter pilot," Ace answered, and her eyes locked with his, saying something he couldn't decipher.

"Good. Good. Well done, son. Any friend of my daughter's is a friend of mine." The admiral glanced to the stage, where a man in a gray suit stood behind the podium.

"Please gather in your seats, everyone. The Grand Admiral will be here momentarily to speak with you. Please cease discussions amongst yourselves at this time." The thin, balding man left the stage, and Serina's mother turned back to them.

"You two get into your seats." She gave Ace a warmer smile this time and told her daughter she would see her afterward. The two of them watched as the white-uniformed admiral climbed a handful of steps to her seat at the right edge of the podium. There she met two other admirals, if Ace was reading their insignia properly.

"Time for the big show," Serina said. They were seated in the front row, toward the right side of the auditorium.

A woman entered from the back of the stage. Her presence took over the gathered troops immediately. She was in the black uniform of the Grand Admiral, five stars sewn onto the collar of the garments. Somehow Ace had expected a thicker woman, one with more character lines spread across her face. This woman wasn't petite, but lithe, and her age was difficult to put a finger on. When she stepped behind the podium, not a single person in the room was making a sound, as if they were all collectively holding their breath.

"Greetings, recent recruits and Fleet troops alike. I'm Grand Admiral Jish Karn, and I'll cut to the chase. There is a threat from a rebel group near Neptune. They've been a quiet conglomerate of terrorists and pirates, stealing ships from inter-system stations, and we think they've been receiving funds from one of the dome manufacturing partners."

Ace heard a few gasps in the crowd. It didn't sound too surprising, but he knew it had to be a big threat if the Grand Admiral was speaking to them about it, instead of funneling the details through the command structure.

"We have it on good authority they're planning an attack in six days. We'll be sending a probe soon, and if they're there, as we've been informed, we'll be sending a covert group of fighters in to take care of the incursion. The names of the pilots and crew have been decided, so please check with your direct report to see if you're included."

Ace hoped he wasn't on the list. He was growing confidence in his own skills, but he didn't want to end up being killed on his first real mission by some run-down pirate ship with more luck than him.

He glanced to the left of the room, where Ceda, the big oaf he'd made enemies with, was talking to an Earth Fleet officer. It looked like a commander, and Ace shrank down in his seat. Ceda was scanning the full room, and he locked on Ace, who'd been trying to make himself as small as possible. The thug pointed to him, and the commander nodded, motioning to a couple of the armed soldiers nearby.

The Grand Admiral kept talking, but Ace didn't hear another word she said. He was busted, and it wasn't going to end well. He took a deep breath and thought about running, but where could he go? It would only delay the inevitable. He waited until the speech was over and the Fleet audience were on their feet, clapping for their leader. The armed guards wound their way across the floor, in front of the stage, to where he and Serina sat.

Flint

Flint was still reeling from his arrival at their secret destination. Fairbanks had done something truly noteworthy, and Flint couldn't believe he was aboard the ship he was going to be piloting. *Eureka* was the best-looking ship he'd ever laid eyes on, and he felt bad for his own freighter when he thought it. She'd gotten him through a lot, and he'd put her through the wringer on multiple occasions, but this vessel was one for the ages.

God, I hope this Shift drive works. He'd heard Benson say it was tested and functional, but he was still sweating bullets thinking about jumping so far, and through a space Rift. They'd arrived half a day ago and were finally given clearance to head onto Fairbanks' ship.

"Flint, I'm so glad you didn't convince them to leave me on Titan. This is so much better," Kat said. She was wearing a brand-new uniform, one sourced by Benson. Fairbanks had foregone the Earth Fleet attire and had produced new uniforms for his staff. Kat's was dark gray, black boot laces tucked under her long pants. It looked sharp. Flint was wearing the same uniform, only his collar was different. He looked down to see his tan boots contrast with the clothing. They'd been with him through a lot, and he wasn't going to part ways with them now.

Rank on the ship still hadn't been explained to him, or where he'd fall into it. Benson had told him they'd be meeting with Captain Heather Barkley and Jarden Fairbanks on the bridge. Flint was as ready as he'd ever be for this new chapter in his life. After the recent scares he'd been through, and the truth about the Earth Fleet being behind his parents' and countless others' deaths, he was looking forward to the adventure. No more hiding was necessary. He was on his new home.

"I hope we can trust these guys. How are you feeling about it all?" Flint asked his younger co-pilot. She looked back at him with a twinkle in her eye.

"Flint, this ship is amazing. Have you ever dreamed of something this great? It gives me hope. After seeing the crappy ruined colony on Mars, and the old cities back on Earth, we've become a race divided into slums and luxury. Maybe we can get in this Fairbanks' ear and convince him to help some of those people. If he has the ability to manufacture the *Eureka*, imagine how many lives he could change. He could rebuild Mars Major…" Kat was ever the idealist, and while Flint respected that about her, he didn't think any of their current paths would lead them to becoming philanthropists.

Flint raised a hand in front of him. "Slow down. You realize we're 'jumping' into another galaxy. We might be hundreds of thousands of light years from home, with no way to return for at least thirty years, if we're to believe the stories we've been told. I don't want to stifle your passion, but Kat… our lives as we know them are over. This is it for us now. We may never be coming back," he said, hoping the point got across to her.

The twinkle was gone, but she still grinned at him. "I know. I'm sorry."

"Don't be," he said as the door to the room slid open, revealing Benson.

"Come with me, if you would," the man said before

turning and walking down a hall.

Flint beheld everything with wonder as they crossed most of the ship, taking an elevator to the bridge ten minutes later. He couldn't wait to have time to freely explore the vessel. He felt like a kid the one time his parents had brought him to a museum in New Boston. He'd wandered the exhibits for hours, soaking up as much of the facility as he could.

The doors to the lift opened, and Flint found himself on the largest bridge he'd ever seen. The viewscreen was at least thirty feet across and twenty high; a few ships hovered nearby in space outside the vessel, stars glimmering in the backdrop.

Three work stations made a first row on the bridge, closest to the screen, and he guessed two to be for himself and Kat, if they took his suggestion. The other was likely to control the weapons systems, and that was to the right of the row. He walked over to them and ran a hand over the console that hung over the lap of the seat. It was unlike anything he'd seen, sleek and white. His own ship had makeshift buttons and switches in a mad array. Compared to this, his freighter seemed to come from another century.

"Can you believe this?" Kat asked another open-ended question. He could believe it, because he had no choice, but it wasn't what he'd expected when he'd first landed on Europa.

"What do you think?" a new voice asked from the back of the bridge, and Flint spun around, seeing an elderly man in a dark uniform. He could only be one person.

"Councilman Jarden Fairbanks. A pleasure to meet you." Flint wasn't sure that was true, but he put himself on his best behavior. He walked over to the man, stepping up to the rear seats on the bridge, past the captain and first officer's seats.

They shook hands, and Flint was surprised by the man's firm grip. "Likewise, Mr. Lancaster. You didn't have trouble finding the place, I hope." Fairbanks' joke hit, and Flint couldn't help but laugh at the timing.

"No. It was a quick jaunt to Europa after getting shot at on Mars, then being boarded by Marines on the way. No big deal." Flint watched for any sign of shock in the councilman's eyes but failed to spot one.

"Good. I'm glad there weren't any issues," the man said without missing a beat. He apparently had a wry humor Flint could appreciate. He wasn't anything like the man Flint had expected.

The bridge's main doors opened off the elevator, and a woman in a pressed white uniform stepped onto the bridge. Her hair was slicked back, pulled into a tight braid, but her eyes had a soft edge to them.

"Captain Heather Barkley, I'd like you to meet Lieutenant Flint Lancaster and Junior Lieutenant Kat Bron." The councilman knew Kat's last name, and that caught Flint off-guard. She wasn't even listed on his own ship records.

Heather walked over to them and shook their hands. "You're the pilot Councilman Fairbanks couldn't live without. I'll be curious to see what you bring that anyone else couldn't."

"So will I. Pleasure to meet you, Captain. You have a beautiful ship here," Flint said.

"Don't for a minute presume to think this is my ship, Lieutenant," Captain Barkley said. The use of his newly given rank hit him in the chest. It sounded strange to hear it. "I may be the captain, but *Eureka* is all the councilman's."

"Be that as it may, you are the captain," Fairbanks said, sitting down in the first officer's seat.

For the first time, Flint noticed someone else on board with them. She stepped out from the office in the back corner of the bridge. She didn't have a Fleet look to her, if there was such a thing. Her dark curly hair was cut short, and she had a gorgeous tone to her skin. The woman cleared her throat and walked toward them, her gaze darting between them.

"This is Doctor Wren Sando, one of our science officers." Fairbanks seemed pleased by saying this, and Flint could tell there was much more to the back story. He didn't press it right now.

"Welcome aboard, Mr. Lancaster and Miss Bron," Dr. Sando said. Her gaze lingered on Flint for a few more seconds, and he wondered if she was feeling the same thing he was. Heavy footsteps emerged from the office, and two glowing orange eyes looked back from the dim corner of the bridge. No one else seemed to pay attention to the lingering android, so Flint ignored it too. Probably on the cleaning crew.

"How long have you been with the councilman's crew?" Flint found himself asking.

She laughed, a quick sound. "Two days."

Kat raised an eyebrow, but no one elaborated. Fairbanks was really throwing together a last-minute effort here.

"Shall we discuss the mission a little more over dinner?" Councilman Fairbanks asked, and everyone nodded.

Flint's stomach was growling, but with everything going on, he wasn't sure he had much of an appetite.

22

CD6 (Charles)

CD6 was among new people, yet he couldn't shake the feeling that he was once again all alone. Wren was tied up with her lab preparations, and CD6 helped where he could. But did he only want to be her lab assistant? He didn't think so. There was more out there for a being such as himself. *A being.* The thought came to him unbidden but sounded right when he thought it.

CD6 was an android, made up of electrical components and metal, but if one thing was sure, he was no ordinary android. What had created him? He wanted to know his origins and had started searching the Interface for signs of another like him. There were plenty of stories from the past five centuries about metal men having consciousness, so maybe it wasn't as far-fetched as it felt. Still, those were stories, and he was real.

He tried to think of himself as Charles, the name Wren had given him, but he couldn't shake the given name of CD6 in his own head. Maybe, with time, he could become Charles. He'd like that.

He walked down a hall; a few uniformed crew members walked by, ignoring him. They wouldn't know he was thinking while they passed by, considering his future, his likeness to a human. They were leaving for their journey in five days, and everyone seemed to be in a panic to get things done. From what CD6 understood, many of the crew had recently found out where they were really heading, or at least that they were on a secret mission. Those who didn't want to partake were being held on a nearby vessel, with no communication out until the *Eureka* was off; then they could go home, if that was their ultimate destination.

CD6 was glad to hear they'd be spared. He didn't know the councilman well, but he assumed a man of his nature didn't get where he was by giving in to others' needs. It was something he'd have to remember moving forward.

Footsteps stopped behind CD6 as he stared out a window along the edge of the ship.

"Beautiful, isn't it?" the man asked. It was the one named Benson. There was a walkway that took you a full three-sixty around the ship, and this was CD6's second round trip this morning alone.

CD6 looked over at the man, unsure who he spoke to. When he saw there was no one else around, he replied, "It is. It really is something. The vacuum of space, death to all organic life, yet we look at it with amazement and awe."

"You're special, aren't you, Charles?" the man asked him.

"I'm not sure. I am unique, if that answers your question." CD6 was uncomfortable with the attention, yet it was nice to be acknowledged by a human other than Wren.

"I think they're one and the same in this case. I hate to ask something of you, with us just having met and all." Benson turned to him, his eyes going soft, and his hands interlaced at the fingers as he spoke. "We left something important behind. When we didn't have Wren with our team, it wasn't quite as valuable, but now, with her research on the subject, we need it again."

CD6 knew a favor was about to be asked of him. He didn't know how to take it. "Go on."

"We have a small vessel, built with one of the new Shift drives. We need you to go to the gathered Earth Fleet and get this subject so we can continue the research. Wren might be the only person capable of saving humanity, and we can't do that without your help."

CD6 felt a rush of excitement. The human race needed *him* to do something. Nothing would make him more accepted than participating in the annals of new history. But a question gnawed at him: "Why can't you send a human?"

"I'll explain the plan, and you'll understand." Benson motioned for them to keep walking, and for the next thirty minutes, he described what CD6 would have to do.

By the end, CD6 was nervous but ready for another adventure. "Take me to the vessel," he said, not wanting to waste time.

"You're doing a great thing here, Charles." Benson clapped him on the back, and CD6 finally began to feel like he was fitting in.

Jish

Three days to go. Jish Karn paced around the near-empty bridge of the *Stellae*. She suddenly felt every year of her age. Her bones ached, and her hips were tight. It was time to send the probe out and have it wait there, taking footage of the Rift. Three days until they'd find out if the Invaders were going to attack. She closed her eyes and saw the image of the alien below deck, scratching red lines through the zoomed-in image of Earth.

Whatever happened, they were ready. She told herself this over and over as she slumped down onto the admiral's chair. "Are we ready for launch?" she asked the lone man on board. He was her most trusted officer: a man twenty years her junior, but as loyal as they came. Henry glanced back at her from his spot at the front of the bridge.

"Probe is ready for launch." He zoomed in on the small vessel five thousand kilometers from their current position.

They'd tested the Shift drive a hundred times on the small probe, tweaking it until it worked properly. She was confident it would arrive at the programmed destination with ease, but that didn't stop her from being as nervous as she'd ever been. This had to work. They needed to have the upper hand on the Invaders, or it was all for nothing. She'd had terrible dreams last night. Hundreds of their gigantic vessels emerged from the Rift; thousands of their alien-manned fighters roamed into the solar system, each with Shift drive capability. Jish was proud of the Fleet's two dozen vessels with the same technology, but there just wasn't enough time. The reverse engineering took far too long.

Thirty years. They needed at least thirty more years. Maybe the Invaders wouldn't be there this time. The Rift could open up, reveal nothing, and close a while later. These were all possibilities Jish had to consider, but deep in her heart, she knew these were dreams she told herself to stay calm. The enemy would be there in force. She had to be ready.

Henry cleared his throat, and she looked down at him from the view of the lone probe against the backdrop of deep space. She took a breath, held it briefly, and sighed it out. "Activate the drive. Send it on its way." She leaned forward in her seat and saw something she'd never expected. It was so outrageous, she started to laugh. Deep racking laughs from her belly turned to sobs, and her hands came to cover her face.

The probe had exploded. Pieces of it were floating in their viewscreen. Henry was ashen, and he muttered something Jish couldn't hear.

Wren

"I'll take a coffee, please." Wren heard the pilot's voice at the bar and looked up to see Flint Lancaster leaning one arm on the countertop and surveying the room. His eyes met hers and he smiled. What was it about this guy that intrigued her? His hair was brown, a little shaggy for her liking. He could use a shave, and he always seemed to be fighting a grin, like he expected someone to tell a joke at any given time.

But still, she could tell he'd taken an interest in her. She used to be blind to that sort of thing, always nose-deep into a research paper or her work, but now, after two years away from any sort of work or men, it was obvious. She wondered how many men had given her the same signals back in New Dallas. Her ex-fiancé Timothy had only caught her eye because he was a doctor, working in the same field. Otherwise, she was sure she'd have stayed alone. The way he'd turned out, she wished she *had* been alone those last few years.

"Dr. Sando," Flint said, approaching the table with a mug in his hand. "Good to see you. I didn't expect any familiar faces here at this hour."

"Please call me Wren. I've always thought that phrase funny. We're in space, far away from a rotating planet around the sun, and days really have no meaning other than a structure for a work shift or sleeping." Wren said this and instantly regretted it. Why did she always feel the need to comment on everything?

He didn't seem to care and grinned in that insufferable yet charming way he had. "I agree, but let's face it. I need a solid three meals a day, and without the clock, I might miss one."

It was her turn to laugh. Who was this man who could so quickly disarm thirty-two years of barriers?

"I guess you do have me there. How did you get here?" she asked impulsively. They'd met, but no one spoke of his back story or his journey here.

"I left my quarters and asked an android for the nearest cafeteria," Flint said, straight-faced.

That was how it was going to be. "Very funny. Seriously, what's your story?" Wren asked.

He glanced at her empty cup. All that remained was an inch of tepid water and some green leaves. "If you want that, we're going to need something a little stronger."

"Deal. How about an ale from the Moons?" she asked, and Flint nodded.

"I just came from there, and can attest they have fine beer." He got up and crossed the room to the bar, coming back with two tall glasses in mere moments.

They clinked glasses, his eyes locked on to hers as they did so. "To new friendships," he said with a wink, mirroring her cheers from the other day. Odd that he'd say the same thing.

Wren took a sip and set the glass down. "There. We have a drink. We made a toast. How did you end up here?"

"You see, I was born… You want the long version or the short?" he asked.

"How about somewhere in between? I have all the time in the world." Wren leaned back as he began telling her an unbelievable tale. An hour later, they were on their second beer, and it was her turn to share her story. She felt so comfortable with him, she didn't leave any detail out. She described being attacked, she told him about the strange man who'd arrived to learn about her connection with Fairbanks, she held back tears as she described Mara dying on the smelting room floor.

His hand reached for hers.

"What are you two up to?" a woman asked, and Wren glanced up through glassy eyes to see Flint's co-pilot Kat there, frowning as she saw their hands touching. Flint pulled away, grabbing his glass instead.

"Just chatting. Why don't you join us?" Wren asked, but the younger woman shook her head.

"I'm heading to bed. See you tomorrow," Kat told Flint without a glance back at Wren.

Jish

Jish had a dilemma on her hands. She had a backup plan if the probe failed; unfortunately, they'd only been able to shrink the size of the Shift drive recently and didn't have a second probe to send. The explosion would be investigated. Jish knew it had to have been tampered with, and she was on a mission to determine by whom.

"What now?" Henry asked.

"We move on." Her backup plan needed a pilot, and from what she'd heard, the recent recruit in a holding cell aboard her ship might be a good fit.

The comm-switch on her seat lit up. "Go ahead," she said.

"Grand Admiral, we have something to report," the

voice said.

She wasn't in the mood for formality. "I don't have time for this. Spit it out!"

"A ship recently arrived," the man said.

"A ship. Okay. Is it one of ours?" she asked, her patience wearing thin.

"No, ma'am. It's an old Recon-class fighter, but it's not coded Fleet. It came into range dead in space. No life signs either." His speech was clipped and rushed.

Her pulse sped up. It might be a trap. "Did you scan it?"

"No explosives aboard, at least not from our scans. We think there may be an android on board, but it appears to be powered down," he said.

"Very well. Secure the ship, and store it below once you determine there's no threat. Let me know what else is on that ship." Jish didn't like it, but it wasn't the first time an unmanned ship had been found floating around space.

She had bigger things to concern herself with. It was time to speak with the boy.

Ace

Ace counted his blessings. It had been a few days and he was still alive. No one had come to him, no accusations were thrown around; he was just led to a cell aboard the Grand Admiral's vessel. They brought him food twice a day, and his cell had a cot and washroom. It was more than he could have hoped for, and a better setup than living on the streets of Old Chicago.

They'd even given him a reader, and he found himself drawn to a fiction book. It reminded him of the old library he used to frequent back on Earth. It was one of the few places he could go unimpeded. He used to sit and read for hours; stories of faraway places distracted him from the monotony and struggle that was his life.

He sat in the middle of the makeshift bed, his feet planted against the stark white floor, when the energy barrier holding him in dissipated. Two armed guards stood outside, each holding blasters in their hands. They stepped apart, and the Grand Admiral walked into the cell toward him.

"Thank you, guards. I have it from here," she said. The guards didn't move for a moment, and she finally turned to them, her back to Ace. He knew then that she didn't fear him, and he was grateful for the action. The last thing he wanted to come off as was a threat. "I said that will be all."

They turned, leaving Ace alone with the Fleet's top officer.

"You're a small one, aren't you." She didn't say it like a question, so he didn't answer. "Who was Edgar Smith?"

Ace had no choice but to be honest, so he told her the story. He didn't leave out any detail. She glanced to his hand when he got to the part about swapping the ID chip, and didn't comment until he was done.

"And then I walked to the recruitment office, and the rest is history." His hands were shaking. It was the first time he'd explained his story, and it was likely enough to be sentenced to death, or at least a lifetime on a prison mine. Ace wasn't sure which was worse.

"You've been through a lot in such a short life. And all you wanted was to come to the Fleet so you could be part of something, and have food and shelter, isn't that right?" Her tone was kind, motherly, and he felt himself drawn to her.

Ace nodded, looking down at the ground.

"We've contacted Edgar Smith's parents and have

sent them a reparation payment. They didn't know he was dead; they only assumed he'd joined the Fleet and they hadn't heard from him. We explained that he was killed in a training exercise on the moon base, and they've accepted the payment without hesitation."

Ace couldn't believe his ears. If they were covering it up, did that mean he couldn't be tried for impersonation?

"What does this mean for me?" he asked hesitantly. He held his breath while he waited for his punishment.

"I have a special mission for you, Ace. Do you mind if I call you Ace?" she asked warmly.

He shook his head. "No. Please do."

"Very well. Ace, you heard the speech in the auditorium, correct?" The Grand Admiral came to sit beside him on his cot. There were no chairs in the room, and the bed squeaked as her small frame joined his on the mattress.

"Yes. You're sending a probe to spy on the terrorists."

Her gaze sank to the floor. "We've encountered an issue, and the probe's no longer an option. We need to send a fighter to scout it for us. We have a modified EFF-17 with the new Shift drive technology ready to go, but it can't be operated remotely. We need a pilot."

Ace knew what she was about to tell him, but as nervous as it made him, he was excited at the same time. "I'll do it!" he said too loudly.

The Grand Admiral didn't seem to notice; she gave him a matronly smile. "Good. I'm glad to hear it. Come on; you don't need to be in this cell any longer. And when you're back, we'll change your ID tag. You can have a fresh start."

Ace liked the sound of that. He walked out of the cell, past the guards, and out of the holding bay. He felt like a new man already.

CD6 (Charles)

CD6 came to life as his timer activated, returning power to his core. The room he found himself in was dark, and he started to panic, worried he was still on the ship he'd come in. He stepped forward and tripped on something, stumbling to the floor with a clatter. He activated his night vision, the room turning black and green in his cybernetic optics.

He faltered back as he stood up, seeing the horrors around him. The space was full of disassembled androids. Torsos hung from the walls, their wiring loose and torn. He averted his eyes from the headless components and found something far worse. To the left was a forty-gallon bucket, apparently full of various models of android heads. One on top stared at him with dead black eyes.

He let out a small scream before catching himself from making more noise. They were only androids, created to serve a programmed function. They'd felt no pain and had no feelings. Maybe they were in a better place now, not having to slave over a task non-stop for a human. But wasn't that what he was doing now? Working for humans? Doing what they asked, instead of what he was programmed to do?

No, he told himself. He was helping a friend and, in turn, helping save the human race. CD6 looked down at himself and remembered he had no clothing on. He was nothing but a plain android here, one with a menial task. Models like his were rarely guards on vessels such as the *Stellae*. Instead, he found the console at the edge of the room and keyed into it. From there, he determined the coding for the engineering androids and changed his series number to match theirs.

If he was caught, he could feign a malfunction, but then he'd clearly be wiped and reused somewhere else. Would he lose himself if that happened? CD6 guessed he'd be nothing more than another simple android, devoid of thought and emotion, if he failed his mission and was apprehended. Or he'd end up in this very room. Perhaps his torso would hang from this very wall and his head would adorn the top of the bucket.

There was no option. He couldn't fail.

With determination, he exited the storage room and found himself in a dim hall. This was one of the floors between decks where the servant androids stayed, and maintenance could be done below each of the ship's multiple decks. This particular vessel had twenty, half of them with these in-between floors.

CD6 didn't need to worry about those, though. He had one location in mind and knew it would be harder to get to than even Benson thought. With *Stellae*'s blueprints downloaded, he couldn't find the secret level Benson told him about. But it was there, according to Councilman Jarden Fairbanks, and CD6 had to consider that as a truth.

He began moving down the corridor, toward the lift where he'd attempt to find the Grand Admiral's largest secret. Benson hadn't told him just what he was bringing back with him, but it was supposed to be hard to hide. CD6 opened a compartment in his chest and pulled out a device. Benson had trained him on how to use it, and he felt confident it would work if the target was willing to come along. If it wasn't, CD6 had a tranquilizer in another partition.

23

Jarden

Jarden Fairbanks couldn't have been happier. He was aboard *Eureka*, the flagship of a new era. With it, he was going to find what lay beyond the Rift. What were the Watchers really like, and where did they live? Perhaps they came from a world thousands of light years from the Rift. Maybe they'd only discovered the Rift a couple of centuries ago themselves and had started to peek through with caution and curiosity.

The Fleet had screwed it all up last time by being there with a force. It was taken as a hostile encounter, and that was after Fairbanks had been told there was to be no contact. It was the moment he lost all respect for Jish Karn. Even then, she'd been an arrogant young woman, the Fleet's youngest admiral. He only wished he could see her face when she found out he'd left the system through the Rift.

August first. One day to go. Jarden stood at the back of the bridge, Benson beside him with his arms folded over his chest. The man had once again proven his value, as he always did, by bringing Flint Lancaster to him. Surprisingly, Lancaster had been amenable to the idea of searching for a colony of humans beyond the Rift. One never knew what someone's reaction to such unpredictable news would be, but Jarden considered himself a fair judge of character. Flint wasn't just amenable to the idea; the adventurer in him was thrilled at the prospect of seeing another system, one with habitable worlds.

Out there, they wouldn't need a colony dome. They wouldn't live in a cold, desolate wasteland, hoping the domes would protect them from the solar storms, radiation, and bone-freezing temperatures. The world they'd found with their probe so long ago was so akin to Earth, Jarden had to wonder if there was intelligent life there.

Just where had the large group of two thousand colonists arrived at, and what were they doing sixty years later? These were questions that had plagued Jarden for countless years, every single day, driving him forward in his single-minded task.

"Activating the Shift drive," Lancaster said from his seat at the front of the bridge. He looked every bit the part in his uniform. An air of casual leadership enveloped the man, and Jarden found himself liking the pilot more each day. He'd picked up the training with no issues. Captain Barkley was impressed with him as well, which didn't come as a surprise.

Barkley spoke now, sitting in her captain's chair. "Set coordinates, Junior Lieutenant Bron. On my mark…" Her hand was in the air, her index finger raised to the ceiling.

Jarden took a deep breath, closing his eyes while she spoke. "Hit it."

When Jarden opened his eyes, the image out the massive viewscreen was totally different, and they were millions of kilometers from their previous location. Lancaster looked back at the captain, then to Jarden, with a smile on his face.

"Nice work, everyone. We wait here until tomorrow. You know the drill," Jarden said, and he left the bridge to get some sleep. With everything that might happen tomorrow, he knew it was now or never.

Ace

It was time for Ace to leave the *Stellae.* He could already tell the Grand Admiral was getting nervous about the delay, but she didn't want to rush his training on the new drive technology. He was confident he could use it to get to the target in time. The idea of folding space around him scared him, but the GA claimed it was as safe as, or safer than, their current technology.

He had no leg to stand on and couldn't very well ask to send someone else. If he did that, he was heading right back for that cell, or maybe for the airlock. He didn't want either of those options, so he stuck with the mission at hand.

A man simply named "Henry" entered his quarters and handed Ace something. Ace felt the familiar rough edges of his playing card hit his fingers, the ace of clubs back in his possession.

"Jish thought you might want this," Henry said, using the leader of the Earth Fleet's first name. It sounded strange to Ace, but he was thrilled to have his memento from his previous life back.

"Thank you," was all he could muster out of his tight throat.

Ace looked around the small room he'd called home for a short period of time, and entered the hall just as a series of alarms rang out. Red lights strobed along the ceiling and floors, and Ace instantly felt stressed and anxious.

"What's that?" he asked Henry, who was fumbling for his earpiece.

"What's going on?" Henry asked someone through his mic.

Ace noticed the man's already pale face turn ghost white. "That's impossible," Henry said, his voice little more than a whisper. "Defend the Fleet. Give us cover on the *Stellae*. We're sending a ship out in a few minutes. Don't let them get it."

Ace could hardly hear the conversation. His heart beat so loudly, his blood was filling his ears in time with each pulse. The klaxons were deafening in the corridor, and he wanted to go back into his room and hide his head under a pillow.

Henry grabbed him roughly by the arm. "Come. We have no time to spare."

"What is it?" Ace asked, still not sure what was happening.

"We're being attacked."

CD6 (Charles)

The elevator door released, and CD6 locked it open before removing the protruding merger-stick from his finger. Anyone looking to use the elevator would be notified it was under repair.

He left the lift and entered the narrow space before him. He scanned the walls and found a hidden compartment where a stunner sat mounted inside. He took the weapon, just to be safe. He still didn't know exactly what was on the other side of the doorway fifty yards away, and he needed to play it cautiously.

Each footstep was too loud as his metal feet clanged on the grated floor. This hall wasn't finished like the ship's main corridors, likely so no one would notice the extra cost and effort to build the secret area. CD6 moved quickly and arrived at the doorway. It didn't open for him. He'd been warned it might have some sort of biometrics reader, and that was indeed the case.

He tapped the left side of his torso and pulled a device from inside. This was one of two given to him by Benson. It was supposed to duplicate the last bio-readout from the corridor, and since CD6 was an android, Benson had claimed it would work. He activated it, and an invisible pulse erupted from the stick-shaped device.

A long minute passed, and CD6 was sure it had failed, when the doors slid open and an alarm rang out. Red lights flashed all around him. He scanned inwardly on the ship's server, which he'd linked up to earlier. He was relieved to know it wasn't him who'd set the alarm off by opening the doorway. The nearby Earth Fleet appeared to be under attack. He had to hurry.

The room was dim, but lights came on as his movements disturbed the sensors. He found his target across the space, where a blue barrier kept the being trapped. CD6 felt trepidation as he crossed the room, arriving a few feet from the barrier. The keypad had the same biometric scanner on it. No one but the Grand Admiral could let the prisoner out.

Before using the device again, CD6 looked past the glowing blue energy field to see a creature huddled in the cell's far corner. It was a thick animal. Even in its crouched position, CD6 could tell it was tall: at least eight feet in height, with long arms and a wide torso. Its head lifted from a resting position, and two black eyes stared back at him.

"Hello," CD6 said. "Can you understand me?"

The creature stood now, and CD6 stepped back in fear.

He tried again. "Do you know what I'm saying? My

name is" – he hesitated before saying the name Wren had given him – "Charles. I came to break you out of your prison." This was becoming a common occurrence for him, only he was sure the alien before him was going to end up back in another prison once it was with Councilman Fairbanks.

The alien used a palm to hit itself in the chest as it stood proudly. It said something unintelligible, which CD6 assumed was its name.

"Pleased to meet you. Will you come willingly?" he asked it, knowing he still had the tranquilizer if necessary. The creature lifted its head and nodded up and down in an exaggerated yes.

The alarms still rang out, but they were muted inside this room. The noise carried to them from the corridor he'd come from. Without a second thought, CD6 tapped the device again and gained access to the console, where he turned off the energy field.

The alien started to move slowly, reaching a two-fingered hand toward the spot where the barrier had stood a second before. When it met no resistance, it made its move. It ran past CD6, knocking him to the ground. He landed on his back and watched the creature race down the hall.

"It's going to be like that, is it?" CD6 said out loud to himself, and picked up the stunner. He ran for the corridor and spotted the alien struggling to get down the tight hall. With hard effort, and probably a few cuts, the alien made it into the elevator.

He couldn't leave without access, and CD6 kept moving, slowing as he neared the lift. The stunner was raised in his hand. This was programming he was used to. They always carried stunners at the prison and were each well-versed in taking a prisoner down if necessary. This was the same act. He leaned on those abilities as he waited for the alien to poke some part of his body into view.

He didn't have to wait long. An arm exposed itself in the elevator doorway, and CD6 tapped the trigger, hitting the thick forearm. The creature fell to the ground, all of his nervous system freezing up. CD6 pulled the tranquilizer pen out and pressed it against the alien's thick gray skin.

CD6 had done it! Wren would be so proud of him. Even though the creature had attempted an escape, he was grateful of one thing. He didn't have to drag its huge frame down the narrow hallway. It was already in the elevator.

He closed the doors and set forth on the next part of his mission: getting off the *Stellae* and back to *Eureka*.

The elevator lifted. CD6 hurried to cover the alien with the energy field and strapped a tarp around it. The end result looked something like a pile of rocks in a bag, but CD6 didn't have to be in the hallway for long. He'd stolen a hovertrolley from a storage room, and he hefted the creature onto it now, the trolley's magnetic base sagging toward the ground under the weight.

When the doors opened, CD6 did his best to look like a maintenance android hauling away a load of refuse. He passed a few people, none giving him the time of day. As he was nearing the hangars, he heard a voice directed at him.

"You there," it said. CD6 turned to see a uniformed officer, hand heading to hip, where a stunner sat holstered.

"How can I be of service, sir?" he asked, using phrasing from his programming.

The man bent down as if to touch the tarp. "What's under here?"

"The refrigerators broke down on deck two. I'm hauling away the rotten meat. Would you care to see it?" CD6 asked, reaching toward the wrapped-up alien.

The man's interest vanished quickly. "No, be on your way."

CD6 watched the man walk down the hall, then took the opportunity to enter the first hangar he could find. A sole ship sat there, one CD6 didn't recognize from his database.

Ace

Henry left him to it, called away on some urgent matter. It was pure chaos out there. Ace hopped into the modified fighter. This one was twice the size of the ones he was trained on. The Shift drive technology took more space than the ones he was used to, and they had an added storage space for passengers or goods behind the cockpit.

He was in the secret hangar alone. The rest of the Fleet didn't know about the Grand Admiral's plans, he was told, and this ship was the backup to the probe failing. He was sure that if there was no attack on the Fleet at that moment, there'd be a full array of people in the hangar with him, making sure he was prepared for departure.

He flipped his earpiece in and turned the ship's power on. Instantly, the screens flashed red, and he zoomed out, seeing a map of their sector of space. There were hundreds of green lights racing around, some in formation, but mostly, they were broken and sporadic. Any non-fleet vessel nearby was red, and Ace was surprised to see as many as there were. Just who had this kind of fleet to attack them with? Were they being invaded by an alien race?

His earpiece buzzed, and he tapped it. "Ace, this is the Grand Admiral. I can't be there for your takeoff, but I'm there in spirit. Regardless of what you see out there, you must leave. Do not fail. Go to the coordinates I've given you. Send the feeds back to us."

Ace strapped himself in, and his chest rose in pride. "I won't fail you, ma'am."

"Very well. Godspeed." The communication ended. He glanced at the console again, seeing green and red lights blink out as they were destroyed. It was a real battle out there.

The hangar was small, only made for a couple of the Grand Admiral's private ships. Now Ace was the only one in the hangar. The modified fighter was the solitary ship sitting there. He tapped the console and the wall slid up, revealing the energy field and space beyond. Even from here, he saw the warzone in the distance. His heart hammered hard as he activated the drive.

"You can do this," Ace whispered to himself and sealed the mask over his head.

The fighter hopped forward, a little touchier than he was used to. The hangar was only a few hundred yards deep, and in no time, he'd breached the energy field and soared into open space. Chaos erupted around him. His console showed ten red icons within a few kilometers' range of his ship, and he arced the ship away from their clusters.

His HUD zoomed in on the ships one at a time, showing him a fleet of derelict run-down vessels. This was no alien invasion. It was a terrorist attack. The Grand Admiral had spoken of an attack coming where the probe was supposed to travel to, and where Ace was destined for now. If the attack had already happened here, what was the point of him even going? He could help his Fleet here by fending them off.

He was about to reach out to the GA, when her voice carried into his earpiece again. "What's the delay, Ace? Get to your target destination. Do it at all costs."

He didn't bother questioning the command. There was a reason behind it, and it came from somewhere far above his pay grade.

Pulse fire erupted around him and he rolled the ship, narrowly avoiding being struck by the enemy blasts. The incoming vessel was an old Recon model from the turn of the century. Ace raced around it, firing at the ship as he tried to escape. He connected with fire to its underbelly, and it stopped dead in space. He kept moving. All around him, skirmishes were taking place. Some of the EFF-17s showed familiar names on his readout, and he silently cheered on the other recruits.

An EFF-17 exploded in front of him, and Ace let out a shout of rage as his ship barrelled through the debris. He had to leave, but it wouldn't hurt to avenge his fellow Fleet pilot first. The attacker was in a clunky freighter, its weapons slow to charge. Ace targeted the thrusters and fired his pulse cannon. Seconds later, the ship exploded, and he curved around the destruction into open space, past the fluttering icons on the screen.

When he thought he was in the clear, one of the Fleet carriers appeared in front of him, and he heard the command in his ear. "Serina Trone, destroy that fighter. It's been compromised!" The voice was clearly that of the Grand Admiral, and it was sent out across all frequencies.

He saw fire from the Earth Fleet vessel begin to race toward him.

24

Jish

Everything had gone to hell. Jish Karn felt her world slipping between her fingers. How did this group find her? She'd told a lie to the troops about a rogue group threatening the Fleet, but she had no real intel that an attack was imminent. Somehow, she felt the touch of Fairbanks on the incursion. She had no idea how he'd done it, but he had to be behind the terrorist assault.

Ace was still in the ship, and she watched as its icon moved on her holoscreen. He had to escape and make it to the Rift watching point. There was no other way to know if the Invaders were coming through. She'd done so much, given up too many years to waste the opportunity. If they failed here, they might have no chance at defending the colonies and Earth. And here they were, the Fleet engaged in a battle with a ragtag group.

She watched as far more red icons flashed out of existence than Fleet green, but any loss was too much at this point. They'd need both Fleet and rogue vessels if they were to hold off a real invasion. For the first time, she noticed the yellow blinking light on her holoscreen.

"What's that?" she asked herself out loud from the seat on the bridge. Her team was active, moving from attacks, and destroying as many ships as they could with her powerful warship. *Stellae* wasn't to be trifled with.

They'd need a lot more than old smuggler ships and run-down rock haulers to destroy her.

Then it hit her. The yellow blinking light was the Invader. She'd chipped it long ago, and since it never moved, the small dot remained synonymous with her hidden floor below deck. Now it was off the ship and appeared to be in Ace's modified Shift drive fighter. Had he been sent here purposely? Had Fairbanks been behind that too? She was furious.

The closest vessel was the EFC-02EP, and she was started to see a new recruit being trained as the captain. The name was familiar, and she knew it to be Admiral Helina Trone's daughter.

She sent the message across all channels. "Serina Trone, destroy that fighter. It's been compromised!" With that, she raced off the bridge as her crew members shouted. *Stellae* jostled from an attack above, and Jish stumbled from the bombing. Alarms rang out loudly in the halls, and she found her footing, heading for the elevator. Inside, she used her code to get to the lower level. The lights in the elevator were dim, as the ship's main power was diverted to shields.

The doors opened below, and she knew he was gone the instant she set foot in the corridor. The stunner door was open, as was the main door at the end of the hall. The only Invader they had under lock and key was free and loose, and in one of their most powerful new fighters.

Ace

"You have to escape," a voice said from behind Ace.

He nearly jumped out of his skin, and his hand jerked the throttle, sending the ship into a roll. "Who said that?"

Ace was strapped firmly down and couldn't see behind him. The cockpit was large enough to house a stowaway or two, but he'd been in too much of a hurry to check the compartment.

"My name's Charles. I'm an android, and I have something back here that will help save humanity," the voice said, and Ace now caught the monotone timbre to the words.

The carrier ahead was sending out EFF-17s toward him, and when Ace looked at his screen, there were few red icons left. Now the Fleet could focus on him. But why? What had changed the Grand Admiral's mind? It had to have something to do with the android talking to him.

Ace tried to get through to the ship. He found its bridge-comm channel and hit it. "Serina! Don't do this. Call them off. It's me, Ace! Don't do this!"

He was being shot at, and he pushed his fighter as hard as he could while the Shift drive charged. It was almost there, but he knew the fighters would catch him before he could activate the Shift.

"Ace?" Serina's voice cut into his ear. "What are you doing? Why is she telling me to stop you?"

"I don't know. It's a setup. She gave me the ship, pardoned me, and sent me on my merry way!" He was running out of time, and he zig-zagged from the incoming fire on his tail.

"I can't disobey her. I'm sorry, Ace." He could hear the frustration in her voice.

"Serina! Trust me. You know me. Let me go. Call them off!" The call was only between their two signals, though he knew the Grand Admiral would be able to hear their conversation later. Clearly, Serina knew this too.

She hesitated, and he looked to see his drive ninety

percent charged. Almost there. When she spoke again, he knew she was talking to the squadron under her carrier's command. "Cease fire. He's one of our own. Cease fire."

One last pulse arced over him, and as the Shift drive finally glowed green finally, Ace spoke into his headset. "Thanks, Serina. I… I love you." He hit the drive, and everything around him ceased to exist.

Wren

Wren scrolled through the files on her holoscreen. It was amazing that she hadn't considered just what she'd been doing back then. She'd been so stupid, working with blinders on. The money had been great, and knowing that the great Jarden Fairbanks was backing the project had been enough to get her on board. Now, seeing how obviously alien this DNA was, she couldn't help but think she'd deserved to be caught.

Anyone finding this mess in her lab would have thought she was creating a biological weapon, because she was, only they were careful to never have the DNA strain details anywhere prying eyes could find them. Even the Earth Fleet wouldn't have known just what kind of research was being done.

If Fairbanks came through, she was going to once again find a way to wipe out an alien race using a virus. She considered the fact that she should feel something on her conscience about it, but she was finding it hard to care. If doing so would prevent her own race from being destroyed, then she'd do it. That was the way of life. Plus, according to Fairbanks, the Watchers had fired first, and in the basic rules of engagement, that gave the Fleet every right to strike back, in any way possible.

A bell rang from the door. Wren closed the files and

got up from the desk inside the office settled at the lab's back corner. It was a great space, one Fairbanks had put a lot of thought into. He hadn't known she was coming, so he must have had plans to have someone else continue her research. She was curious who it was and what had happened to them.

She tapped the door open and found Flint Lancaster standing there. "I thought I'd find you here. Want some company?" he asked nonchalantly.

They were hitting it off, and she worried about getting too close to a stranger like this. She wanted to tell him she was busy, but his intense eyes gave her other thoughts. "Sure. Come in."

"What's all this?" he asked, motioning to the tables and different sections of the lab. On the left of the room was a glass room with an energy-barrier wall, which sat deactivated. What was that for? She hadn't gathered enough nerve to ask Fairbanks yet.

"This… is a biology lab." Wren said it as if it were the most obvious thing in the universe.

Flint walked around, touching tabletops and running his hand over a tray of beakers. "I don't get out much. I was never much of a student either."

"I find that hard to believe. You seem like a smart guy," Wren said. Was this her way of flirting? It had been so long, she felt off her game.

"Sure. Space smart, but that's about it. Maybe people smart too. You know, emotional and social I.Q., but not much else. What are you going to do in here?" he asked.

She didn't know how much to tell him, but Fairbanks hadn't asked her to keep it quiet. "I told you my story the other night. I was busted researching for the councilman. Apparently, one of the Watchers was left behind thirty years ago, and he got a sample of its flesh for me to study."

Flint raised an eyebrow, evidently not believing that was all she was doing with it. "Study for what purpose?"

Wren cleared her throat. "To create a life-ending virus."

He changed the subject, and she wasn't sure if they connected in his mind. "Do you really think we're going to a colony over there?"

The thought hadn't crossed her mind. "Of course. What else are we doing?"

"We only have what Fairbanks is telling us to go by. I've seen the videos, so I know there's indeed a Rift. Or someone doctored those videos, and this is all a big screw-around. All I'm saying is, maybe there never was a colony ship. Fairbanks might never have been married, and God knows if he had kids. I couldn't find anything on the Interface about his personal life."

"Come to think of it, Charles didn't find many useful details either. I think we have to trust him, though. In the end, what other options do we have?" she asked.

Flint shrugged. "Not many, but I can't help but feel like a puppet in all of this. They set me up to get here. That's clear to me. But you, you came without them ever suspecting it. You throw a wrench into it. But still…" He tapped his lips with an index finger, deep in thought. "He conveniently had a lab for you, with all of your old files to sort through, I bet."

Wren nodded.

"Are you sure this android doesn't work for him?" Flint asked.

"No way. He's been at the prison for forty years," she said.

"And you know this how?"

"He told me," Wren answered, but she was suddenly

catching on to his line of reasoning.

"He told you so. Could he be unaware of it? Maybe programmed to think he'd been there that long?" Flint asked.

Wren had to sit down. Her head was spinning. "He broke me out of prison. He was the one who tracked down Fairbanks' secret location when even the Fleet didn't know where he was… oh my God, you could be right."

"I'm not saying this for a certainty, but I want us to consider the possibility that Fairbanks gathered all of us here for a reason. He's a cunning old fox, and if he wanted us here, he managed to do it." Flint walked over to her and crouched down, setting his hands on her knees. "Let's make a deal. We need to watch out for each other."

She almost laughed at him, but he was right. Wren leaned forward into her hands. "How did I not see this? Here I was, actually admiring the man. Have I always been such a naïve fool?"

"He's done the same thing to me. Let's keep him thinking that we're on his side, but in the back of our heads, we're in this thing together. Deal?" Flint asked, sticking his hand out. She locked eyes with him. He did have kind eyes.

Her hand met his, and they softly shook. "Deal," she whispered. A thought crossed her mind. "Flint, have you seen Charles around lately?"

"No," Flint answered. "I thought he was with you."

25

Ace

Ace couldn't believe it. The Shift drive had worked. He'd been sure he was about to be killed, and when he activated the drive, he was sure it was going to blow up like the probe had. He found himself patting his own chest and legs, making sure all of him had made the trip.

"Very well done," a voice from behind him said, and Ace remembered the android was back there.

"Let's do this again. Who are you?" Ace asked, undoing his seat straps. He craned around to see the basic android staring back at him. Behind the android, a glowing blue energy field wrapped around another figure: a huge one, by the looks of it. Ace found he'd lost his voice and swallowed hard.

"I am CD6, more recently known as Charles. This is one of the Watchers, an alien race who will undoubtedly be the downfall of all humanity. We need to get him to the *Eureka*, where Dr. Wren Sando can study him and create a virus that will be deadly to his kind, so humans have a chance at survival." The android said all of this quickly, and Ace's head reeled from the information.

"You're telling me that aliens are invading, and that's one of them?" he asked.

"The only one in our solar system, yes," Charles replied.

"And where did you find this alien?" Ace couldn't believe the secured lump behind him was really an extraterrestrial.

"On the *Stellae*. Grand Admiral Karn has had him stowed away in a secret room on her ship for the last thirty years." Charles seemed to believe what he was saying, or at least he was programmed to. What kind of android was this? Ace had never seen a model so boisterous.

"Thirty years? You expect me to accept all of this?" Ace asked.

The orange eyes stared at him, and the android nodded. "I would prefer it that way. We don't have much time. The Rift opens tomorrow. We must get over to the *Eureka*."

Ace spun around, sitting heavily into his seat. His hands set over his mask, and he considered what he was hearing. The Grand Admiral must have had the alien tagged, and that was why she'd turned on Ace so aggressively. His life wasn't worth the alien's escape.

"Where is it?" he asked, unsure of his next move.

"Young man, may I ask your name?" Charles asked.

"Ace. Just Ace."

"Ace, there is much you don't know transpiring. Tomorrow, a Rift opens in space, not far from here. It's likely why you were being sent here. As surveillance. The councilman claimed he sabotaged the probe."

The probe. So it had backfired because of sabotage. That was why Ace was here now; otherwise, he might be dead after the attack. It hit him then. The same person responsible for the probe's destruction had set up the attack on the Earth Fleet. Who would do such a heinous crime?

"I know what you're thinking. It was the only way. The councilman has humanity's best interest at heart,"

Charles said.

"And what would an android understand about heart?" Ace asked, frustrated with his dilemma. No sound came from behind him for a minute, and Ace found himself feeling bad for his comment. "I'm sorry."

"It's all right. It's a consideration I've made for many years. I don't seem to be like any other androids," Charles said, and Ace could tell from the short conversation that he was correct.

"If I go along with this, what's the next step?" Ace asked, still not having made up his mind. If this councilman could save their race, did he want to oppose him? Especially if the key was bundled in an energy field in his ship at the moment.

Charles was up, crouched over in the short ceiling of the cockpit. "We cut the feeds back to the Fleet before moving an inch. We remove your ship's ID transponder and head to the *Eureka*'s location."

Ace endured an internal battle. The Grand Admiral had seemed so kind, but he knew this was only because of her predicament. She wanted a grateful, disposable pilot to scout this Rift Charles talked about. She didn't care about his little life. Then there was Serina. Was he betraying her if he did this? Or was he helping ensure her safety?

"Let's do it. How do I kill the feeds?" Ace asked. He didn't have full clarity on the situation, but he'd made up his mind. He was going to bring the alien to this councilman, and to the doctor who might be able to help save them all.

He hoped it was the right decision.

Benson

Benson waited for news from Shadow but wasn't holding his breath. The militant leader wouldn't be there for the actual attack on the Earth Fleet. She'd be hiding – in the shadows, as it were. No wonder she'd given herself that name. It was an apt description of the coward.

But to the woman's credit, Benson knew he'd avoid the battle as well, were he in the other's shoes.

It was almost time. Benson had put a lot of eggs in this android's basket. But even if they didn't get the captive Watcher, he'd still go ahead with his plan. In the end, Fairbanks wouldn't have a choice but to go along with him.

"The student becomes the master," Benson whispered to himself.

Soon. Soon they'd be on the other side of the Rift, and the next chapter would be upon them. Benson imagined the Grand Admiral's smug face as the Fleet was under attack. She was so arrogant, so sure that no one would be dumb enough to consider such a thing. She'd always been short-sighted, focusing only on the Watchers' imminent invasion, just as Fairbanks solely thought about his family and the lost colony. It was up to Benson to cover the rest of the ground.

He walked the halls, wondering if this Charles was really going to be able to pull off the impossible.

Flint

The jump was seamless. Flint was enjoying his position with the crew of the *Eureka*. It had been a long time since he'd been part of something larger than himself, or larger than his ship and Kat. Even when he'd been with the Fleet, they'd never felt like a solid unit. He'd mostly resented them and what they stood for. Now he understood he had good reason for it.

The hours of waiting were growing tiresome, but Jarden demanded he be ready to move should any issues arise. With the new Shift technology, a vessel could pop up to you in an instant, and you had to be ready. Flint didn't want to fight a war against a race full of these ships. It would be chaos exemplified.

The bridge was quiet. Kat sat in the seat beside him, just five feet away, and he caught her staring absently into space out the viewscreen. A weapons officer stood at the edge of the room, typing away on a holoscreen. Otherwise, the bridge was empty.

"Hey," Flint said, getting Kat's attention. "I'm sorry you ended up mixed up in this."

She gave him a soft smile, one that gave her dimples and caused her eyes to crinkle up just a little at their edges. "You're all I've ever had, Flint. Did you know that? I was a kid when they died. You took me in, made me who I am today. I'll forever be thankful, even if this crazy mission ends with us dying tomorrow." She reached a hand out to him, and he took it.

Her speech hit him hard, and he blinked away a forming tear. "You're my family, Kat. You and me. And we aren't dying tomorrow. I'll make sure of it." Flint glanced at the viewscreen. "You know, in a weird way, I'm looking forward to seeing what's on the other side of this Rift."

She laughed then, a familiar sound from his co-pilot. "So am I. What's wrong with us? Everyone else just wants a good job with a roof over their heads, and that wouldn't be enough for either of us. We need adventure and space chases, don't we?"

Flint nodded. Kat was right. He'd been that way since he was old enough to run. Flint was about to comment, when an alarm buzzed on his console. The holoscreen projected in front of him, and he spotted the reason. A single ship was heading toward them, within reach of the ship's powerful scanners.

Kat was typing away. "Two life forms on board."

Flint had been told no one was allowed near them. He got the weapons officer's attention. "Lieutenant Tsang?"

"Already targeted. I've sent a message to the captain," Tsang said.

They watched as the fighter approached. A bead of sweat dripped down Flint's forehead as the doors to the bridge hissed open and Captain Barkley strode in, finding a standing position behind Flint and Kat.

"Zoom on the target," Barkley said, and Kat did.

"That's an EFF fighter, but modified," Flint said.

Captain Barkley set a hand down on the back of Flint's chair. "So it is. Curious."

"Don't you dare fire on that vessel." Fairbanks' voice carried from the door to his office. "That will be Charles, back from his mission."

Flint glanced back at their old leader. "You sent the android on a mission? Where to?"

Jarden smiled and rubbed his hands together, as if they were cold. "He rescued something from the Earth Fleet for me. Please tell me there's a life form reading on board."

Tsang answered, "Sir, there are two."

"Two? Let them in but use precautions. I'll send Benson with some guards to greet them." Fairbanks left as quickly as he'd arrived.

"Sending the clearance now," Kat said.

Flint had a bad feeling after seeing the Fleet symbol on the side of that modified fighter.

Ace

"They aren't going to kill me, are they?" Ace asked the android nervously. He was second-guessing his choices as the ship sealed into the huge vessel. The *Eureka* was like nothing he'd ever laid on eyes before. He'd thought the *Stellae* was impressive, and it was, but this ship was something new, something special. He noted there were no Earth Fleet markings on it.

"They will not harm you. I have seen nothing from them to indicate they would harm another human. Also, my friend Dr. Wren Sando is working with them, and I trust her implicitly." Charles stood as the cockpit door hinged open. Ace glanced at their "guest" inside and cringed as it moved, struggling to break free from its confines. He couldn't get a good look at it yet, and wasn't sure he wanted to.

"Great work, Charles," a deep voice said, and Ace spun to see a man in slacks and a blazer enter the room. He grinned at them, his face composed and friendly. "And who's this?"

Ace didn't fail to notice the four armed guards enter behind the suit. The front two pointed stunners directly at him.

Charles placed a hand on Ace's shoulder. "This is Ace. He brought us here. Please do not harm him."

The newcomer lifted a hand, and the guards lowered their weapons. "My name's Benson. Why don't you come on down from there, and we'll get you settled?"

Ace did as he was told, climbing down the fighter and

jumping the last three rungs to land on the ground with a clang. His mask came off with a snap, and he tossed it back into the cockpit, narrowly missing Charles. "What is this?" Ace asked, not specifying on purpose.

"This is the future. It looks like you've bought a free ticket on the most priceless train ever built." Benson smiled again, and Ace found it unnerving. Benson had avoided giving a real answer, he noted.

Soon Charles was down on the ground, and the guards rushed forward, heading into the ship where the alien lay trapped.

Ace was ushered out of the hangar by Benson, who placed a hand on the small of his back and directed him away. "Come with me, Ace. Is that your first name or last?" Benson didn't hold back laughing at his own joke.

Ace didn't think it was funny. "What about Benson? Is that your first or last name?" he asked the older man, and the laughter ceased momentarily.

"Touché," the man said; yet, again, Benson hadn't answered his question.

They entered a wide hall. Smooth polished floors ran in both directions, and everything looked and smelled so new. Wherever they were going was a long time coming. This ship had to have taken an extended time, and more money than Ace could fathom, to build.

Ace followed Benson's long steps down the corridor and into an elevator, where Benson chose the seventh floor. "Where are we going? Charles here said something about a Rift opening, but didn't elaborate on it. I only entered the Fleet a few weeks ago, and now I'm going to be blacklisted. If I'm stuck here, I'd like to know what that means."

"That will be disclosed very soon. I'll take you to your room, and then we can figure out what to do with you.

You seem to be a resourceful young man. How… how old are you?" Benson asked, looking Ace up and down.

Ace swallowed and considered lying like he had to the Fleet. "I'm sixteen. I think."

To Ace's surprise, Benson didn't press him on it. Instead, he gave a quick nod and strode out when the door opened, beckoning Ace and Charles to follow him.

There were a lot more people here, walking the halls, talking amongst each other. There was a nervous but excited energy in the air. Ace felt younger than his sixteen years as he walked through these officers and crew members. Most of them were twice his age, and he knew he'd stand out like a sore thumb in their midst. Back on the moon, side-by-side with eighteen-year-old recruits, he only looked like the runt of the litter. Here, he'd look like someone's kid.

"How's this?" Benson asked, opening a door to reveal a huge room. The lights turned on, a soft white glow over the small space. Inside were a living room, a couch and table, and a small kitchen; two doors led him to his own bathroom and bedroom.

Ace was speechless, but he finally found his tongue. "All of this? For me?"

"Yes. The *Eureka* is state-of-the-art, and one thing our benefactor believes in is crew comfort. What do you think?" Benson asked.

Ace turned away, not wanting the man to see his reaction. He couldn't remember ever having his own room before. When he glanced back, Benson was at the door, and Charles between them.

"I… thank you," Ace was able to muster out.

"Think nothing of it. You've done humanity a great favor, and we're happy to have you on board. Charles, please fill him in on any details he requires. And show him where to get food, if you don't mind." Benson stepped into the hall, and the door slid closed before Charles could reply.

"Would you care for a moment to get situated?" Charles asked, eyes glowing dim orange.

Ace liked the android. It might have been lower on his list of surprises over the last forty-eight hours, but it was there. "I'd like to take a shower and change." He glanced to the bed, where a stack of clothing sat. How did they know his size? They moved quickly on this ship.

"Very well. I'll wait in the hall," Charles offered.

Ace shook his head. "Stay here. One thing first, though."

"Anything," Charles said.

"Are they really going to invade?" Ace asked.

Charles stared at him for a moment before speaking. "It is likely. I only know what I've been told on the subject by humans, so there is a lot of conjecture and trust in my views on it. I have seen an alien, and that in itself proves a lot to me. I have not seen the Rift yet, but we will tomorrow. Flint Lancaster claims to have seen evidence of the Rift. And he is trustworthy… for a smuggler."

Ace had no idea what the android was going on about, but if Charles believed it, then so did he. "What are you?"

"I am… I don't know. Different."

"So am I," Ace said, feeling a kinship to the robotic man.

Charles moved for the door. "Anything else?"

"The destination. On the other side of the Rift. Do you know it?" Ace asked. His heart beat harder in his chest. He wanted options.

"I don't think they would care for that to be spread

around," Charles said. "What do you want it for? I see no path that leads you to using that information."

Ace had to be careful. Instead, he decided to be honest. Charles seemed to appreciate that. "I'm scared. I just joined the Earth Fleet, and I left all my new friends back there, one in particular. If what you say is true, they're going to be decimated. I want to warn them."

"I don't think that's a good idea. The diversion was used to prevent the Fleet from interfering with the councilman's plans."

"Then give me the location, so I can help them when the Rift opens. I'll take my ship back and follow *Eureka*." Ace thought the plan might work. At least, a small part of him did.

Charles looked deep in thought as he considered the situation. Ace wondered how the thought was processed inside his positronic brain.

"I will give you the location, but promise me you will only use it for yourself. Not the others." Charles crossed the room to the desk and opened up a holoscreen, entering some information into it. "There. Use this, but I urge you to come with us and forget what you know. There is no helping them. Not one young man against the coming Watchers."

Ace got goosebumps as the android used the name for the aliens.

"Thank you. I'll be out shortly." Ace was thrilled Charles had given him the information. Now he just needed a way to get that information to Serina. She deserved his loyalty.

26

Wren

Wren drained the remaining coffee from her mug and finished off her runny eggs. It was August second, the day everyone had been waiting for. Jarden's life had been building up to this moment for thirty years – actually, sixty – and his obsession was clear. Nothing felt different for her. She was on borrowed time. If Charles hadn't broken her out of prison, she'd still be hauling sheets of metal used to produce more Fleet ships, and eventually, she'd have died or been killed from toxin inhalation due to a faulty mask in the smelting room.

Wren sat for longer than she would have back in New Dallas and listed off things she was grateful for this morning. She was grateful to be alive, for the fresh coffee she'd just had, for meeting Charles, for the forward thinking of a man like Fairbanks, for her ex-fiancé saying all those horrible things about her so she didn't have to worry about him any longer, for meeting Lancaster.

She considered the last thought, which had come unbidden. There was something about the way his chestnut eyes bore into her, and the sideways grin that was always ready to show itself off.

With a shake of her head, Wren pushed back and got up. The cafeteria lounge was quiet. Everyone aboard was nervous, and likely there were a few uneasy stomachs this morning. Wren grabbed a coffee to go, smiling at the ability to do so, and made her way toward her lab. On a ship this size, it took her a good fifteen minutes, but she took her time, saying hello to half a dozen crew members along the way.

Eventually, she wound her way to the lab, where two guards stood perched on either side of the door. They moved to prevent her from entering the room, and Wren had to bite her tongue to keep from telling them off. It was her lab, according to Jarden, so why would they try to stop her from going in?

"I'm Dr. Wren Sando. What's going on?" She stretched her hand out, and one of the guards scanned her before stepping aside and lowering his gun.

"Sorry, ma'am. Just following orders," the one on the right said, and she passed by, opening the solid sliding door.

It was dark inside, so the blue light emanating from the left side of the room instantly caught her eye.

"It's funny, Doctor." Wren jumped at the sound of Jarden's voice. She could hardly make out his shape where he sat on a table in the middle of the lab.

"What is?" she asked hesitantly.

"I got a sample a few years ago but had no success with a potential virus until I hired you. That damned Karn found out and shut it all down. We could have been ready for the invasion otherwise. I never expected to see you again, but here you are, in the very same room as myself and the subject. That's what I call a royal serving of ironic situation." Jarden's voice was lighter, more wistful than she'd ever heard it sound before.

"What do you mean, the subject?" Wren took her gaze from his shadowed back and looked at the energy field covering the front of the glass cell in the lab. Something was inside it. "Oh my God. You didn't..."

She kept walking until she stood a foot away from the flickering wall of light. Behind it was the creature: the one her DNA map drew out, or a very close representation. "The Watcher," she whispered. It heard her and met her eyes from the corner of the cell. She instantly felt sorry for the being. It was trapped far from home and had been for the last thirty years.

Wren knew what it was like to be stuck in a cage and had the urge to let it free. She pushed the thought away, because that wouldn't do anyone any good. Who was she kidding? She was going to use its samples and find a way to destroy every last one of its kind, should they decide to attack the Earth Fleet.

"Impressive, isn't it? I still can't believe Karn managed to keep it hidden from her crew for so long. Do you know how close I was to whistleblowing on her after you were caught?" Jarden let out a low whistle, as if this would prove something.

"But you didn't."

"No. I trusted my gut, and look where it got us. All three of us, together in one place. Wren, today is August second. It's the big day, and I expected to be a ball of anxiety and stress. But I'm not. I'm the opposite. Today, I'll see another galaxy: one where my... the one the colony ship traveled to so long ago," he said, and she looked back at him to see him staring at the trapped Watcher.

He looked far younger in the dim blue glow of the energy field, and she imagined him at an impulsive forty, finding out his children and wife had left through the Rift. She admired his tenacity and dedication.

"I have to go now, but if you don't mind getting started, there's no time like the present. You need to continue your work, and quickly. We don't know what we'll find over there, but I want to be ready for it. The *Eureka* won't go down easily in a fight, but if we find the colonists are held as slaves, or dead by the Watchers' hands, they'll regret ever poking their heads through the Rift. Is that clear?" Jarden was up now, closer to her, and he looked every second of his age again.

"Clear as crystal."

"Good. Now find a way to kill them." With that, he left her alone in the lab with the lights off, and an extraterrestrial a few feet away from her.

Jish

The tumbler broke as it hit the door, sending shards of glass spraying around the entry of her office. Who the hell did the little twerp think he was? The Invader was gone, the damned little kid was gone, along with her backup to the destroyed probe. How the hell had the alien escaped? It didn't add up.

Jish picked another glass and threw it hard against the wall, this one also shattering. Almost unconsciously, she grabbed the decanter of Scotch and drank too much for her mouth to hold, spitting some of it out as she tried to swallow it down.

What kind of leader had she become? Their Fleet was amassed together for the first time in a century, and she was throwing a tantrum in her office while they waited for her decision. It was a risk. She had no intel on the Rift at all now, and they needed to know if the attack was coming. She'd waited too long, and it was now only an hour away.

Jish dropped the near-empty decanter of Scotch and wiped her mouth with a sleeve. She was in no position to lead the Earth Fleet, but there was no one else with enough balls to make the tough calls. Except for Jarden Fairbanks, and he was the reason she was in this mess in the first place.

She got on the communicator and made her announcement. "All Shift drive vessels to the *Stellae*. We make the jump in twenty minutes. Bring every EFF-17 you can fit. Today, we fight for Earth." Jish ended the call and sat back in her leather seat, the room spinning slightly.

This was it. Either the Invaders would be there or they wouldn't be. She wished she could give the odds at fifty-fifty, but her gut was one hundred percent sure they'd arrive and soon find a fleet of enemies nearby. She needed another thirty years but didn't think she was going to be that lucky.

After cleaning herself up, she took an injection to help process the alcohol and pulled her disheveled hair into a slightly professional ponytail. When she arrived on the bridge of the *Stellae*, the crew were scattered, and she could smell their nervousness.

The ships were in formation and ready to go. Jish hit the comm-switch for the entire Fleet to hear. "Today, we stand together as Earth Fleet. But more than that, we're going to protect the entire system: each colony, and every human alive. We'll bring the fight to the enemy before they can bring it to us. I'm proud to be Earth Fleet because of all of you. Today, we fight for humanity." She paused and noticed her own crew sitting straighter and standing taller. "Activate Shift drives. On three."

She watched out the viewscreen as the handful of carriers, corvettes, and warships vanished, the *Stellae* a split second behind them.

Flint

Flint was startled as the Earth Fleet vessels appeared near the Rift's eventual opening. He counted fourteen large vessels in total. A lot of firepower, but potentially not enough, if Jarden's predictions came to fruition.

"I knew they'd still come," the councilman said as he paced to the front of the bridge. "Don't engage in communication with them. Stick to the plan, do you all understand?"

The entire crew said "Yes, sir" in unison, including Flint.

Jarden was still in front of them, staring at the massive screen from two feet away. Flint followed his head angle and saw the blue dot appear. "It's here," Jarden whispered.

Flint glanced over at Kat, who was sitting still, her mouth opened slightly as she took in the image. When Flint looked back, the Rift was opening wider. There was nothing coming through it. He let out a sigh of relief. Maybe the Watchers weren't going to make their move after all. He started to smile, when he heard a gasp from behind him.

The image on the viewscreen zoomed in, but they were too far to keep a crisp image at this distance. It didn't matter. Flint could still see the familiar boxy shape of the Watchers' ship as it entered. He'd seen the same thing on the footage they'd found aboard his ship, only this time, there wasn't just one. Vessel after vessel poured through the Rift, which had to be five kilometers wide at this point.

"Stick to the plan. Flint, get ready to punch it," Jarden said, never averting his gaze. He was so transfixed on the viewscreen, Flint doubted anything would break the old man from staring at it.

"Yes, sir. Destination is locked, and we're ready to Shift." Flint sat there watching the imminent battle unfold, his finger ready to tap the icon on command.

Ace

Ace could see the image from the viewscreen through his feed in his quarters. He pocketed the datastick with the Shift coordinates and ran for the door. Serina was on one of those carriers, and he couldn't let her get killed. He'd slept like a baby last night, at peace with his decision to stay on board the *Eureka* and go with them through the Rift. Now, seeing the Fleet arrive and the aliens coming to destroy them, something broke inside him.

He raced down the halls, winding his way toward the small hangar, where the Shift-modified fighter sat empty. He made it there quickly and was surprised to find the hangar unguarded. It was dark and quiet in the room as he hurled himself into the fighter's cockpit. His mask was where he'd left it, and he threw it on before closing and sealing the ship.

The hangar wall lifted as the engine started, a nice technologic advancement that made his exit easier. Ace kept worrying the *Eureka* would jump, and he'd exit into space to find they were already on the other side. He hurried, lifting the fighter up, and passed the blue containment field into space. He let out a sigh of relief when his sensors picked up the Earth Fleet vessels a few thousand kilometers away.

Ace raced toward them, pushing his thrusters as fast as they would go. As he approached, he heard chatter in his earpiece from the crew of the ship he'd just escaped, but he ignored it.

"Where are you, Serina?" he asked himself and spotted the carrier she'd been in the other day by its ID number. She'd still be there. He had to get in touch with her, and he searched for her private line.

He'd been so preoccupied, he hadn't seen the thousands of alien ships rushing toward the Earth Fleet lines. Ace felt the urge to bank the ship away from them and run back to the *Eureka* with his tail between his legs. The battle began to unfold before his eyes.

Earth Fleet fighters tore through space, entering into dogfights with the enemy ships. They were clearly outmanned and outgunned, and Ace noticed some of the alien fighters blink out of existence. They were using their Shift drives to do small jumps. There was no way the Earth Fleet could compete. The attacking fighters were squat, wider than the Fleet's, each of them moving swiftly and with purpose.

Large pulses shot from the Watchers' largest ships, blasting against the Fleet's warship shields. They would only hold for so long.

Finally, he found Serina's line and tried to reach her. "Serina! It's Ace. They're shifting mid-flight. You have to get out of here. Move back to the rendezvous and regroup. Tell them what you found here. You'll all be destroyed!" His words came quickly and erratically.

"Ace? How's this possible? Where are you?" Serina's voice hit his earpiece, and he grinned despite the chaos around him.

He could give her the location Charles had passed him. While he considered this, he ensured the Shift drive was charging and set the destination into the fighter's console.

"I just got here. It's hopeless. Look. They're still coming." Ace zoomed in on the Rift; more and more alien vessels were entering through the opening in space. It was real. They were really being invaded, and Ace knew there'd be no way of stopping them. Charles swore this Fairbanks character was going to save humanity, but Ace didn't know how.

"We can't let them invade!" Serina sounded scared, and he didn't blame her.

"You're overpowered here. Retreat. For me. Tell them what's happening!" Ace saw the Rift shrinking. He glanced to the right edge of his viewscreen and saw that the *Eureka* was gone. It had jumped.

Serina didn't reply, but he noticed the carrier she was in under heavy fire. He raced toward it, firing at an enemy fighter along the way. It shifted away, his pulse cannon missing and hitting empty space where it had been a moment before. As he approached, hundreds of the EFF-17s still battled around him. One of the huge enemy warships arrived a thousand kilometers away, and he knew what its target was.

"Serina, they're targeting you. Retreat now. Shift out of here!" he yelled as the blasts cut through space. Just before they hit the carrier, it vanished, and Ace let out a sigh of relief.

That was, until he saw he was under fire of his own, surrounded by a half-dozen alien fighters.

He arced away, checking the Shift drive with the corner of his vision. It was charged. At this point, the Rift wasn't a tenth of its largest size, and he closed his eyes as he activated the drive.

When he opened them, the *Eureka*'s location flashed on his HUD, and Ace let out a sigh of relief at the sight of the massive vessel. He pressed the throttle and made for the hangar.

27

Jish

Ten minutes. It had only taken ten minutes for Jish Karn to be sure they were doomed. To be honest, it had only taken seconds, but for the next few minutes, she clutched to the hope that something would turn the tide. It didn't.

Thousands of enemy ships swarmed the space around them, destroying the Earth Fleet fighters like they were mosquitoes around a campfire. Jish cringed as the Fleet's most powerful corvette exploded, an anticlimactic end to a thousand lives. She slumped down in her seat, the crew of the *Stellae* looking to her for answers.

"Leave. Jump back. I just need three minutes." She got up, and when a series of questions flew at her, she yelled over them. "Retreat and give me three damn minutes. We're going to lose today, but not without some pain on their end."

Jish ran from the bridge, tears streaming down her face. She almost laughed at how tired she was after keeping this pace for half a minute, still feeling the effects of the Scotch from earlier. Her private hangar door opened as she approached, and she ran for the solitary ship. It was small, but she knew it would pack a punch.

The original Watcher fighter hummed to life, and she wasted no time in strapping herself in and lifting it out of the *Stellae*. She saw her fleet retreating, the Shift drives activating, leaving the invaders to fire at empty space instead of the Earth Fleet. She spoke into her earpiece as she flew away from her ship.

"Captain, get out of here. Now!" she yelled and watched her console as the *Stellae* disappeared. The enemy ships looked confused. They hadn't expected the humans to have their own technology. She had one last surprise for them.

Jish Karn wasn't a young woman any longer. She'd lived a good life, a long life. Her years as the Grand Admiral of the Fleet had been her finest, even though they were marred by the prediction of this invasion. The pressure of knowing she held the only live alien in a cell below the decks of her ship had been enough to drive her a little crazy at times. But as she entered the enemy lines, she did so unimpeded, as if she'd piqued the Invaders' curiosity.

Jish found herself the last Fleet ship in the whole region, a needle amongst the haystack of devastation coming to Earth and the colonies. The Invaders let her pass their ranks, and she made for the largest cluster of warships.

She half expected them to attempt communication, but she knew it was pointless. Jish wished she could wipe the tears from her mask-covered cheeks, but it didn't matter anymore. She might not have always done the right thing at each moment of her life, but she knew she was going to die proud of what she'd accomplished. She was going to sleep eternally sound.

The antimatter bomb had cost the Fleet more credits than she cared to think about, but at this moment, she knew it had been worth the price.

The countdown started on her console. Ten. Nine. Eight.

She took a deep breath before closing her eyes, saying the numbers out loud as they ticked away.

When the countdown reached one, she smiled momentarily before being torn apart. She may not have stopped them, but she'd damn well die happy, taking as many of the bastards with her as she could.

Wren

The noise was terrifying at first. Wren had been working, which meant organizing all her files from the lab back in New Dallas from a few years ago. She was impressed with most of the results, though they hadn't quite nailed it down. One moment, the room was silent; the next, the Watcher was screeching. It caught her off-guard, and she dropped her coffee cup to the ground, the metal container splashing the brown liquid on the floor before rolling away.

The screech turned into a howl, and Wren knew they'd made the jump. They were on the other side of the Rift, and the alien had somehow sensed it. That was very curious. She made sure the event was being recorded and walked over to the cell.

"Stop yelling. You're fine," she said, and it ceased howling momentarily. But just as quickly as it stopped, it began again, and she had to put her palms to her ears to muffle the noise.

This continued for a while longer, and then it switched from howling to speaking. It spoke in a series of clicks and groans, a sound quite unlike anything she'd ever heard. It was animalistic, but wasn't every language essentially an animal talking?

"What is it? I can't understand," Wren said, watching it stand in the cell, its dark eyes pleading with her.

She couldn't stand to see it and decided to leave the room. "It's making a racket in there. Just be aware," she told the guards in the hall and made for the bridge.

No alarms rang out, and she took that as a good sign. Clearly, they hadn't emerged in the heart of a Watcher fleet. Her steps quickened as she got closer to the bridge, and Wren tapped her foot impatiently, waiting for the lift to bring her up. When she arrived, there was no sound other than the soft chiming of different computer systems running their functions.

Jarden Fairbanks was standing at the front of the bridge, his gaze plastered to the gigantic viewscreen. The star patterns were unfamiliar; a purple nebula danced slowly in the distance, catching Wren's eye in the top right corner of the screen. Otherwise, there were no ships, no planets or moons in sight.

She crossed the space and stood beside Captain Barkley, who noticed her and looked up to smile. "We made it," Heather said.

Flint

Flint's racing heartbeat finally began to slow down. Seeing the Watchers emerge through the Rift was disturbing, like a scene from a holohorror. From the moment he and Kat had seen the footage of the Rift from ninety years ago, he'd been hoping it was a fake. He'd thought Jarden might have actually been a delusional eccentric with too many credits and power. But it was all true: the Watchers, the colony ship, the Shift drive capability.

He tried to determine where they might possibly be by having the system scan for any familiar star patterns. The diagnosis quickly came back with no results. They were far from home.

Home. It was a strange word to Flint, and to many on board, he suspected. The Earth Fleet troops rarely had families, since they didn't have time to settle down and grow roots.

"Setting destination," Captain Barkley said from her seat. Jarden finally broke his locked gaze from the viewscreen, a look of elation in his eyes. His excitement was palpable.

Flint almost inquired how far it was but found their trajectory mapped out. Thirty-three hours. He wanted to ask why they wouldn't use the Shift drive to get there, but he knew the answer. The drive showed four percent charged. The extreme distance they'd traveled had drained whatever source powered the ship's new drive.

Excited chatter passed between Tsang and Barkley, Kat joining in. Flint stayed quiet. Whatever they were about to stumble into worried him. It felt too empty here, as if the expanse of space had changed. He couldn't put it into words; everything felt upside down. The metaphor didn't work, but it was something along those lines.

He spent the rest of his shift in silence, cautiously scanning the viewscreen for incoming enemies.

Six hours later, he found himself in the same lounge where he'd spent a few hours with Wren the other night, and to his surprise, the doctor was sitting there, her hands wrapped around a beer. She didn't notice him, so he stood there watching her. She looked tired; of course, the entire ship's population was tired at this point. Still, he was drawn to her sad, withdrawn eyes.

"Flint, how very nice to see you here," a voice said from the hallway. Wren looked up from her glass and caught him watching her. He turned away to see the android Charles standing there with a young man beside him.

"Hey, Charles. What's shaking?" Flint asked.

"Nothing is shaking, Flint. The ship is constantly vibrating, if that's what you mean," Charles said. He was the smartest, most unique android Flint had ever seen, but he was still easy to pull a fast one on.

"Never mind. Who's this?" Flint asked, taking the boy in. He was just a kid, all arms and legs, like a puppy growing into his body. He had a long face and close-cropped hair that looked like a butcher job from the Fleet. Flint knew the hairstyle only too well. It was one of the reasons he'd let his hair go so shaggy to this day.

"Ace. Nice to meet you." The kid stuck his hand out, and Flint shook it – three solid pumps – and let go.

"Ace. Nice call sign. I haven't seen you around." Truthfully, there were a thousand people on *Eureka*, and Flint hadn't met many of them.

"I just got here." Ace grinned, and Flint felt like he was missing some pertinent information.

"Ace helped me bring the Watcher from the Earth Fleet's *Stellae*," Charles said matter-of-factly.

Wren's ears must have perked up, because she called to Charles and waved them over. "What's this all about? You were the one who brought my subject in? How's that possible?"

Wren was introduced to Ace, and the four of them took seats around the square table.

"I need one of those," Flint said. "Anyone else?" When no one replied, he nudged the kid. "How about you, Ace? You look like a guy who has a story to tell, with something to wet your whistle." Flint knew he was still a kid, but when you witnessed an alien invasion and were millions of light years from home, what did it matter?

"Sure. Thanks," Ace said.

Flint already found himself liking the guy. He reminded Flint of himself as a teenager. He wanted to tell the kid that it was going to be all right, and that he'd grow into those shoulders eventually.

"How about you, Chuck? Pint of fission core?" Flint said it straight-faced, and a second later, Wren let out a laugh.

"I don't see why that's funny," Charles replied.

Flint left, bringing back two beers before plopping down in a seat beside Wren. Kat entered the cafeteria lounge and meandered over to their table, stealing a sip of Flint's beer with a smile.

"What are we talking about?" she asked with a chipper tone. Flint was glad to see her in good spirits. Despite all the crazy events leading them to this table together, their mismatched group felt right.

"We're telling our stories. If we're going to be living together for the foreseeable future, we may as well get to know each other." This from Wren, who was still nursing the beer she'd been staring into when Flint arrived.

"I'm game," Kat said, and Flint was glad to see her opening up to the others.

"I, for one, need to know what's going on with our good friend Charles the android," Flint suggested.

"I'm not sure there's much to tell, if I can be honest." Charles sat at the end of the table, his arms hung down at his sides.

Wren took this one. "He's a complicated android, but I owe him my life. Without Charles, I'd still be rotting away at the Uranus Mining Prison for Women. I never quite noticed how much of a mouthful that is to say."

Flint didn't know she'd come from a prison. "Now this is going to be interesting."

He sat back, took a pull from his beer, and they talked well into the night, regaling one another with stories of their pasts: first Charles, then Wren, followed by the heart-wrenching tale of Ace. Flint wanted to hug the thin boy, to tell him life was going to get better, but that wasn't a promise Flint could give him, not after everything he'd witnessed in the last few days. When it came time for Kat, she talked about the attack that had killed her parents as well as Flint's.

Flint stopped drinking after two beers, knowing his shift would start in six hours.

Everyone stopped talking for a moment when Ace spoke. Flint noticed the room was empty except for their small group, and he was grateful for it.

"Are they going to destroy Earth?" Ace asked. It was a simple question at its core. Were the Watchers going to turn into Invaders, as the Fleet called them? Flint guessed they never really were Watchers. They were Wait-until-the-right-timers, and when it was time, they'd sent a fleet large enough to take over.

"What do you think? You were with the Fleet. Can they fend off the attack?" Wren asked.

Ace's sad eyes turned down as he answered. "No. They can't win."

Flint hated to say it, but he agreed. "The Earth Fleet has never dealt with anything close to this magnitude. There's a big difference between space pirates and idealist groups attacking small outposts versus this invasion. Come to think of it, we recently learned that most of the terrorist attacks were commissioned by the Fleet in order to prove their own value and necessity."

Ace paled further, and Flint felt bad for the kid. He'd grown up wanting to be a pilot with them, and by sheer luck, he'd ended up doing just that, only to find out they were corrupt and about to be destroyed.

"We need to find a way to stop them," Kat said, and

all eyes turned to her.

"To stop who?" Wren asked.

"The Watchers. We can't let them have Earth." Kat sat up straighter, the tiredness gone from her face.

Wren slammed a hand down on the table. "I agree. We're going to kill the bastards."

Was Flint the only rational one in the group? "How do we do that? We're on the other side of the Rift, far from home. A Rift, need I remind you, that only opens up once every thirty years."

"We'll find a way." This from Ace. Flint really did find himself liking the kid.

Wren raised a mostly empty glass in the air. "To resisting!" She gave them a wry smile, and Flint couldn't help but finding himself grinning with her.

"To the resistance!" they all echoed.

28

Jarden

Jarden paced the back of the bridge, trying to make it look more casual than anxious. The crew needed him to be strong. He was the unflappable Councilman Jarden Fairbanks, the reason they were on the other side of the Rift, approaching a new world where life was abundant, water fresh, and air breathable.

Jarden saw the system's star in the distance, a glowing hot yellow ball of gas. This planet had the right parameters for an Earthlike world, but this was old news. Their probe had told them this ninety years ago when Jarden had been just a little boy, staring into the night sky outside his family's farm in desolate middle America.

While he was dreaming of traveling into space to escape the harsh life of a poor farmhand, he never could have guessed that one day he'd be among those distant stars, exploring a new world. As he paced the bridge, he tried to remember that little boy, to see the viewscreen with his optimism and delight, but it had been too long ago. Too much had happened to Jarden since then.

"Any luck on the sensors?" he asked for the tenth time since he'd woken up.

"No, sir." Tsang answered this one. "Maybe something in the atmosphere's messing with the pulse, or maybe the colony lost power to the beacon."

All good reasons, but Jarden feared worse. *Leona Fairbanks, are you still alive? Nik and Oliv, are my children okay?* As much as he'd tried to push their names and faces from his memory for the last sixty years, he couldn't. They were there every night when he closed his eyes, and he could almost smell Leona beside him on the bed when he woke in the morning.

The planet appeared on the viewscreen. It was zoomed in as much as they could while keeping the image crystal-clear. As the hours passed, the shape grew, until they could see wispy white clouds, deep blue seas, and high mountain ranges. Jarden became calmer as the planet grew nearer.

Flint took them closer as the last hour dragged on, seconds ticking by in Jarden's internal clock.

"Bring us into orbit," Captain Barkley said.

The viewscreen showed the rounding of the world above, and Jarden hadn't ever felt this nervous in his life. It hit him like a brick wall, and he found his knees giving way, himself falling to the floor. At first no one noticed, but seconds later, Heather Barkley was at his side. "Sir, are you all right?"

He was, he tried to tell her, but no words came out.

"Captain, I'm picking up a signal. It's weak, but it's there," Tsang said.

Jarden found his breath and sat up as Heather left him there, too drawn by the news. "Is it…?" he finally croaked out.

"It's the beacon, sir. It's faint." Tsang couldn't keep the excitement from his voice. "It's the pattern you were waiting for."

Jarden pulled himself up on the arm of the captain's chair and pulled himself into it. *Don't fail me now, body. Not while I'm so close.* "Attempt communication," he said, his nerves shot while he waited.

"Nothing, sir," Tsang said.

"Keep trying." Jarden knew there could be many reasons for them not answering. The equipment could be damaged or they might have turned it all off. Hell, sixty years was an awfully long time to be waiting for a rescue, and they might be afraid of who else was listening.

A few minutes later, there was still no answer to their communication, and Jarden made a decision.

"Kat, take Flint's seat. We're going to the surface." Jarden watched the scans of the planet, showing minimal electrical readouts. Whatever was down there, it wasn't alien cities and technology.

Flint Lancaster got up and followed him off the bridge. "I'm coming, Leona," Jarden whispered.

Benson

Benson caught his reflection in the mirror, and fixed his collar. He'd always hated wearing a uniform and was glad Jarden allowed him to dress as he pleased. Benson had done a lot of favors for the man over the years and knew that if he could make himself invaluable, he would have free rein over Fairbanks. It had worked even better than he'd imagined.

He read a message from the bridge saying they were in orbit of the colony world. Years ago, Fairbanks had dubbed the world Domum, Latin for *home*. Benson had never liked the name, but that didn't matter.

He walked by a few crew members on the way to his destination, and he paused to chat with a delightful young woman before carrying on. He stopped in the cafeteria, grabbing a much-needed coffee, and kept moving.

Benson was in a fantastic mood. The buildup had

taken a lot of effort, but they were here. He approached the laboratory where Wren Sando was working. He had it on good authority she was still eating breakfast. With a wave of his hands, the two stationed guards nodded and vacated the doorway.

Before entering, he pulled a palm-sized device from his blazer's inside pocket. With the tap of a dim icon, it began working. Benson stepped into the room, knowing the recording feeds would be on a loop. If anyone watched this feed, they'd see nothing but the same five minutes over again, where the room sat empty and nothing moved.

The glowing blue energy field drew him toward it, and he grinned as he saw the crouched Watcher in his cell. The alien stood tall as he approached, not making a noise.

Benson spoke to him then: at first a low growl, then a series of clicks and groans.

The creature was silent for a moment before answering the question.

Benson lost his smile.

The End

ABOUT THE AUTHOR

Nathan Hystad is an author from Sherwood Park, Alberta, Canada. He writes science fiction and horror.

Keep up to date with his new releases by signing up for his newsletter at www.nathanhystad.com